SHARK AND OCTOPUS

Shark and Octopus

A novel

by

JC SULLIVAN

Adelaide Books
New York/Lisbon
2020

SHARK AND OCTOPUS
A novel
By JC Sullivan

Copyright © by JC Sullivan
Cover design © 2020 Adelaide Books

Published by Adelaide Books, New York / Lisbon
adelaidebooks.org
Editor-in-Chief
Stevan V. Nikolic

For any information, please address Adelaide Books
at info@adelaidebooks.org
or write to:
Adelaide Books
244 Fifth Ave. Suite D27
New York, NY, 10001

ISBN-13: 978-1-952570-93-3

Printed in the United States of America

TO MY DAUGHTERS,

KIRA AND MEREDITH

One

July 4
5:10 am

For a long moment, Griffin Gilmore sat in the passenger's seat of the Malibu, cradling the box.

"You don't expect to see him waiting, do you?" Kit asked. "It's still too dark to see much of anything."

"Even if you could see," Griffin Gilmore replied, "he's way too cautious to be standing out in the open. But he'll be watching me and I want him to know I'm alone. No cops in sight. He's more than eager for what he thinks is in this box. But he won't take foolish risks. If he spots a police car, he'll bolt."

They sat a while longer.

"Don't forget the box," Kit said. It was, Griffin understood, a gentle push to get him moving.

He grabbed the box and opened the door. "Kit?" Griffin stayed in the safety of the car a bit longer. "You know, I can't be sure how this meeting is going to go," he said. Admitting he was not completely in charge of events was not something Griffin did easily.

"What will you do when he finds out the box doesn't have what he wants?"

Griffin did not answer Kit's question. He wasn't sure what the answer to that question was.

He walked up Dumbarton Road toward the softball field, where the meeting was to take place. The day was muggy already. As planned, he arrived a few minutes early. The darkness was lifting enough he was sure the field was empty. Along Dumbarton Road he could see the grey outline of row houses. Somewhere in those houses were Baltimore County police and federal officials following his movements. Carrying the box, Griffin reached the softball field and waited.

Griffin was aware that in his nervousness the minutes would pass with unnatural slowness. Still, it seemed several eternities before his wait ended.

★

His wait ended with the ringing of a phone, which he found taped to the bottom of a bench by the softball field. He yanked away the tape and hit the button to answer the phone. He was greeted by a formal, smoothly gracious, Latin-accented voice. The voice was unmistakable, though he'd heard it only once before. "Good morning, Mr. Gilmore. I trust you are well. You are Griffin Gilmore? How are you, sir?"

Griffin could not quite manage to reply, so the voice resumed.

"I have been watching you for the seventeen minutes since your arrival. You are attired in a red shirt, blue slacks, and running shoes, which you will need momentarily. I have also observed that you have a habit of rubbing the left side of your face. You did so throughout our conversation when we met at the museum one month ago."

Finally Griffin spoke. "I only do that when I'm nervous."

"You have been doing so the entirety of the time you have been here."

"Well, yes."

"You are alone, I see."

"I am. You'll be coming here to me to handle our transaction?"

"No, Mr. Gilmore. I will not be joining you. You will be joining me. Now, listen attentively."

"I'm listening."

"Turn around and face the other direction."

Griffin did as ordered.

"You are now facing Stevenson Lane. I will meet you on Stevenson Lane, Mr. Gilmore. You have sixty seconds to get here from the termination of this phone call. If you are not here in that time, I keep driving. If the contents of the box are damaged in any way, there is no sale. You understand my terms?"

"Yes."

"You accept them?"

"Yes."

Griffin was then told, "Put down the phone. Hold onto the box. Start running, Mr. Gilmore. You have sixty seconds."

And the call ended.

★

Unbalanced by the box, Griffin stumbled twice but reached Stevenson in under a minute, he was fairly sure.

He saw no cars moving in either direction. He had no idea what would happen next. Could he have missed the deadline?

Directly across the street the headlights of an ordinary, small grey car switched on. A window powered down and that same accented voice called out, "Do be careful with the box crossing the street. With haste, please, Mr. Gilmore."

Griffin got into the front seat of the car, the box resting between his knees. The man driving wore the same outfit he'd worn the only other time Griffin had seen him, at a museum fundraiser one month before: white gabardine slacks, white suit coat, ivory colored shirt, and marble-white tie. Then, he had been wearing a Panama straw hat, also white. In the intervening month Griffin had learned the man's name, but still thought of him as he had that night – the man in white.

Griffin looked into the back seat and spotted the Panama hat. He also saw what looked like an oversized, bulky pair of sunglasses. That, Griffin decided, must be the night vision equipment enabling the man to watch him by the softball field.

The man reached into the pocket of his white suit coat and withdrew a small rectangular block of wood. On the box were four switches. He pushed one of the switches forward.

A loud explosion instantly followed. A car on Dumbarton Road blew up with a crumping noise. The flames must have leaped twenty feet into the air. The flames reached high enough Griffin could see them from Stevenson Lane, hundreds of yards away.

The man in white hit another switch and there was another crump and explosion, further up Dumbarton Road. The two flames burned a bright yellow and red against the background of the still-dark houses.

He flicked the third and fourth switches and two more explosions resulted, these on Stevenson Lane. A car ahead and another behind Griffin suddenly burst into flames.

The exploded car ahead of Griffin was no more than one hundred feet away. This close, the explosion was loud and Griffin watched sections of the car tumbling into the air. Chunks of roof and bumper cascaded into the street with thumps and scraping sounds. Car alarms were going off up and down the road. Griffin could not believe how high the flames were reaching. He could not pull his eyes from the fire, which gave off a *whooooo*shing sound.

There was another explosion on Dumbarton Road. Griffin figured a car must have been parked close enough to an exploded car that its gasoline tank blew up.

"A bit of a distraction," Griffin was informed. "Now you must be frisked. That is the American word?" Griffin nodded that he understood. "Get out of the vehicle and place your hands against the hood, Mr. Gilmore. If you would be so kind."

He got out of the car, still holding the box.

"If that box contains what you have promised, you have nothing to fear. I am a man of my word. You will be paid, generously."

A tracking beeper was taped inside Griffin's left armpit and the tape keeping it in place covered less than a square inch of skin – but this frisking was so thorough Griffin knew it was inevitable the beeper would be discovered.

The man's hand worked its way up the left side of Griffin's torso. Griffin tried shifting his body slightly to the side. He hoped by doing so the man would miss the beeper. He did not. With a single sharp yank he pulled away the tape and beeper. Griffin let fly a yelp of pain as the tape was torn away from his skin.

"A beeper in the armpit is standard procedure, Mr. Gilmore. I am afraid your law enforcement associates will hereafter be unable to track your whereabouts."

Griffin knew that was true. The Baltimore County PD and the feds would not know where he was going. He did not know either.

"Return to the car, Mr. Gilmore, please. We must leave immediately."

They pulled away from the curb.

Two

June 4
8:27 pm

Griffin Gilmore had met the man in white exactly one month earlier. On that night as well the man's slacks, suit coat, shirt and tie had all been white. He wore a Panama straw hat, also white, but with a gold band. The hatband was the only non-white part of the ensemble and flashed all the brighter for it.

When Griffin first saw the man in white he was taking an hors d'oeuvre from Griffin's girlfriend Annie. Her role was as a server at the Baltimore Museum of Art fundraiser. As the man in white took the last prosciutto crostini he gave her a courtly head bob of thanks. Then he slipped away into the thick crowd. At the time Griffin did not give the man another thought.

On her way to the kitchen for another tray, Annie stopped to speak to Griffin.

"So. Another five minutes?" she asked.

"Four," Griffin replied, without needing to check his watch.

"Have you heard from Kit?" Annie asked next.

Griffin tapped his ear piece. His role tonight was privately hired security. The real museum guards had been told he'd been hired for this occasion only and to be left alone. This gave him the chance to go into other parts of the museum, which he was about to do.

"Kit says he's parked right where we planned. He assures me the limo engine is running and the champagne is chilling. Remember where he is?"

"Surely," Annie answered, and Griffin knew felt himself relax. No one else could do that for him.

"I'll meet you in the limo," he said. "It's almost time for Bobby's big moment."

They both looked at Bobby Lowell, the fourth member of Griffin Gilmore's team. Bobby's gig was as a magician entertaining children at the fundraiser.

Bobby was making animals from balloons. He twisted a few balloons into a dachshund. Then he made a bouquet of flowers. He airwalked the dachshund over to the bouquet, and lifted the dog's rear leg, as if the animal were relieving himself. The kids circled three deep around him shrieked with laughter.

Sensing Griffin and Annie's glance, Bobby looked over. He turned his shoulder slightly, so his young audience couldn't see. He stuck an index finger into his throat, as if forcing himself to vomit. Bobby, an actor since his high school days with Griffin, Annie and Kit, despised children's theater.

"Please, Griffin," Bobby had pleaded, when Griffin handed out assignments. "Don't make me work with kids. I'm a classically trained actor. I'll do anything other than perform for children, please. Let me be a server."

"Annie's got that."

"I'll wear a dress."

"No, you'll wear a tux. We can't take a chance on any kids wandering off into the rest of the museum, Bobby. The fundraiser is supposed to be restricted to the first floor of the museum, but you never know where people might go. Kids especially.

13

"I need five minutes alone in the room with the display of The Life of 18th Century Italian Nobles. You have to keep the kids entertained and occupied and out of the exhibit while I'm in there. And you have to give me the signal when to leave."

At the fundraiser Griffin was waiting for Bobby to give that signal.

Bobby reached into the pocket of his tuxedo. He withdrew a waxy looking grey lump of something, size of a gumball. He showed it to the children, who waited expectantly. He threw the grey lump against the floor. And he disappeared in a puff of sky blue smoke.

The children erupted into cheers and applause. A few seconds later Bobby emerged from the smoke, bowing, ten feet to the side. All eyes were turned toward him, away from the stairs leading to the second floor of the museum.

By then Griffin was halfway up those stairs.

No one challenged him, to all appearances someone in security checking out the second floor. He moved quickly but did not run. A running man attracts attention.

The Life of 18th Century Italian Nobles exhibit took up the first two rooms on the right side of the second floor hall. He went to the second room.

The entrance to the room was barred by a sign stating NO ADMITTANCE, EXHIBIT UNDER REPAIR. The sign had been placed there at Griffin's request, as part of his preparation for this assignment. Museum officials had been convinced to cooperate, although they were never informed why their assistance was needed.

Griffin strode past the sign, through the doorway and into the room, which held five waist-high glass display cases. He headed immediately to the case in the far corner. When he reached the display case, he glanced at the room entrance, empty. Seems he'd gotten here without being followed, or even noticed probably.

From his preparation, Griffin knew that breaking into the display case, with its basic pin and tumbler lock, would not be difficult. A sergeant with the Baltimore County Police Department had tutored him in the fine art of picking locks. A pair of four inch lengths of copper wire, tension pliers, practice, and a steady hand were enough.

No, the challenge would be dealing with the spring-loaded alarm, set off by any change in the weight within the display case. On display were twelve keys, eleven from Italian counts, dukes and princes of the 1700s; one key belonged to a jailer in the employ of a Duke. The keys were arranged in four columns of three keys each. If even a single key were removed from the cushion inside the display case, the decrease in weight would cause the alarm to sound.

Griffin, though, was not planning to remove a key. He was going to exchange one.

★

Griffin picked the display case lock in under ninety seconds. His teacher, Sergeant Ahearn, would have been proud. He pushed back the glass lid of the case.

Griffin glanced again at the doorway, still empty. Sounds from the fundraiser floated up to him. He could hear more applause for Bobby's performance. Bobby was killing them, no doubt to his dismay. From the other end of the fundraiser he could hear the musical entertainment, a jazz fusion trio, starting back up after their break.

Griffin reached into the pocket of his suit coat. The coat was the brown of a lunch bag and about as stylish. He didn't want to draw attention to himself by overdressing for his part as hired security.

From his suit coat pocket he removed a key. The key appeared to be an exact replica of one of the keys in the display case – the one identified as belonging to an unknown jailer in the employ of the Duke of Arazzo.

In fact the key Griffin held was not a replica. It was the original. He paused for a moment, contemplating the irony of stealing from the exhibit a worthless fake and replacing it with the valuable original.

Griffin again eyed the doorway. Empty. Another minute and he'd be back through that door, his assignment accomplished.

With the most extreme care he could manage, Griffin brought the original key into the open display case. Then, moving with even greater slowness, he brought the round end of the original key into contact with the display cushion. He did this with his left hand.

At precisely the same speed and at exactly the same time, with his right hand he pulled the replica away from the display case. Mastering this skill had required far more practice than learning to pick locks.

Once the keys were exchanged Griffin held his breath, listening for an alarm. But all he heard was that sweet, sweet sound of silence.

He did not exhale until the replica was inside his coat pocket.

From the doorway someone called out, "Bravo, Mr. Gilmore." It was a man dressed entirely in white, nodding appreciatively at Griffin.

★

"How did you know my-" Griffin began, then stopped himself. Reverting to role, and in his best head of security tone, he informed the man in white, "Sir, I'm sorry, but the second floor is off limits to guests of the fundraiser."

"As I have been informed. Nevertheless, Mr. Gilmore, I am here."

Trace of a Spanish accent, Griffin decided. But European Spanish, not this hemisphere, not New World.

"I am sorry, sir," Griffin persisted. "You will have to leave."

He noticed the man in white wore an oversized silver signet ring on his index finger. There was some sort of design on the front of the ring, which Griffin could not quite see.

Summoning up his most authoritative voice, Griffin insisted, "You will have to go back downstairs."

And how, Griffin wondered, do you know who I am?

"Alas, Mr. Gilmore. I do not believe that will transpire."

Griffin noted the man spoke with the formality of someone fluent in, though not completely comfortable with, English.

"And why not?" Griffin asked, curious now.

"I regret the strong arm tactics, Mr. Gilmore. Honestly, I do."

The man in white nodded toward his left hand. Griffin followed his gaze and saw the gun there.

Instinctively Griffin took several rushed steps backward, until he edged into something. The impact sent him tumbling. He broke his fall by grabbing the arm of the champagne-colored sofa he'd backed into. With gracious patience, the man in white waited to speak until Griffin righted himself.

"Mr. Gilmore, do you know who first owned that sofa?"

"The Contessa of Este."

The man tilted his head in an understated, aristocratic gesture of appreciation.

"You are as thorough in your preparation as I was informed you would be," came the reply. He sounded to Griffin like someone praising an expensive vintage at a wine tasting. "Yes, the Contessa of Este. Reputedly the most beautiful woman in Europe. Her portrait hangs in the Prado in Madrid. The Contessa was most admired for her flawless neck. Are you aware of how the Contessa died?"

"Poisoned."

"Do you know for what reason she was poisoned?"

"She was poisoned by a rival for the king of France's hand in marriage."

Another head bob. Despite his fear and the circumstances, Griffin enjoyed the respect the man was giving him. Where all this was going, Griffin had no idea.

"Indeed. She was poisoned. The cyanide burned a hole in her lovely throat. The Contessa died on that sofa directly behind you. She died," with his gunless hand he pointed, "right there."

Griffin heard a *fluuff*fing sound behind him. Turning, he saw what he realized, after a few seconds, was a bullet hole in the sofa where the man had pointed. Griffin needed a bit more time to realize the shot must have passed through the few inches of airspace between his arm and suit coat.

"Forgive the theatricality of my gesture, Mr. Gilmore. I trust my point is taken."

"Yup."

Conversation ceased for a few seconds. Music drifted up from downstairs. The jazz fusion trio was launching into Coldplay's "Viva La Vida." Griffin was watching the man in white's face. When the Coldplay began – following something classical—the man winced. He was too well mannered to be blatant about his displeasure, but his dislike of the pop rock replacing classical music was unmistakable.

"What do you want?" Griffin asked.

"Your American directness is appreciated, Mr. Gilmore. Our time here by necessity must be limited."

The man took two steps forward. He moved with a limp. The man pointed at the display case. In the movement his gold hatband caught the overhead lights and gleamed.

"You will repeat the process," he told Griffin.

"I'll what?"

"You will take the replica from the pocket of your suit coat. You will return the replica of the jailer's key to the display. And from the display case you will retrieve the original key, which you will then hand to me."

"Do you have any idea how hard that is to do?"

Griffin spoke reflexively. He was not trying to be confrontational – he wasn't that foolish. Nor was he angry, though he was not at all pleased with the way this scene was trending. More than anything else, Griffin was being informative. He figured the man in white ought to know.

"I am," the man paused, in search of the proper word, "cognizant of the difficulties posed by my request. Nonetheless, you have proven yourself quite capable."

Cognizant? Griffin thought. He tried to recall the last time he'd heard that word. His mind tended to pinball around at entirely the wrong times. He needed to focus. He looked at the gun pointing in his direction. The barrel seemed the width of the Harbor Tunnel. His focus improved greatly.

"I'm not sure I can do that again," Griffin admitted. "If I make a mistake – if at any point the weight inside the display changes, changes at all – the alarm goes off. I listened to a tape of the alarm being tested. It's ungodly loud."

"I am confident we will not need to concern ourselves with the alarm. I am confident in your skills, Mr. Gilmore."

Griffin said, "You are aware the key that I put back into the display – the original jailer's key – is the least valuable of the twelve keys in the display?"

"I am."

"You know that several of the other keys have appraised values ten times that of the jailer's key?"

"Yes."

"But this is the key you want?"

"It is. This is not about money, Mr. Gilmore. I need that key and you shall give it to me."

"If the alarm goes off," Griffin said, not stalling but genuinely curious, "what will you do?"

"I shall endeavor to exit the museum prior to the arrival of security."

"I'd like to see you try," Griffin said, happy to score a verbal point in their exchange, "with that limp."

"You would not see me try, Mr. Gilmore. You would be shot dead."

Griffin did as instructed. From his pocket, he took the replica and exchanged it for the original jailer's key. He could feel beads of sweat working their way down both sides of his face as he switched keys, again. When he was finished, as he had the first time, Griffin slipped the key into his coat pocket.

"No, Mr. Gilmore. You will kindly hand me the original key. Our business is now complete. I regret we could not meet under more congenial circumstances. May I inquire? Has your client perhaps mentioned he is himself of ancient Italian nobility?"

"Every chance he gets," answered Griffin, no longer surprised at the extent and accuracy of the man's knowledge.

The man in white responded with a bemused smile. He pulled a pair of latex gloves from the pocket of his suit coat.

As he put on the latex gloves, he explained, "It's true. He is a direct descendent of the first Duke Ferlinghetti, whose father was a Borgia pope. Did he tell you he needs the key to avenge his family's honor?"

"He did."

"That too is true. At least in the Duke's eyes. His father, the previous Duke, acquired substantial gambling debts at Monte Carlo. He sold the original key – the one you are still holding, despite my request – to a collector to help cover the debts. When the father was asked to contribute the key to a Rome museum, his nobleman's pride did not permit him to admit the key had been sold. He had an identical, though worthless, copy of the key made, which he then donated to the museum. That key became part of this exhibit.

"The son's vices are not as expensive as the father's. The son, the current Duke, was able this year to buy back the key from the collector, who himself had fallen on hard times. Now the Duke has the real key but wants – is *needs* too strong? – to give the key to the exhibit. In his mind placing the real key in the exhibit restores the family honor. The current Duke is quite determined to satisfy his family honor, no?"

"Yes."

"Hence, when the exhibit of Italian keys traveled to Baltimore, your services were engaged by the Duke to switch the keys. Mr. Gilmore, I fear he will not be pleased when you meet him this evening with empty hands. Your fee arrangement is half payment in advance and the rest upon delivery of the duplicate key, I believe."

"Yeah," Griffin replied, thinking, Why aren't I surprised he knows that?

"My profuse apologies for your financial setback. But, alas."

But alas, indeed, thought Griffin.

The man limped forward to receive the key. Again the room lights caused the gold hatband to shimmer brightly.

He accepted the real key from Griffin, then motioned with the gun for Griffin to step back and to sit. Which Griffin did, on the spot where the Contessa of Este had died of cyanide.

"I shall see myself out, Mr. Gilmore."

The man limped backward out of the room. Griffin remained on the sofa until the man in white reached the hallway. From there to the door at the end of the hallway was no more than twenty feet. The man was through the door before Griffin reached the hallway.

Griffin considered but decided against chasing the man down the steps. Doing so might invite getting shot. Instead Griffin ran back into the room and went to the window at the far end. He arrived in time to spot a car, an older Buick-sized vehicle, a real land yacht, stop by a curb. In less than five seconds the man in white reappeared and got into the car. The car sped away. Griffin caught most but not all of the Maryland license plate: something, something R 187.

A few minutes later Griffin collected Annie and Bobby and started on the long walk to Kit in the limo. He wondered what the client would say, when Griffin arrived with what the man in white had called, far too accurately, empty hands.

Three

June 4
9:41 pm

"I am not looking forward to this," Griffin said. "First time I met the Duke he tossed a pheasant from room service out the window, because it was undercooked. This was twelve stories up, mind you."

"Just like that he heaved it out the window?"

"I got a couple seconds warning when he cleared his throat, Kit. Then the pheasant went flying."

It was half an hour later. Griffin, Annie, and Bobby were riding in the limo to Duke Ferlinghetti's hotel room. Kit, Griffin's best friend since kindergarten, was driving. The champagne remained unopened.

"I am not looking forward to this," Griffin repeated. No one else said anything. Griffin knew they weren't looking forward to this either.

"What I can't get over," he said next, "is how much he knew about me. My name, our client's name, our arrangements for payment, why we'd been hired. He knew everything he needed to know."

"Did he know about us?" Covington "Kit" Carson asked over his shoulder as he turned onto Pratt Street. Doing so, he cut off an SUV, whose horn blared in protest. Griffin suppressed the urge to cower beneath the dashboard. "Did this man in white know about Me, Annie, Bobby?"

"Hey, Kit? Amigo?" Bobby yelled over the SUV's horn. "I thought you said you had a chauffeur's license."

"I said I was *thinking about* getting a chauffeur's license," Kit answered. "I did watch some YouTube videos on limo driving."

"Did this man in white know about the three of you?" Griffin asked, repeating Kit's question. "Annie, how many servers were working the museum fundraiser tonight?"

Annie bit her lip as she thought. "Seven."

"And you served him, just before I went upstairs to switch keys."

"A couple times I served him. He walked past other servers to get to me."

"Which tells us he knew you were with me."

"He was so well mannered, Griffin. That perfect gentleman you hear about and never meet. At five hundred dollars a ticket you'd think the guests would be better behaved. I wish. There was so much grabbing for the grilled curried shrimp half my tray got spilled. I barely managed to avoid getting it on my clothes."

"I wasn't so lucky," Bobby said, pointing to a greenish-yellow blotch on his right tuxedoed leg, mid-shin. "I played Ibsen in summer stock in these pants. One of the brats pelted me with a hors d'oeuvre. Twice."

"A token of the child's appreciation for your performance tonight, I'm sure," Griffin told Bobby. Neither of them smiled. "Annie, by any chance did the man in white touch a glass?"

"Not that I saw."

"I'm not surprised," Griffin said. "That he never touched a glass. He put on latex gloves before leaving the room. With his limp he'd have to use the railing getting down the stairs. That might have left fingerprints. He's too careful to leave prints.

"The Hotel Monaco's up here, Kit. Hang a left on Charles Street."

Kit did, causing an MG convertible, top down on this warm summer night, to slam on its brakes. A pair of middle fingers emerged over the windshield, pointed in the limo's direction.

"Oh, come on," Kit said, pulling into a parking space after bouncing off the curb. A doorman who had been on the sidewalk flattened himself against a wall to avoid becoming the limo's hood ornament. "It wasn't that close."

"Yeah, it was," Bobby said, climbing out of the limo as quickly as he could.

"I'm not looking forward to this," Griffin said again.

★

Griffin hesitated before knocking on the hotel room door, so Annie knocked for him.

"Best to just get it over with," she told him.

"You may enter," Duke Ferlinghetti called from inside. "There is wine to toast your success."

The four of them stepped inside the suite, Kit taking up the end of their reluctant parade. The lights were off. The only illumination came from a dozen candles, which sputtered and gave off a smell faintly reminiscent of a backed up toilet.

"These candles," the Duke explained, his back to them, "were made on my family's Tuscan estate during the Napoleonic invasion. With no other source of tallow for the candles, the servants were forced to use the carcasses of diseased cattle."

Which may explain the smell, Griffin thought.

Griffin had endured the candle lecture before, so he could let his mind wander to the man in white. The obvious questions *Who is this guy?* and *How does he know so much about me?* did not hold his attention long.

Of greater interest to Griffin was the point the man had made: *This isn't about money*. What then, Griffin wondered, is it about? For Duke Ferlinghetti it was about his family's honor. What was it about for this man in white?

The lecture on the Napoleonic candles was at full bore. On both sides of him Griffin could see Bobby and Annie standing with an appearance of feigned interest plastered on their faces, like students waiting out a principal's lecture.

Griffin asked himself how much he knew about the man in white. Spanish, knowledgeable, refined – Griffin recalled the man wincing when the jazz fusion trio started performing – and certainly well mannered, as Annie said. His age? Uncertain, anywhere from mid-forties to sixty or so. Thinking back, Griffin realized he hadn't felt threatened, though he never doubted the man would have shot him if necessary.

The candle lecture had apparently ended. Duke Ferlinghetti, still with his back to them, announced, "Fill their glasses, Gretchen, dear. It is time to toast our success. The Ferlinghetti honor has been restored."

To the Duke's right, a tall blonde, spilling out of her low cut silvery gown poured wine into four glasses. In the uncertain candlelight Griffin could barely see the bottle's label, which showed a drawing of the key now in the possession of the man in white.

Griffin looked at the woman pouring the wine. Her hand was shaky and more wine wound up outside the glasses than in.

He tried to remember if this was the same blonde he'd seen when meeting the Duke in Manhattan in the spring to discuss the assignment. Griffin doubted it. Wasn't her name Ursula? To his recollection she'd also worn a silvery, cleavage-y gown. Apparently the Duke liked his women tall and Scandinavian and scantily clad. He seemed to have an assembly line and this was the latest model.

"That wine is also from your ancestral Tuscan estates, isn't it?" Griffin prompted, delaying the moment a bit longer.

"It is," Duke Ferlinghetti answered, and went off on a lecture explaining the superiority of grapes grown within sight of the sea.

Griffin felt himself smiling, and not only at the Duke's self-importance, so easily manipulated. Griffin could not help but admire how effectively the man in white had managed the heist of the key, and the style with which he had done so.

Griffin heard the Duke go on about how "temperamental" grapes are and how "shy" they can be. He listened with half an ear to the Duke's lecture. Griffin was focusing on the huge and ancient car the man had escaped in. The choice of vehicle left Griffin puzzled. The car seemed downmarketly out of character for the man in white.

"The grapes, you understand, must be protected from the rot which has ruined so many vineyards of inferior —" Duke Ferlinghetti stopped abruptly, as if he'd slammed on his verbal brakes. Griffin knew the man was not a total fool. He was sensing Griffin's efforts at delay.

Duke Ferlinghetti spun around to face the four of them. Griffin was surprised, as he had been meeting the Duke, how commonplace he appeared. Average height, average build; chubby faced. He could have been an accountant or bureaucrat or anything. His only unusual physical feature was the hair which stuck out from the side of his head, too much like Bozo the clown to be ignored. The blue blood of nobility? Griffin wasn't impressed.

"I would like you to give me the replica of my family's key now, Mr. Gilmore."

"I'd like to give you the replica, too."

"I beg your pardon?"

"I very much wish I could give you what you hired me to retrieve," Griffin said. "But I can't."

His answer angered the Duke, who placed his wine glass on the windowsill behind him. He grabbed a pint of Etrusca bottled water from the table in front of him. He put the Etrusca on the table but kept his hand on the bottle's neck.

Griffin asked, "Do you know a Spaniard, dresses entirely in white, good, very formal English but with a bit of an accent, walks with a limp?"

The question was so unexpected, Griffin had no doubt the man answered honestly.

"Spanish, you say? Not Italian?"

"Spanish."

"No. I know no such individual that you describe."

"It'd be better if you did, since he's got the real key. The museum still has the replica."

"You have failed me, Mr. Gilmore?" Duke Ferlinghetti asked, through clenched teeth.

He looked Griffin up and down with blatant disgust. Now I know how a cockroach spotted on the kitchen floor feels, Griffin thought.

The Duke tightened his grip on the bottled water. At this point Griffin knew he was in a race. If he explained what had happened at the museum fast enough, the Duke's noble anger might be restricted to screaming. Otherwise, the water and whatever else was within his reach would go airborne.

Griffin, always a fast talker, spoke as quickly as he could. To his ears he sounded as speedy as a legal disclaimer at the end of a commercial. But he was not fast enough, not nearly.

He was describing the man in white's climbing into the huge, ancient car when the Duke cleared his throat and the bottled water came tomahawking in Griffin's direction.

The Estruca spun in around chest high. Griffin was able to sidestep the incoming bottle, giving it a clean olè, but Kit never saw the bottle coming. The Etrusca hit his chauffeur's cap, sending it flying.

Griffin knew he should have simply left at that point, or at the very least kept his mouth shut. But prudent behavior had never been his strong point.

"You sure you don't know this man in white?" he asked. "He sure knows a lot about you."

Next object airborne was a glass of wine, heaved in Bobby's direction. Bobby easily avoided the glass, but wine flew everywhere, including onto his slacks.

"Tell me," Bobby said. "Does your ancestral wine go with grilled curried shrimp?"

The Duke heaved another glass, aimed at Annie, but which caught Gretchen on the jaw.

"Get out," he ordered.

They did not have to be told twice. From the hallway they heard Duke Ferlinghetti yell, "Forget about your money! Forget about my key!"

As an exclamation point, a bottle slammed against the door they had stepped through minutes earlier.

"I'll forget about the money," Griffin said, loudly enough for Annie, Bobby, and Kit to hear. "But I'm not forgetting about the key."

Four

The next morning the four of them were having coffee in the living room of Annie and Griffin's house in Parkville.

"From now on," Griffin told Annie, Bobby, and Kit, "we're working on contingency. I can't even guarantee that. If none of you is interested in continuing with this, I'd understand. But I want – I badly want – to get that key back. And I can't imagine doing so without your help."

Kit, who lived in a renovated garage behind the house, answered quickly, flashing his gap toothed grin, "Nah, I'm in." Annie said, "So of course." Bobby nodded to show he was in as well. He poured himself another cup of coffee. Bobby had gone cold turkey on the booze earlier in the year and Griffin knew some mornings were difficult. This seemed to be one of those mornings. Bobby's cup shook as he sipped.

"So. What do we do now, Griffin?" Annie asked.

Griffin paced by the open screen door. Temps had already slammed past 90, by nine o'clock. Another hot, muggy Baltimore summer day was muscling in.

Griffin explained, "This morning I'd like the three of you to call on our contact in the federal government."

"You mean Grace," Annie said.

"Sure. See Grace in Washington. Tell her what happened last night. Duke Ferlinghetti is obnoxious and condescending, but he's got clout in Italian politics. He's a steady ally of American interests in the European Union. Grace helped arrange the museum's cooperation for last night. She'll want to know how it went down anyway.

"If you can, find out from Grace who this man in white is. Why's he so interested in the key? He's Spanish, we know that. Does the Ferlinghetti family have some kind of beef with some Spanish noble from centuries ago? Gotta say – the man in white carries himself like a count or baron or whatever. Whoever he is, he went through enormous trouble – and would have killed me if necessary – to get that key. We need to know why.

"Is he a collector of historical artifacts? Does he buy and sell and steal them for a living or a hobby? Why else did he go through all the trouble he obviously did? Grace can contact Interpol or whoever handles trade in stolen artifacts in Europe. We can't give her much of a description to work with, but ask anyway. Find out anything you can about him.

"While you're at it, have Grace request a ballistics report on the bullet the man in white so skillfully sent in my direction. He didn't leave behind any fingerprints, but he did leave that bullet. A shell casing, too, I assume. Let's hope that will tell us something about who he is. Tell Grace everything I've told you, but don't tell her two things."

Griffin looked out the screen door. The morning sun was blasting off the windshields of cars parked on the street.

Holding up one finger Griffin said, "Don't tell Grace what the man in white said: *This isn't about money*. If we can learn what it *is* about, we're a lot closer to recovering that key. That's for us to find out. If we can."

He held up a second finger. "One other thing I don't want Grace knowing. I saw some of the letters and numbers of the license plate of the car the man in white rode away in. I'm going to trace that plate. That's doable online, but my computer skills aren't up to it. I'll need some help."

"Who you thinking of going with, Griffin?" Kit asked.

"Remember Saif Venkatesan from high school? Shy, smart, orderly, do your homework first thing every afternoon kid. Remember him?" They all did. "Serious computer jock. Absolute genius at the computer keyboard. Several standard deviations of talent better than mine. He's an assistant professor of statistics at Johns Hopkins University. I'll see him while you're in Washington.

"The license plate's our starting point for getting to the man in white, who stole the key from us. The man in white is right – this isn't about money. Not to me anymore it isn't. We were hired to do a job and we're going to finish the job."

"But, Griffin," Annie said, "why not tell Grace whatever you know about the license plate? The government could trace it easy enough. Don't forget, without Grace's help in December? Those charges against you that were dropped might not have been dropped."

"Which kept me out of jail. But since then Grace has been promoted along with her boss. Her plate is not only bigger, it's a lot fuller. We'll only ask her for the things we can't get ourselves. I think Saif can do this. Hope so at least. Any other questions?"

There were none. Kit said, "Alright! This week I'm leasing a Porsche 911. My ride is seven speed, got self-dimming mirrors. I wanna let it rip out on I-95."

Bobby slugged back the last of his coffee. He put his cup down with a nervous chinking sound, and pleaded, "Can't Annie drive?"

★

From outside the office of Professor Saif Venkatesan, Griffin watched his old high school classmate at work. Saif's fingers were nearly blurry with speed sliding over the computer keyboard. Saif paused to study a graph on his computer monitor. Immediately he shook his head, typed a few seconds. Another graph appeared. This he studied a bit longer, before shaking his head again.

"Is that for 'The Inexactitude of Econometric Analysis'"?

"Yes," Saif replied, eyes still on the computer screen. Turning in his chair he continued speaking, "Yes, this is for my doctoral-" His dark brown eyes widened in surprise.

"Griffin Gilmore! Griffin, how have you been?" Saif scrambled out of his chair to shake hands. "Griffin, I haven't seen you since, since you, since you were, ah..." He trailed off.

"Since I was arrested last December. The feds dropped their prosecution against me for interstate transportation of stolen goods. State charges for burglary and theft were dropped as well. Once I had retrieved what it is they wanted back."

Griffin had a quick memory from December, six months earlier. He was standing in falling snow with Grace and her boss, along with Annie, Kit and Bobby. Their assignment was completed. They had recovered and returned what the government needed returned. Griffin had a very clear picture of holding the paper charging him with burglary and theft. After Grace nodded her approval, he ripped the pages into tiny pieces and let the winter wind carry them away.

"Saif, I'm in business now, which is why I've here today."

Griffin looked around Saif's office. Floor to ceiling text books and scholarly articles. The books were arranged alphabetically by author and the journals by publication date. On the wall was a picture of Albert Einstein on a sailboat.

"I checked you out online before coming here, Saif. Inexactitude is a word I hadn't heard before, but I think I understand what it means. Who are econometricians?"

"Charlatans, mostly. Griffin, it's great to see you again. You were the smartest guy in our high school class."

"When I bothered showing up for class."

"I'll never forget." Saif leaned back in his chair, smiling. "That time senior year when you went to AP Physics class with me. The teacher gave a pop quiz. You got the highest grade, a 99. The teacher took off a point for not showing your work."

"I didn't need to show the work, Saif. I could do it in my head."

Saif shook his head with admiration. "And you weren't even in the class, you just showed up that day."

"Annie was home sick that day. I had nothing better to do."

Saif glanced at the room crowded with books and journals, a very mixed expression on his face. He told Griffin, "I'm sorry, but I have-"

"A summer session class in ten minutes, I know. As I said, I checked you out online before coming here. This isn't just a drive by, Saif. Here's what I came to ask. You remember our classmates Bobby Lowell, Kit Carson, Annie Knaack?"

"Sure do. You guys were always so tight. You're still with Annie?"

"Still am. The four of us have a kind of business where we help folks retrieve whatever it is they need back. And we do so without anyone knowing it was ever gone. Last night I was working at the Baltimore Museum of Art and a man showed up very unexpectedly."

"You're not telling me everything, are you?"

"Not just yet. This gentleman left in a car with the item I was paid to retrieve. I managed to see some but not all of the car's license plate."

"How much of the license plate have you got?"

"Here's what I saw of the plate: Maryland tags. Something, something, R 187.

"What can you tell me about the car the plate belongs to? Car make and model. And the owner – date of birth, family, address, prior arrests, whatever public information is readily available. I know some of the websites with publicly available information cost. We'll reimburse for expenses. Doable?'

"Doable, sure, with limitless time and resources. Here's the problem, Griffin. You've got two alpha variables here. The two missing letters. That's way too many potential combinations to search. I mean, the plate could be AAR 187, ABR 187, all the way to AZR 187. Then it's BAR 187, CAR 187, and so on. I could give you the total number of possible permutations."

"Won't be necessary. Would it help if I narrowed the field?"

"Immensely," Saif replied. "Parameterization would be very helpful."

Griffin thought back to the car as it pulled away from the curb. "The vehicle's got to be more than fifteen years old. Could be much older. Huge car, maybe eight cylinders, from way back in the day. Likely American made."

"I can do this between classes today. I'll work through lunch."

"Annie and I have a house off Harford Road. Kit, Annie, and Bobby and me'll meet you there at six." He handed Saif an index card with the address. "I know you're busy, with your classes and doctoral defense coming up, but can you make it? I can assure you Annie, Kit and Bobby would love to see you. And we need your help. You still like the pepperoni with extra cheese from the place over on Joppa Road?"

"I haven't had one in years, but, yes, I assume so."

"There'll be one waiting for you at our house. If we get paid, we'll share the money with you. Can't promise that, though."

Saif again looked around the room. The mixed expression returned to his face.

"Don't worry about my getting paid," he told Griffin. "It's enough to get together with you guys again."

"See you at six."

★

Annie waved a pizza slice at Griffin as he came up their sidewalk. She stepped away from Kit, Bobby, and Saif on the porch and waited for Griffin at the top of the steps. Her blonde hair seemed to catch the sunlight. Annie had on sandals, pink tee shirt, golden earrings more than an inch across, cut off jeans and her long, long legs. The earrings shook cheerfully as she waved. She also wore a smile that Griffin – who could read her smiles with satisfying accuracy – meant *Saif's fitting right in.*

Kit was saying, "Remember our history teacher, ninth grade?"

"Mr. Hackett," answered Griffin, walking up the steps. Annie passed him her pizza slice. He bit off the bottom third of the slice before passing it back. The pizza tasted of Saturday nights the five of them spent together in high school.

"You know he had an affair with the French teacher?" This was Annie. "Remember how he'd drive off at lunch and get back to school just as lunch period was ending. She'd show up at the same time, in her car. Like we were all too dumb to figure out what was going on if they just drove separate cars. His shirt would be unbuttoned; hers wasn't tucked back into her slacks. He and the French teacher used to go out to Loch Raven reservoir at lunch and park."

"Remember Phys Ed class freshman year?" Griffin asked. "When we played Shark and Octopus on the football field? One student was selected the Shark-"

"Usually you," Bobby reminded him.

"No doubt because he was the most disruptive," Annie said, laughing.

"All the other students were an octopus. The shark – and you're right, Bobby, it was always me – had to tag someone. Once a student got tagged the student became a shark too. The sharks kept tagging other students who became sharks until only one student had not been tagged. I can remember every time we played Shark and Octopus I felt like I was going to drop I was so tired from running around so much. There were classes I thought I'd never be able to last long enough to get everyone."

"But you always did," Kit told him.

"I did because the four of you helped me. Not sure why I thought of Shark and Octopus right now," Griffin said. Annie looked at him, a smile of understanding forming.

They tore into the last pizza. The stories continued until the pizza boxes were empty. Kit smoked a Cuban cigar.

"C'mon inside," Griffin said at last. "We got business."

Five

Griffin placed an 8 by 10 photo on the coffee table in front of Saif, who sat on one end of the living room couch. Bobby sat on the other end, Annie between. On her lap slept a calico cat she had rescued from a snow storm that winter. Griffin had named the cat Dr. Eckleburg, after a character in his favorite novel, *The Great Gatsby*.

Kit leaned against a windowsill. There were no chairs in the living room. The couch and coffee table were as far as Annie and Griffin had gotten in their house decorating.

"This," Griffin explained to Saif, while pointing at the picture, "is the key we're trying to retrieve. Eight and a half inches long. Heavier than it looks; exactly fourteen and a half ounces. The key was originally the property of a jailer in Arazzo, Italy, whose name is lost to history. Made 1715, or thereabouts. The unknown jailer was in the employ of Duke Ferlinghetti, whose duchy includes Arazzo.

"The count's present descendant hired us. Here is a picture of the current Duke Ferlinghetti. The picture was taken this year at a Parisian restaurant. The blonde sitting with him, I'm pretty sure, isn't Ursula or Gretchen, who I've both met."

"I don't care what her name isn't," Kit said, eyeing the picture intently. "She comes to Baltimore? Somebody let me know, wouldja?"

Griffin resumed. "At the Baltimore Museum of Art right now there is a touring exhibit about life among the Italian nobility in the 18th Century. Part of the exhibit are twelve keys from that time and place. Last night we went to a fundraiser at the BMA."

Saif tapped the first picture. "To steal – I mean retrieve – this key?'

"You'd think so, wouldn't you?" Griffin said, impressed with Saif's ability to jump ahead in his thinking. "But no. Strange as it seems, we were hired to take a worthless replica of this key from the exhibit and replace it with the original key."

Griffin explained to Saif how Duke Ferlinghetti had felt the need to avenge his family's honor by replacing the fake key with the real one. His account was quick but thorough. At one point he even lowered his voice a bit, as if inserting a footnote into the text. This was when he mentioned the "This isn't about money" line.

"Then, last night – when I'm no more than seconds from a clean getaway with the replica key in my pocket and the real key safely in the display case – a man dressed all in white shows up.

"Annie, Kit and Bobby spent the day in Washington with a contact we have in the federal government. They're trying to find out about this guy in white. Who pulled a gun on me, by the way. And took the key from me, after I'd done the hard work of switching keys. He made me switch the keys back. Bobby? Tell me and Saif about your day in Washington."

★

"This won't take long, amigo," Bobby said, leaning forward on the couch. "We worked all afternoon in DC with Grace. We didn't learn anything about the man in white."

"And Grace sends you her best," Annie added.

"And Grace sends you her best," Bobby said, leaning back on the couch. "Sorry, Griffin."

"Don't worry, Bobby. I spent all afternoon online until I was on the verge of retina burn. Came up with zero also."

Griffin looked out the living room window. The sky was sliding into twilight. The evening was warm, though no longer hot. Still looking out the window, Griffin said, "You're telling me we don't know anything more about the man in white than we did last night?"

"Fraid not."

"Bobby, we have no idea how he learned we'd been hired by Duke Ferlinghetti? And all the other details he knew about me? He wasn't guessing or speaking in generalities. He *knew.*"

Bobby Lowell, an actor who randomly practiced accents, replied in the voice of a Kentucky colonel.

"Well, suh-" he said, nodding at the picture of Duke Ferlinghetti and the unknown blonde in the Paris restaurant. "Suh, maybe we do know" – *know* was two syllables somehow – "somethin' about that."

Griffin looked directly at Bobby. "What do we know, colonel?" Griffin asked.

Bobby replied not in an accent, but in his own voice, a voice flattened with sadness.

"Look at the woman's eyes." Everyone in the room did. "Look at her stare. No life there; none at all. She's gone. She's physically in the restaurant, sure, but that poor woman's not really there. She's on her way to her next fix or next drink or next whatever it is she needs to keep going. I know that Duke Ferlinghetti is an obnoxious turd – forgive my language, Annie."

"No, you can say it. He's a turd."

"It seems the turdish Duke Ferlinghetti has a regular supplier of tall, model-y blondes. Remember the blonde last night, in the hotel suite? Pouring the wine she kept missing our glasses. Even at the time I could tell her problem wasn't the candlelight. Her hands shook." Bobby paused, looking at his own hands.

"I assume the Duke bankrolls each blonde's particular habit, in exchange for what we can all guess. Is there anyone here who doubts the Duke would resort to that? And addicts – whatever their particular poison – are the world's worst secret keepers. The blondes probably then turned around and sold what they knew to the man in white.

"I-" Bobby hesitated, and when he spoke his voice came out clear but distant, the voice of a man looking at himself and not caring for what he saw.

"I couldn't admit it to any of you – and I know this isn't my best profile – but in the fall I tried rehab for my drinking. The key word there is tried. I snuck out of rehab in the middle of the second night. Hit a North Avenue liquor store on the way home. I wasn't ready." He pointed again at the woman in the picture. "I saw plenty of those lifeless stares in rehab. I saw one when I looked in the mirror.

"Then, Griffin, you called me just before Christmas last year. You asked if I could help you and Annie and Kit with something. If that worked out, you said the feds would drop their case against you. You didn't know it but having some-thing to do that mattered kept me out of my jail too. Haven't had a drink five months now. Hardly even want one anymore."

"No worries," Griffin quietly said.

Annie reached over, touched Bobby softly twice on the forearm. It was, Griffin knew, the perfect, understated gesture of support.

The silence stretched comfortably a few seconds, broken by Griffin saying, "I'm sure you're right, Bobby. That's how the man in white found out Duke Ferlinghetti had hired us and knew what we planned to do last night. Through the Duke's blondes is how he knew. They passed along to the man in white all our plans as I so conveniently explained them to the Duke."

"You going to tell the Duke about that?" Annie wondered.

"Tell the Duke *he* caused the theft of his beloved key?" Griffin said. "I'd have to wear full body Kevlar armor to do that. God only knows what would go flying in my direction. Besides, what good would it do? I don't know anything about those blondes, even their last names."

"And I doubt the Duke does either," Bobby finished for him.

"And even assuming Duke Ferlinghetti could track down these blondes," Griffin went on, "how much could they tell us – women who sold information to the man in white while they sold their companionship to the Duke. These ladies would be close to useless. And the man in white, if I am any judge, wouldn't be careless enough to put himself in a position where they could hurt him. No, unfortunately, the blondes will get us no closer to finding out who the man in white is. Grace didn't help. Let's hope we can find out about the man in white from another direction.

"Guess you're on now, Saif. What can you tell us about the license plate of the car the man in white drove off in last night?"

★

"Griffin, here's what I learned about the partial plate you gave me," Saif began. He'd printed out his notes but did not need to consult them.

"You had all but the first two letters of the license plate. Turns out the plate is *DNR* 187. You said the car was an old land yacht, and it is that – a 1996 Buick Riviera. The vehicle was owned by a Miss Andrea Marie Platts. She was the original and only owner."

"Was? Not is? You mean the car was stolen?"

"That too."

"Ah, Saif-"

"Griffin, the car owner, Miss Platts, is dead."

"Meaning we can safely assume she wasn't driving last night."

"Safe assumption. I knew you'd want to know, so here's what I can tell you about her. She never married. No children. No sibs. No prior arrests. No bankruptcies, no debts. She resided the last fifteen years of her life at the Oakecrest Village retirement community. Died March 16 of this year, age 86.

"With no close relatives and no will, there was some squabbling about which second cousin would inherit the estate. Lawyers got involved, there was a one inch, single paragraph article about it in the Baltimore *Sun* newspaper on April 12."

"What was in the estate?" Griffin wondered.

"Besides the Buick? Some stocks. A bit of cash. Oh, and several dozen salt and pepper shakers she liked to collect."

Griffin motioned for Saif to continue.

"April 16, four days after the article appeared in the paper, the Buick Riviera was stolen from the Oakecrest Village parking lot. You know Oakecrest?"

"Sure. It's just a couple miles from here. My grandmom's at Oakecrest."

"Then you know how big the place is, Griffin. The car theft wasn't noticed for a couple days. I accessed a report filed with the Baltimore County police. One of the guards at the place thought he'd seen someone in the parking lot who didn't seem to belong there. All he remembered of this guy is that he had tattoos on both arms and reeked of what the guard described as a 'strange mix of Aqua Velva and whiskey.' Strange must be putting it mildly. That's it. That's all I could find."

"Well played, Saif."

Griffin looked out the window once more. The sky was streaked with red-rimmed clouds; another hot day tomorrow.

"Okay, let's walk through the time line," he said. "I think better when I can see it in writing. Kit, hand me that empty box, will you?"

"You're going to write on a pizza box?"

"Abraham Lincoln wrote the Gettysburg Address on the back of an envelope."

"Somehow," Kit said, giving Griffin the pizza box, "it sounds almost logical when you say it."

★

"First off, March 4." Griffin made a mark and wrote the date on the pizza box, "I get a phone call from Grace. She's been contacted by an obnoxious Italian duke nobody likes. But he's a strong ally of our country, so she's got to help him if she can. The Count has this somewhat weird request – put a real key into a museum exhibit in place of a fake one. And do it without anyone knowing it's been done. His Ferlinghetti honor is at stake. Obviously this isn't something the federal government can touch, so they have to go off the books.

"That same day, Grace contacts me. Which makes sense, since this is just the sort of thing we do, retrieve stuff without anyone noticing. Besides, the exhibit with the key to be switched is coming to Baltimore on its tour of American museums.

"On March 16, poor Miss Platts departs this life." Griffin wrote the date in a pepperoni stain on the box. "On April 12," another mark, this in a streak of tomato sauce, "the article in the *Sun* appears about the squabble over the estate of Andrea Platts. The estate consists of her big, old car and not much else of interest. I'm assuming no one but the dearly departed cared about the salt and pepper shakers."

"Safe assumption," Saif agreed.

"By this time I've been in frequent contact and even met with the Duke. Whichever blonde he's with at the time is aware of this. She's there when the Duke and I are on the phone. She's there when the Duke and I meet. She would know what I'm planning and that Bobby, Kit and Annie will be working with me on this.

"Whatever the blondes' addictions, addicts need money, right?" Bobby nodded. "The man in white seemed to have lots of it. He could find out what we've been hired to do easily enough, through buying off the blonde du jour. All he needed to know about was the Duke's interest in the key. Which he told me last night he knew about."

Griffin continued and another mark went on the pizza box.

"On April 16 the Buick Riviera is stolen from the Oakecrest parking lot. As you noted, Saif, the retirement community is huge. The disappearance of one old car isn't likely to be noticed right away. Apparently this guy with the tattoos and Aqua Velva and whiskey boosted the Buick without a key.

Hotwire the car; jam a screwdriver into the ignition. With a car this old? Certainly very doable.

"We know next to nothing about the man in white, but we can be sure he's from out of town. He knew he'd need a car. Not something he rented or bought, which would leave a traceable paper trail. Once he saw the article in the *Sun,* he figured the Riviera was right for his purpose. He wouldn't even have to be in Baltimore for that. The paper can be read online from anywhere in the world. He'd hire someone to steal the car. Then have the car sit someplace safe for a while."

"Wouldn't the police be looking for a stolen car?"

"Months after it was stolen, Saif? Not likely. "At the museum fundraiser?" Griffin pressed on. "While I was watching the man in white ride off into the night? His choice of getaway car surprised me. A huge, ancient American car? He seemed a brand new Maserati or Bentley type. But now his mode of transit makes sense, for the reasons we've just gone over."

Griffin tapped the pizza box against his knee. It was a soft, contemplative tap.

"The Oakecrest Village car thief – our Aqua Velva and whiskey man – likely hid the car someplace until last night, when the man in white needed it. My guess is he drove the man in white to the museum fundraiser."

More tapping of the pizza box against Griffin's knee. This was a harder, anger-flaring tap.

"The man in white wouldn't cab or Uber or Lyft to the fundraiser. Their riders can be easily traced. And a guy as distinctive as the man in white would be remembered.

"Last night I couldn't see the driver and obviously I couldn't smell him, but it wouldn't surprise me to learn the driver had tattoos and reeked of Aqua Velva and whiskey. It's logical to use the same man for both the theft of the getaway car and the getaway itself. Fewer people mean fewer problems, fewer chances for betrayal if anything goes wrong. It seems the man in white hired this Aqua Velva and whiskey guy as his car thief and his driver."

"Who is he, Griffin? And where is he now, do you think, the man in white?" Kit asked.

Griffin did not even attempt to answer the first question. To the second he replied quietly, "Somewhere in the world."

Griffin banged the pizza box against his knee with enough force the box bent.

"The man in white lets me do all the hard work – the planning, the learning how to pick locks, learning how to exchange the key without setting off the alarm. Once the man in white knew our plans, all he had to do was keep an eye on me at the fundraiser. Which he could do easily enough in that crowd. When I left for the second floor, he waited a few moments, then went after me. We do all the work and he gets the key. Truth is, he played us. Me especially. That's a slap in the face. We just can't let that go."

"Everything you mentioned, Griffin, took place in March and April and this is June," Bobby observed. "Seems the man in white has been planning this for a while."

Griffin agreed that was certainly true.

"And he's got brains enough and money enough to pull it off," Kit noted.

Griffin conceded that seemed to be the case.

"This key, it matters hugely to him," Saif concluded.

It must, Griffin said.

"But what," asked Griffin, who crumpled the pizza box some more. "What does the man in white want with the key? Is he a thief? Some people rob banks, some rob convenience stores, he robs museums?" Griffin quickly answered himself.

"That can't be the explanation. He knew that key is the least valuable of the twelve on display. But he wanted it anyway. What does he want with *that* key?"

Griffin began stabbing the box repeatedly with his pen "Why is he after the key? And what happens after he has the key, what does he want to do with it?"

Annie took the pizza box from Griffin. She said, "What does anyone want with a key?"

"I give up. What?"

"To open something that's locked."

Six

June 5
7:14 pm

"What you're pointing out," Griffin said, beginning to pace once more, "is that the man in white wants to get in somewhere."

In the rugless room, Griffin's pacing – he was always a clomper – echoed harshly. The calico, Dr. Eckleburg, scurried to safety behind the couch.

"So, Griffin? What was the key made to open?"

"Annie, it was made for the jailer in the Arazzo Castle, when the Ferlinghettis lived there, way, way back in the day. This was about 1715, remember. The key was made for a room or a jail cell, I suppose. But where? The jailer's not around to ask."

"He's not, but could the jail still be around?"

Griffin stopped his pacing. The question had not occurred to him.

"I knew there was a reason I liked you," he said to Annie. This earned him a smile and a mock curtsy. "That must be why the man in white wanted the original key – to get into someplace in the jail. The replica wouldn't do him any good. The replica wouldn't open anything. It's just a replica."

"Could the jail still be around?" Annie asked again.

Griffin gave a maybe yes, maybe no tilt of his hand.

"The jail still could be, I suppose. That's a big could. The castle was sacked by Napoleon and flattened by Allied bombing during the Second World War. The Ferlinghettis haven't lived there in generations. The castle has been partially reconstructed into a tourist destination. It's kind of a fantasy camp for folks who want to live like a duke for a day. The brochure for the castle doesn't say if the jail survived."

"You got any idea how we can find out if the jail is still there?"

"I can help with that, Annie," Saif said. Everyone in the living room turned to hear Saif's unexpected contribution.

He said: "There's a professor at Hopkins. Saul Silverman. He's been emeritus for years now. One of the world's leading authorities in Italian history, Renaissance to Italian Unification. Almost eighty now, but he still keeps office hours every weekday morning. He'll be your starting point if you want to learn about an Italian castle that was around in the 18th century. Nobody knows more than Saul Silverman. I can introduce you."

Griffin said, "I agree that's our starting point, Monday morning. Bobby and I will go see him. But I don't want you introducing us. Time for you to get back to being a professor."

Saif's face crumpled in disappointment.

"Saif?" Griffin said, but seeing the hurt on Saif's face, he could not continue. Griffin tried again. "Saif, how long before your doctoral defense? About a month?"

"A little less."

"Only three weeks or so before you become Dr. Venkatesan."

"Likely."

"If I know you at all, Saif, there's no *likely* about it. That result is an absolute lock. Unless … Unless, of course, you're

50

spotted on the campus of Johns Hopkins University consorting with a man arrested just last year for committing a felony. Who would be me. And who happens to be engaging in the illegal activity of attempted theft of an historical artifact. Which is exactly what I want to do – steal back that key.

"Saif, we appreciate your help, enormously. It'd of taken me days to dig up what you got in an afternoon. But you can't afford to be seen with me."

Saif looked around the living room, almost furniture-free.

"Griffin, do you known how lucky you are this place is barely furnished?"

"What? Why?"

"Griffin, you and Annie can decorate this room however you want."

"And?"

Saif threw his arms out, as if trying to embrace the possibilities of the empty space.

"And you can hang purple drapes. And put zebra striped shag carpeting on the floor if you want. Or on the ceiling, if you want. My life is nothing like that. Ever since I can remember, I've been on a kind of highway, taking me to where my career is now. It's what my parents expect of me. I'm okay with that. I'm their only child. It's fine, really.

"But you guys aren't highway guys. You're off road guys. Let me be part of this. We'll keep a firewall between you and me at Hopkins; what you say makes sense. But I want to be part of this. It's fun to go off road occasionally."

"That it is," Griffin replied.

"Just don't tell my Mom and Dad."

"Done," Griffin agreed.

Saif leaned back against the couch contentedly.

Griffin said, "Here are Monday's assignments.

"Kit and Annie, go to Oakecrest. Pretend you're looking into an apartment for an elderly relative. See if you can talk to the security guard who saw the car thief, our Aqua Velva and whiskey man. Could the guard know something about the thief that didn't make it into that one inch *Sun* article?

"Bobby? Monday morning you and I go to Hopkins. Maybe we can learn a bit of Italian history."

★

June 8
9:29 am

"Do you have a scheduled appointment this morning?" the History Department secretary asked. She was a short, squareish woman wearing a sweater the red of a brick wall.

"Nothing scheduled, no."

"If you don't have an appointment scheduled, I'm afraid you won't be able to see Dr. Silverman. I could certainly schedule an appointment," the secretary said. She spoke in a tone that left Griffin certain that while she *could* schedule an appointment, she'd rather eat that red sweater.

"Allow me to explain," Bobby said, then dryly chuckled. "I'm Dr. Rob Robertson, of Cornell."

The night before, searching for a role Bobby could play, Griffin learned there actually was a Dr. Rob Robertson of Cornell. Dr. Robertson was presently on sabbatical in the Amazon Rain Forest and unlikely to complain about Bobby Lowell appropriating his name this morning.

"Dr. Silverman and I met my junior year abroad. What was that, twenty years ago now?"

Bobby chuckled again. Griffin thought the chuckle was the perfect, credible detail for a WASP-ish Ivy League professor.

Bobby wore thick glasses with rectangular frames. His tie was askew and carelessly knotted, just enough of the absent minded professor to be believable.

"The years certainly fly past, don't they?" Bobby said, touching the hair at his temples, which he'd dyed grey.

He went on, "Twenty years ago I was spending my junior year abroad in Florence, Italy. A long, lonely year. Dr. Silverman befriended me. He and Mrs. Silverman. They were spending his sabbatical year researching his book on trade between the Italian city states and the Muslim world. That book would win the Herbert Baxter Adams prize, as you may well know."

Griffin had studied Saul Silverman's biography and provided Bobby with those details. Griffin glanced at the secretary to see if Bobby's performance was winning her over. There was no thawing in her glacial look of distrust.

"Dr. Silverman impressed me so much I decided to enter academia myself. Well, long story short, Dr. Silverman left me with an open invitation. If ever I was in Baltimore..." That chuckle again. "Well, here I am. Stopping in. Twenty years later."

The secretary remained unmoved.

"I'm sorry," she said. Not a bit was she sorry, Griffin knew. "You can't just show up and barge in on Dr. Silverman."

"It's hardly barging in, Marjory," came a frail voice to their right, Griffin looked at the nameplate on the woman's desk: Patricia Ann Knightsbridge. "I don't often have visitors."

"Dr. Silverman, I'm not Marjory. Marjory hasn't worked here in-" the secretary was saying as Bobby and Griffin hurried over to Professor Silverman. They directed Saul Silverman back toward his office before his secretary could object.

Their progress was slow. Bobby and Griffin flanked the professor. Each kept a hand near the man's elbow in case he needed assistance to keep moving, which he did several times.

Once inside the office, Dr. Silverman motioned for his guests to sit. Griffin studied the man's eyes. The best word to describe those brown eyes, Griffin decided, was faded. The backs of the man's hands were dotted with constellations of dark aged spots.

Dr. Silverman began, "I am sorry, Dr.- Who are you?"

"I'm Rob Robertson, Dr. Silverman," Bobby responded.

Griffin looked around the office. Maps yellow with age lined one wall. Books with papers sticking out overfilled shelves. There was an unmistakable sense of neglect about the room, completely unlike the precision of Saif's office.

"Don't apologize for not recognizing me, Dr. Silverman, after all these years. In my Florence days" – Griffin knew Bobby had never been east of Ocean City – "I had a beard, typical scruffy undergraduate thing."

Dr. Silverman said, "I enjoyed my year in Florence very much. My wife Susan joined me. It was 2004."

At the mention of his wife, Saul Silverman paused, struggling to continue. Griffin could tell Bobby noticed as well.

"This," Bobby said, pointing to Griffin, "is my co-author on a book we're writing. The work covers some ground in the area of your expertise, which is why we're here today."

"I'm William Haydon," Griffin said, rising to shake hands. He noticed Dr. Silverman's white shirt was fraying at the cuffs. Griffin said to him, "We're most interested in whatever you can tell us about Arazzo Castle."

★

"The castle in Arazzo?" The professor smiled. "Susan loved it there. We visited several times."

The smile faded. Saul Silverman stopped talking. Griffin heard the secretary on the phone, speaking pleasantly, nothing like the suspicious tone she'd hurled against Bobby and Griffin. Griffin understood her attitude now. She was protective of an elderly man in need of protection.

"Professor," Griffin prompted eventually. "What can you tell us about Arazzo Castle? How much of the original castle remains?"

"That was the last trip Susan could take abroad. After that, her troubles began." In a whisper, more of a gasp, Griffin thought, Dr. Silverman added, "It was pancreatic cancer."

After a few long moments, Dr. Silverman blinked, as if rousing himself.

"You asked about Arazzo Castle. I have some pictures here."

He reached for a desk drawer, but was unable to open it.

"I don't often open my desk these days. Still, the house seems so empty when I'm there."

While Griffin was puzzling out the disconnected sentences, Bobby leaped from his chair and slid the drawer open. He removed a book of photographs encased in plastic and placed the book in front of Dr. Silverman.

"Let's see," Dr. Silverman said, turning each page with what was to Griffin infuriating slowness. "You asked about St. Mark's in Venice."

"No," Griffin corrected him, "the Arazzo Castle."

"Of course. Susan loved Arazzo Castle. We visited several times," he replied, unaware he'd said that already.

He turned some more pages. Griffin feared the man had forgotten what he was searching for. More pages turned, even more slowly it seemed to Griffin. After an excruciating five minutes Dr. Silverman said, "Here we are."

This time Griffin scrambled to the other side of the desk much faster than Bobby.

"The picture was taken in Arazzo Castle. That's Susan," Professor Silverman explained.

"And that's you beside her," Bobby said.

"That was Susan's favorite dress," Dr. Silverman went on. "Cornflower blue. I got it for her birthday."

"Where?" Griffin asked.

"Here in Baltimore."

"No, professor," Griffin said, aware his voice was rising, but unable to stop himself. "Where was the picture taken?"

"The dungeon of Arazzo Castle. It was a sort of jail at one time."

"When?"

"October."

"No, professor," Griffin asked, as loudly as before. He really needed to dial back his impatience. "What year was the picture taken?"

"2004," Bobby answered, recognition dawning in his eyes. "My year in Florence."

"Meaning the dungeon survived Napoleon and the Second World War?" Griffin asked, but Saul Silverman did not hear, lost in the picture.

Griffin was staring at the picture as well. The Silvermans were standing in front of a large, very thick and very old door at the back of the dungeon. Between the Silvermans, Griffin noticed a metal bolt, shoulder high, on the door. After a few seconds he saw, barely visible, a metal keyhole.

To Bobby, Griffin said, "That's what the key is for."

Seven

June 8
10:03 am

From the middle of Charles Street, Griffin phoned Grace.

In lieu of hello, Grace said, "I've heard from the Duke. Again. Not at all is he pleased. You know, he's always been a steadfast supporter of our EU policies. For years now. We'd like him happier." In words that were at least as much demand as question, she asked, "You're still working on getting his key back?"

"I am," Griffin replied, now across Charles Street. He stepped onto the sidewalk alongside 33rd Street. Bobby was forced into a near-jog to keep pace. They approached empty tables outside a bookstore. At ten in the morning it was already too hot to sit outside. The sun was so bright it seemed to burn all the color from the morning.

At St. Paul Street they turned right. Over his shoulder Griffin could spot the cherry trees in front of Union Memorial Hospital. The trees were a gift of Al Capone, who'd come to Union Memorial to have his syphilis treated. Unsuccessfully, as it turned out. The gangster died not long after. The trees were a bit of Baltimore trivia Griffin liked to point out to visitors.

When he did and mentioned the syphilis, he was always quick to add, "Which Capone contracted *before* he came to Baltimore."

"Grace," Griffin said, "we're going to need your help on this one. We just met with a Hopkins history professor, an expert on Italian castles. He's gotten us started. From you I need whatever you can find on Arazzo Castle in Italy. Specifically, the Arazzo Castle dungeon. And we need whatever you can get right away. You remember the man in white who Bobby, Kit and Annie told you about?"

"Yes?"

Griffin reached his car, parked in front of Cold Stone Creamery. He said, "Pretty sure that's where he's going with the key – the dungeon of Arazzo Castle. There's a room in the back of the dungeon the man in white wants into. That's what the key is for. To unlock that door. We need to know what he wants in the dungeon before he's gets there and takes it."

June 9
7:00 pm

Thirty three hours later, Grace called Griffin back. She had said she would call at seven with the information about Arazzo Castle he asked for. She did, calling precisely at seven. As was her wont, Grace did not bother with preliminaries.

"We're too late," she started right in.

"You're on the speaker phone, Grace," Griffin replied. "I'm here in our dining room with Annie, Kit, and Bobby. You remember them. And our high school friend named Saif Venkatesan is here as well. And we're too late for what, exactly?"

"Your man in white has come and gone, Mr. Gilmore." Her tone was one Griffin had not heard in his phone calls with Grace. Was she gloating?

"He went to Arazzo Castle?"

"Yes."

"He went into the castle dungeon?"

"Yes."

"He went into the room at the back of the dungeon?"

"Yes."

"When was this?" he asked.

"Saturday afternoon."

"The museum fundraiser was Thursday night," Griffin pointed out. He was clueless where Grace was taking him with this. "He's plotted carefully. What did he take?"

"Nothing." There it was again. Not gloating as much as an I-know-something-you-don't- know tone. "He entered the room at the back of the dungeon. As you predicted he would. But he didn't take anything at all."

"Then why go through all the trouble of-"

"He wanted to take something, your man in white. I'm sure of it. Whatever it was, it wasn't there. He left empty handed."

Griffin sat on one side of his dining room table, Annie across from him. With no other chairs, Saif, Kit, and Bobby stood. Nearly empty cartons of Chinese food covered a table-cloth sandy with spilled rice.

"Grace?" Griffin started, then broke off, distracted when he glanced over at Kit. Who was shoveling in the remains of his shrimp fried rice with more speed than accuracy.

Kit wore a Hawaiian shirt. This was the third straight day of Hawaiian shirts, a streak that began when he watched a "Magnum, PI" marathon. Today's shirt showed a well-tanned castaway snoozing beneath a coconut tree.

"Grace," Griffin started again. "What makes you say that this guy – *my* man in white, as you call him –wanted to take something, but didn't? How can you know such a thing?"

"Because I've got the pictures to prove it."

★

From someone else, Griffin might have assumed the reply was a joke. Coming from Grace, whom Griffin knew to be hu-mor-free, it had to be a literal statement.

"You have pictures?" asked Griffin. He motioned for Bobby to pass him the last egg roll.

"We have film." Griffin tore open a packet of soy sauce while Grace continued. "As you know, Arazzo Castle, once the home of the Ferlinghetti noble family, is now a tourist place."

Griffin poured the soy sauce onto the egg roll, spilling some on the tablecloth. He peered down at the soy sauce spill, a series of black dots in need of connecting.

Grace went on, "There are cameras all over Arazzo Castle. Forty in all. The Europeans are much more aggressive about security than we are."

"You have some film of the man in white in the castle?"

"Not *some* film, Mr. Gilmore." That tone, Griffin thought, that tone returneth. "We have him from the time he walks to the front doors of the castle until thirty seven minutes later when he walks through those same doors and away. He was part of a tour, for those without the time or money to enjoy the castle's Be A Duke For A Day fantasy camp. He is out of camera range no more than a few minutes."

"Those few minutes?" Griffin asked, biting off the end of the egg roll. Strips of cabbage joined the soy sauce stains on the tablecloth. Annie, looking up from her lo mein, rolled her eyes.

"Those moments when the man in white was not on camera. Were they while he was in the dungeon?"

"Yes. There are no cameras in the dungeon. For that matter there is no electricity in the dungeon. There is no need. The dungeon is not part of the tour and there is nothing in the dungeon but dust."

"Any idea where he went in the dungeon, while off camera?"

"We know exactly where he went in the dungeon."

"Where?"

Grace ignored the question. "To get into the dungeon your man in white had to slip away from the tour he was part of. He must have ducked into the dungeon. I mean literally ducked. He was far too tall for the dungeon doorway. You didn't mention he's six foot five."

"I didn't notice." Griffin took another bite of egg roll. "My thoughts were elsewhere. On the other hand, I have a most vivid recollection of the barrel of the gun he was pointing in my direction."

"He limps."

"That I noticed." Griffin took a final bite of the egg roll. He chewed for a long moment. Grace waited, which Griffin understood meant she was waiting for him to figure something out. By the time he swallowed the last of the egg roll, he had it. "The dust. You knew where he went in the dungeon by studying his footprints in the dust."

"I knew you'd think of the dust," Grace said. "The dust was so thick there is simply no question where he went."

"Where?" Griffin asked again. "The room in the back of the dungeon?" Griffin remembered the picture of Dr. Silverman and his wife in front of the door to that room.

"Exactly. Your man in white went in a straight line to the door in the back wall. That door had not been opened within the time of anyone associated with the castle operations. The assumption was that the door *couldn't* be opened."

"Still, you're certain he could open the door?"

"Could and did open the door, but he could not shut it. The door is still open. The door had not been opened in so long it came off one of its hinges and could not quite be closed. The door is very old and very heavy. Solid oak. It was too heavy for the rusty hinges when he opened it."

"I've seen a picture of the door, Grace. The door is exactly as you describe. The door is probably from 1715, when the key was made."

"Quite possibly, Mr. Gilmore. Yes, your man in white opened the door. With the key he got from you at the museum."

"Which means the key was the right key, at least to open that locked door." Griffin gave Annie a nod of appreciation. "That's why he wanted the key. To open that particular door."

Griffin, who'd been staring at the rectangular speaker phone through the entire conversation, now looked up at the far wall of the dining room. The previous owners of the house had painted the walls pencil yellow, with emerald green baseboard trim. It was an eye-assaulting combination. Griffin hadn't yet had the chance to do any painting around the house.

"Describe the room behind the door, Grace. The room the man in white wants so much to enter. Was it a jail cell at one time?"

"If so, it was a very small jail cell. There are bigger closets. But I cannot answer your question, Mr. Gilmore. The historical record, at least as we have it now, is blank. The room could have been a wine cellar. Perhaps storage. Could have been a buttery, one of our experts believes – a storage room for wine. Could have held a prisoner or two from Napoleon's invasion. Whatever it was used for, it's the most secure place in the entire castle.

"The dungeon walls are three feet thick. The walls around the room at the back are even thicker. The castle was damaged in the Second World War. The dungeon survived intact. It was so safe the Ferlinghetti family huddled there during air raids."

Griffin pushed himself away from the dining room table. Annie often accused him of having the sitting still skills of a kindergartener. He began circling the table.

"Grace?" Griffin called as he moved. "Can you hear me now?"

She missed the joke, as Griffin would have predicted. Grace was the place humor went to die. She asked, "You have a question, Mr. Gilmore?"

"The room is well outside camera range, right?"

Grace conceded it was.

"The man in white wasn't searched after ducking into the dungeon, was he?" Griffin asked. "I mean, why would he be? When he was there Saturday afternoon, no one at Arazzo Castle had any reason to believe he was anything other than a tourist like everyone else."

No, he wasn't searched, Grace allowed, for the reason you suggest.

"Then how," Griffin concluded, in what Annie called his Any Moron Can See So Why Can't You voice, "do you know he came out of that room empty handed?"

"Because-"she began, and Griffin finished for her, "because you have the pictures to prove it."

"This will be easiest," Grace said, "if I send the film electronically. You ready?"

"Bring it, Grace."

"Are you sure? It's a somewhat sophisticated software which shows the film while allowing us to maintain a video link. Are you sure can you handle that?"

"Well, I, uh-"

"Why don't I take that," Saif offered. "I'll save the film to your hard drive, Griffin, in case you want to look at it again. Let me handle this."

"Good idea," Griffin agreed. "I'll clear the table. That's something I'm sure I can do just fine."

Eight

June 9
7:12 pm

"This film," Grace explained, as it began to run, "has been spliced together to show this man, still John Doe to us, continuously. Our tech people had a busy time putting this together."

"That's him," Griffin said, as he watched the man in white approach the castle doors. "No question."

Griffin and Annie were to the left of Saif; Bobby and Kit to Saif's right. Saif had the chair. The other four crouched. Five sets of eyes watched the screen on Saif's laptop, which rested in the middle of the dining room table where the speaker phone had been.

On the film, the man walked from the parking lot, across a wooden drawbridge over a moat, and through the portcullis into the castle. He walked in the midst of a good-sized gaggle of tourists. He moved with a limp. The tourists wore fanny packs and tee shirts which did not always cover their jiggling stomachs. Some were in sweatpants. The tape gave a slightly greenish tint to the scene.

"That's a different suit than he had on in the museum," Griffin told everyone. "Different cut."

"Italian," Kit said. "That suit is *not* off the rack. Love the Panama hat, by the way."

"It works for him, doesn't it," Bobby agreed. "He's making himself inconspicuous by standing out in a crowd." Bobby was clearly enjoying the man's performance. "Look at the glances the older women in the group are giving him."

Bobby smiled, then touched the screen.

"See the woman right here?" Bobby pointed to a heavyset woman, round as a muffin, pushing fifty. She was so overweight she wore baggy sweatpants and sweatshirt. "See the lust in that woman's eyes? Before the tour is over I predict this woman makes a play for our man here."

By this time the man in white had entered the castle itself. He limped past suits of armor, which he towered over. The woman in the baggy sweatpants and sweatshirt steadily edged closer.

On the film the tour began.

★

"What you can't quite get from the film," Griffin said, "is how he carries himself. Like an aristocrat. He wore a ring. In other circumstances, you'd think you were expected to kiss it."

"It's a role, Griffin," Bobby stated confidently. "That's a role he's playing. He's carrying himself in a way that projects an image of aristocracy. He's not born to it."

"Grace?" Griffin interrupted. "Bobby has studied actors and acting as long as I've known him. If he says this is a performance, then that's what this is. A performance."

"Then what's his real background?" Grace asked. Her voice caused her picture to break into the upper right corner of the screen. She was sitting at her desk, in her hyper-upright way, her body a rigid L-shape. "He's a blank sheet of paper to us. What's his background?"

"Not aristocratic. Something very, very different," Bobby answered. He shrugged. "That's all I can say now."

They watched the film some more.

"That gentleman standing to the side as the tour passes?" Grace said. "That's a security guard. When Arazzo Castle is open to the public, there are at least three and as many as five security guards on duty. When the castle is closed there are one or two guards at all times."

The woman in the baggy sweatpants and sweatshirt edged closer to the man in white. The tour stopped by a large painting, a battle scene. The tour guide gestured at the painting as he spoke. Someone in the tour asked a question which caused the guide to shake his head, unable to answer.

"See that?" said Bobby, pointing to the man in white. "Grace, can you run that again?"

"Will do," she said.

Her picture flashed again on the screen briefly. Griffin wondered how he'd describe Grace's way of sitting. By no means was she *perching* on the seat. And Griffin strongly suspected Grace had never *lounged* or *lolled* and certainly not *plopped down* anytime in her life. The best he could up with was the phrase *like a statue sitting*.

The film returned to a few seconds earlier, then Grace froze the action.

"See his face," Bobby said. "The man in white knows the answer to the question, doesn't he?"

"He does," Griffin agreed. "He clearly does. The tour guide didn't know the answer to the question about some 18th century painting. But our guy did. It took some self-control to keep from supplying the answer. Still, he stayed silent. He doesn't want to call attention to himself. Grace, can you send me that picture we're seeing right now? That's a nice full shot of his face. Might be I'll need to show the picture to somebody, see if anyone can ID him."

Grace agreed she would.

The tour went on. They passed through a chapel and the kitchen and into a gallery with floor to ceiling paintings filling the walls. In this gallery were two harpsichords. One man stood by each harpsichord. Another man was opening a violin case.

Grace explained: "These men are part of a quartet who will be entertaining at a private party after the tour is over. The castle is sometimes rented out for private parties."

Griffin asked, "Grace, you think he was aware of the cameras?"

"Had to be," she replied. "The security cameras aren't too terribly obvious, but they are spottable. And this guy is thorough, incredibly so. I've watched this film three times now, and I've never seen him touch anything. No fingerprints left behind. And he puts on surgical gloves later."

She kept going. "There are microphones scattered around the castle, wherever the tour goes. But he never speaks when he's with the tour. In fact, he only says three words total. They're coming up. That's not enough for voice recognition. Without fingerprints or voice recognition, without a name or an alias, there is simply no way to even begin finding out who this guy is."

Remembering the accent, Griffin offered, "He's probably from Spain."

"With a population of how many million, Mr. Gilmore? We'll need far more than that before we can begin to track this guy down. Unless you have something more precise in mind?"

Going one on one with Grace in this way wasn't a good idea, Griffin knew, but he couldn't stop himself. He wanted the man in white badly. Griffin offered, "He limps. You've pointed out he's six-five. He's a key thief."

"A specialty which did not even exist before this, I have learned. We are pursuing the angle of a European trading in stolen artifacts. Nothing yet, but we will keep looking. I have my doubts it will yield anything. We are also pursuing the evidence he left in his confrontation with you at the Baltimore Museum of Art."

"The bullet. The shell casing."

"The bullet and the shell casing. The ejection striations tell us the bullet was fired from a Bulgarian pistol."

"Bulgarian? Isn't that unusual?"

"Not as unusual as you might think, Mr. Gilmore. The pistol was a Makarov PMM semi-automatic. Made in Bulgaria, circa 1990, based on the old Soviet model. Spitcurl trigger. 26 ounces, a little over six inches long."

"It looks a good bit bigger when it's pointed at you."

"Fires twelve rounds," Grace went on, "from a detachable magazine. It is accurate up to 50 yards. The Makarov is often the pistol of choice for those who need to conceal their weapon. As your man in white had to at the museum fundraiser. That much makes sense."

After a pause Griffin replied, "By your last comment, can I conclude there is something about the pistol that surprises you?"

"You can so conclude. The Makarov is old enough it is considered a relic by the Bureau of Alcohol, Tobacco, and Firearms. Why would someone who has planned as thoroughly as he obviously had use a weapon more than two decades old?"

Griffin thought a few seconds and then a few seconds more.

"I have no idea, Grace. Any theory from where you're sitting?"

"Not yet. For now, the Makarov is being looked into further. But don't get your expectations up. The pistol is unlikely to help identify the man using it."

"It probably doesn't help, Grace, but he was an excellent marksman. And thank God he was. He put the bullet between my arm and hip. The space could not have been more than a few inches."

"His marksmanship is noted. Do you have anything else to add?"

Griffin admitted he didn't.

Grace summed up: "To return to your question, Mr. Gilmore. Sure. He knew about the cameras."

"But he went to the castle anyway," Annie said.

"Whatever he's after must be worth the risk to him," Grace told them.

This isn't about money, came back to Griffin. They watched the tour resume.

"Do you see the security guard walking through the hallway there?" Grace pointed out. "The guards generally are very active. They keep moving around quite a bit."

In the film the woman in baggy sweatpants and sweatshirt pushed closer to the man in white. Her cheeks shook like jello in the effort. Soon after, the man in white slipped away from the tour for the men's room. When he emerged from the bathroom he was alone in a hallway. By this time the tour must have been well ahead.

"What's he doing?" Griffin wondered aloud.

The man on the screen walked down one hall, then turned into a narrower hall. As he moved he pulled a pair of surgical gloves from the pocket of his suit coat.

"He did that in the museum," Griffin said.

"That was on his way out," Grace explained. "This is on his way in."

★

The man in white then did something unexpected. He grabbed the handle of a chute protruding from the wall. While still walking he pulled the handle open slightly.

"Is he nervous?" Griffin wondered, without much faith in the question. The man in white had been nowhere near nervous in the museum.

"Could be," replied Grace. She didn't sound especially convinced either. "Not sure why he did that, pulling the chute handle. I can tell you the chute leads to the basement incinerator. The chute was installed in the mid-eighteen hundreds, when garbage removal was still dealt with by burning."

Without slowing, the man in white headed down a set of stone steps. Grace stopped the tape with the man's Panama hat barely visible.

"Those steps lead to the dungeon," she explained. "Three minutes and fifty seven seconds pass between what you're seeing now and his reappearance."

"In those nearly four minutes off camera," Griffin said, "here's what we believe happened: Let me know if you don't agree. He descended the rest of the steps and crossed the dungeon floor. He used the key he got from me at the museum to unlock a door so old it fell off a hinge – as it was opened for the first time in who knows how long.

"Next he looked around in the small room at the back of the dungeon for whatever he came for. And he came back up, limping all the way, in three fifty seven. Tight, I suppose, but doable. He knew what he was looking for and where it was supposed to be."

"Whatever he was looking for wasn't there," Grace said.

"But how do you know that, Grace?" replied Griffin with some heat, "Why are you so sure that when he reappears he's empty handed? He's completely out of camera range in that room at the back of the dungeon. We have no clue what he's looking for. Could be it's small enough he just stuffed whatever it is in his pocket."

"Keep an eye on his face when he emerges from the dungeon, Mr. Gilmore. You tell me if your man in white got what he came for."

The film started again. The man came back up the steps. Grace froze the action and enlarged the man's face to fill the computer screen. The look of disappointment on that face was crushing and unmistakable.

"Is he acting, Bobby? Putting on a performance for the cameras he knows are there?"

Bobby brought his face close to the screen before replying.

"Not a chance is he acting, Griffin. See how the tendons in his face are flexed like little ropes? That's not special effects or acting skills. That's disappointment, disappointment so brutal he either forget or did not care he was on camera."

Bobby kept staring at the frozen image of the furiously straining face, fascinated.

"He was expecting something to be in that room at the back of the dungeon, Mr. Gilmore. We don't know what he was expecting – but whatever he was expecting was *not* there."

Griffin eyed the laptop screen and said, "That tells us this is about more than the Duke's key. The man in white already has the key. What is he after with the key?"

Griffin next asked Grace, "Is the rest of the film worth watching?"

That If Only You Knew tone bounced back into her voice. Even more so: she was in an Until Now Everything Was An Appetizer, But This Is the Main Course mode. Grace said, "Oh, yes, the rest of the film is well worth watching," and started the film again.

★

They watched as the man in white slipped the surgical gloves back into his pocket. From the same pocket he withdrew a phone.

"Here's where your man in white made a mistake, Mr. Gilmore. I've given the matter some consideration. Why did someone as careful as this man make such a glaring mistake? Maybe he was, as Bobby Lowell suggests, so distraught with disappointment he didn't think or care.

"Maybe, and this is my belief, he didn't understand that the 40 cameras are placed around the museum so that many areas are covered by two cameras. At this time he's in one of those areas. No amount of preparation could have taught him that. It's a bit of luck for us."

Grace continued her narration as the film resumed.

"He pulls out his phone. See him look up over his shoulder and spot the camera there? He turns his back to block the camera's view of what he's about to do."

Grace stopped the film once more.

"He is, as we all see, about to make a call. What he doesn't understand is that even with his back turned he is within camera range of another camera down the hall. Watch as I slow down the footage from the camera he didn't know about. And we'll enlarge the picture, centering on the phone."

When she restarted the film, the man's phone and fingers filled the screen. He wore an oval signet ring, the same ring he wore in the museum. The ring had some sort of design that Griffin could not quite discern, since the man's hand was partially turned away from the camera. The ring was too big for the man's finger, that much was clear. Griffin wondered why such an otherwise stylish gentleman would wear a ring that did not nearly fit.

Everyone in the dining room saw the number the man in white was dialing.

"That's his mistake. We can see who he is calling. The area code is New York, Mr. Gilmore. We know the number he's dialing. It's a company called Future-Ride. We've tracked the location. 54th Street in Manhattan. Now watch."

"He's waiting for the answering machine to pick up," Grace went on. "He'll say three words when it does. He speaks English, which, Mr. Gilmore, you already knew. Here it comes."

As he spoke, the man's anger and desperation were unmistakable. Everyone in the dining room said the words along with the man in white: "Call me. Now."

Nine

June 11
10:48 am

Thursday morning; Bobby and Griffin were on the Amtrack train to Manhattan discussing their previous client. "I can still remember our client, going" —Bobby shifted into a stiff British accent, 'On behalf of her majesty's government for services most ably rendered, thank you, sir.' A check to Kit. 'Thank you, sir.' A check to you. 'Thank you, sir.' A check to me. A sizeable chunk of change, it was too. 'Thank you, mu'um.' A check to Annie.

"Absolutely loved that *mu'um*. Remember his bowler hat and umbrella? It was like this bloke strolled into our lives from a Gilbert and Sullivan musical, asking us to recover a sword for the British Museum."

Griffin looked outside the window. New Jersey, at least that part visible from the train, was more rusted out than he had expected from the Garden State.

"Time I got into character," Bobby announced. He picked up a briefcase from underneath his seat. "Hey, I didn't ask. You going to that party tonight at Saif's parents' house? He's anxious for you to be there."

"I know. Seems his mother's been ramping up for it all week," Griffin replied. "She's trying to fix him up with someone, but won't say who. All she's told Saif is, 'She seems nice.'"

Bobby: "Nice! She's got a good personality? That's the kiss of death."

Griffin agreed he would go and Bobby promised, "I shall return anon" and went to change.

Griffin watched Bobby on his way to the men's room. Several seats in front of Bobby a child suddenly and ear-splittingly burst into tears. For much of the trip, and from half a train car away, Griffin had endured the kid complaining about everything. His beleaguered father finally quieted the squalling by giving the child two coins to rub together. That brought the train car a few moments of relieved quiet.

That quiet was now shattered as the kid shrieked, "My money! My money!" His two year old voice seemed to bore directly into Griffin's teeth.

The quarters the child had dropped rolled down the aisle in Bobby's direction. Without breaking stride he scooped them up, said, "Super abra-ca-dab-ra!" and seemed to pull them from behind the child's ears. He handed the quarters to the child. The tears and screaming immediately stopped.

"If you're not quiet," Bobby told him, "next I'll make *you* disappear."

The child did not say another word.

★

Griffin and Bobby emerged from surprisingly well air conditioned Grand Central Station into the heat of the New York day.

"This is my third trip to New York." Griffin told Bobby. They were both blinking rapidly in the hard sunlight. "Neither of the first two trips went well."

"I was there for one of them," Bobby said. "Ninth grade school trip to the United Nations. You wound up suspended, didn't you?"

"For mere youthful exuberance. I simply corrected the grammar of the delegate who spoke to the class."

"Griffin, the delegate was French and you addressed him as Monsieur Grand Moronn? I was taking Spanish and even I knew what you'd called him. What was the other trip?"

"The other trip?" Griffin said, looking around for a cab. "The second New York trip was last year. It ended with two FBI agents greeting me with handcuffs when I stepped off the train in Penn Station in Baltimore."

★

A cab stopped and Griffin and Bobby climbed in. Griffin told him: "We certainly could walk to Future-Ride, but men of our distinction don't walk we cab to destinations. You do remember our roles?"

Bobby put on a pair of battered, rimless glasses held together at one end with blue duct tape. He angled his head slightly and the sun caught the lenses of the glasses, making his eyes disappear. He wore faded blue jeans, work boots, and a tangerine-colored polo shirt, with the collar popped, very much the exemplar of geek chic.

Bobby said, "I'm playing Walter Briggs, the brilliant, somewhat eccentric and always frugal inventor of a process that miniaturizes fiber optic cable. You're my lawyer, Charles Wales. We're looking to invest with Future-Ride the money I made from my patent."

"Exactly. Future-Ride buys up struggling companies, strips away their unprofitable divisions, and repackages the company for sale. About half the businesses they've bought are American and the rest European. In order to buy these struggling companies Future-Ride needs investors, so they'll want to see us."

"You're sure this is a real company, Griffin? Not a front?"

"Future-Ride is legitimate. That much we know."

Griffin had been busy the past two days with Grace working out details. The patent existed. The actual inventor had been convicted of tax evasion and Grace had erased any official record of his incarceration. To the world, the man was not in jail but was currently riding in the backseat of a cab in Manhattan.

"We have how much to invest with Future-Ride?"

"Bobby, their minimum investment is $750,000, to keep out the riff raff. We're coming in with twice that much to get their attention. Grace will actually wire the funds to Future-Ride should we agree to invest. That will not happen today. When this search for wherever the key leads us is over, Grace will pull the money back out. But today we don't want to give in and sign with Future-Ride too easily."

"They won't respect us in the morning?"

"Bobby, today is just a meet and make nice. When I set up the meeting I told them we only had thirty minutes. We're in town for a telecommunications conference. Which we have both registered for, in case they check us out. I pitched this to them as a get acquainted kind of thing. Today, we want to learn whatever we can about Future-Ride's connection to the man in white and the key he stole from me. Right now, Grace hasn't a clue about any of that and neither have I.

"The key didn't bring the man in white whatever it is he wanted. When that happened, first thing he did was call Future-Ride. From Italy he calls a Manhattan investment company? The very first call he makes when he's good and mad?

Why did he call Future-Ride? The call was certainly not for everyday investment advice. There's got to be a connection between him and the company, but what is it?"

Bobby asked: "You think the connection is whatever the man in white was expecting in that room in the dungeon?"

"Got to be. But who at Future-Ride did he call? The call went to an alcove phone that isn't listed to anyone in the company. The phone is located between the office of two women, Alexandra Webb and Deborah Miller. Future-Ride is a small shop. Their analysts are part time and probably wouldn't be there late on a Saturday afternoon. The likelihood is that the call was for one of those two ladies, but which one?"

"The company is legit, but one of the ladies running it isn't?"

"Looks that way, Bobby. During today's meeting we need to keep a close eye on both of these women we're chatting up. Maybe one'll give herself away. Kit will be helping us out on his end by calling the alcove number. The trip's nothing like a sure thing, but it's worth taking.

"It's not like we're overwhelmed with other clues."

"No, Bobby, we most certainly are not. This is the only path to pursue to the man in white right now. What we'd most like to get out of this meeting is some idea which of the two ladies got the man in white's call."

Bobby had little interest in any of that.

"We don't get to even touch the million-five?" he asked.

"Sorry."

"Doesn't Grace trust us with that much money?"

"Would you? Bobby, can you make this work?'

"Griffin, I can make this *sing*."

The cab pulled over to the curb. The building they were about to enter was nearly all smoked glass. The glass reflected the sky and clouds, leaving the glass an unfriendly dark. Griffin reached into his pocket for the fare.

With an extended arm Bobby motioned for him to wait. He looked out the cab window. Griffin knew Bobby didn't see any of the world outside. His breathing became quick and shallow. He was, Griffin knew, preparing for his performance. He gestured for Griffin to pay the driver.

Griffin gave the cab driver a twenty. "Keep the change," he told the driver.

"Don't even think about it," Bobby said, now in character. To the driver he ordered, "We'd like three dollars back. You can keep the $1.80."

★

"Gentlemen! Gentlemen, do come in, please."

Griffin heard the voice, a smoothly flowing, deep Georgia drawl, before seeing the speaker. He and Bobby ventured into the Future-Ride conference room as the speaker rose to greet them.

"I'm Alexandra Webb, president of Future-Ride acquisitions," she said, in her easy, pleasing Georgia accent. Sweet faces don't always go with sweet voices, Griffin knew, but this one did.

He guessed her age to be mid-fifties. She wore a powder blue dress and blouse. Her hair was swept back from her ears, revealing a pair of lovely, old fashioned earrings. She exuded graciousness.

"I'm Charles Wales," he said to her. "And this is Dr. Briggs, our inventor looking to invest."

Bobby crossed his arms, signaling Alexandra Webb he did not care to shake hands. She nodded, her graciousness undimmed.

Still holding onto Griffin's hand, she turned to the woman rising from her chair and said, "Gentlemen, this is my assistant-"

"Deborah Miller," Griffin said, to show he'd prepared for this meeting, a lawyer ably representing his client.

"Actually," the woman corrected, "my name is pronounced De-BOR-ah. Stress the second syllable. The incorrect pronunciation is a common mistake."

By emphasizing the word *common*, she left little doubt how she felt about Griffin's mistake. De-BOR-ah had an intense, unblinking stare behind her black-rimmed cat's eye glasses. Griffin would keep his eye on her but keeping an eye on De-BOR-ah would not be pleasant.

"How did you gentlemen hear about us?" Alexandra asked, gesturing for Griffin and Bobby to sit.

Griffin answered, smiling, the woman's voice was so pleasing: "We saw your rate of return for your investors last year was well above the national average for investment firms of this type."

"One point eight times the national average," De-BOR-ah said. Griffin could tell Bobby was also closely watching De-BOR-ah. With the light in the conference room slanting off his glasses, the women could not have known that he was.

"Since we were in New York for a conference anyway," Griffin went on, "we're taking the time to stop by."

"And we are certainly glad you did," Alexandra said. "Would either of you care for some tea? Coffee?" she offered.

"Tea?" Bobby responded in a near-shriek, playing the eccentric card with gusto. "Tannic acid will kill you."

"I'll take some coffee," Griffin said.

Alexandra went over to a silver coffee pot and poured two cups. When her back was turned, Griffin glanced at his watch. At 3:15, Kit would call the number the man in white had called Saturday, the alcove phone. With any luck one of the women would get up to answer that phone. Or at least she'd give some indication the ringing phone was of particular interest to her.

For the first time De-BOR-ah asked a question. "Why do you want to invest in the tech sector, Dr. Briggs?" De-BOR-ah had an absolute gift for firing off questions in an antagonizing, smashmouth tone. "Your lawyer said that was your preference. We're pushing companies making electric car batteries."

"Cars are so twentieth century," Bobby replied, matching De-BOR-ah's stride for disdainful stride. He bent down to re-tie a broken shoelace, the kind of attention to detail that made Bobby's performances so believable.

While Bobby retied his shoe, Griffin noticed the conference room rug was a shiny bright gold color. It was, he couldn't help but remember, the same gold as the hatband in the man in white's Panama.

"We're talking an expected rate of return in excess of twelve percent," De-BOR-ah went on in her dislikeable, foot-in-the-door style. "The tech sector cannot come close to matching that in this economy."

She sat dagger-straight in her chair, almost daring contradiction.

"Alexandra," Griffin said, "what are your thoughts about the best place for Dr. Briggs to invest his money?"

Alexandra Webb spoke for a few minutes. Griffin caught little of what she said. Her words seemed to be coated in honey and soft Southern nights. Maintaining eye contact with Alexandra was a pleasure.

In mid-sentence the phone rang down the hall; Kit calling at 3:15. Neither woman moved.

"Do you need to get that?" Griffin asked, careful to look at both women. Neither betrayed any reaction.

"The alcove phone? All the phones have their own answering machines," said Alexandra. Had she spoken just a bit too casually? Griffin couldn't tell one way or the other. At 3:23 – Griffin was asking about debt-to-equity ratios, a subject he'd had to bone up on – the phone down the hall rang again.

At the time Alexandra was reaching for a corporate prospectus and did not notice Griffin glance at his watch. He was certain De-BOR-ah had seen him look at his watch, but she said nothing. Her stare at Griffin could have corroded metal. Kit was calling on schedule. The phone rang five times and went silent. Again, neither woman reacted.

A few minutes later the meeting ended.

"This has all been very impressive," Griffin said, in a we've-got-to-be-going voice. "I'll be in touch. Dr. Briggs is not one to invest hastily."

Bobby adjusted the duct tape on his glasses, as if proving the point. He gave his head an almost imperceptible shake. To the women, the shake was just another eccentricity of Dr. Briggs. Griffin, though, knew its meaning: I can't tell which of the women took that phone call from the man in white. Griffin couldn't tell either.

Griffin exchanged business cards with the two women.

"Promise me you'll call," Alexandra Webb insisted. Her voice was delightful, especially compared to De-BOR-ah, whose speaking style made a jackhammer seem shy by comparison. "Whenever you make the decision about investing. Even if you decide to invest elsewhere."

"We'll be in touch," Griffin promised.

The women handed him the most recent Future-Rid annual report, a glossy brochure on the company, and documents listing companies Future-Ride had repackaged and profitably sold in recent years.

He and Bobby left New York knowing no more about the man in white than they had when boarding the train in Baltimore.

Ten

June 11
8:58 pm

Annie and Kit were waiting on the sidewalk to the Venkate-san's house on Purlington Way in Homeland when Griffin and Bobby arrived from their unproductive trip to New York.

Annie wore black earrings that hung down like half moons. Kit wore another Hawaiian shirt, this one with an oversized mug of beer with foam frothing down the side of the mug.

"Anything to report?" Griffin asked Kit.

While Griffin and Bobby were journeying to New York, Kit and Annie had returned to Oakecrest Village to question the security guard about the theft of Andrea Platt's ancient car.

"We may have learned some—"

Before Annie could finish, Saif stepped onto the front porch. When he spotted Griffin, the relief on Saif's face was luminous.

"Where you been, Griffin?" he said, loudly enough that for Saif it qualified as a shout. He was decked out in a blue blazer and charcoal grey pants, an outfit Griffin was sure Saif's mother had chosen for him. "I wasn't sure you would make it."

Griffin explained, "We were stuck on the train without moving for half an hour outside Newark. You know, if we had political prisoners in this country, that'd be the sort of punishment they'd have to endure."

He could tell Saif hadn't heard a word.

Saif said, "You have to meet ..." He trailed off, hesitated, then added in a barely audible voice, "meet my date."

They stepped into the house. Saif threw a jerky nod in the general direction of the fireplace. Saif's date was not hard to spot.

By the fireplace stood a woman in grey wool skirt and white blouse. She was short and chubby. By the way she hunched her shoulders and kept her eyes downward Griffin could tell she was not only shy but painfully so. She leaned a chunky arm on the fireplace mantle in an effort to look relaxed, but her attempt was so blatantly staged she appeared all the more nervous. On the mantle was a gleamingly polished bronze statue of Lakshmi. Lakshmi, Griffin knew from his reading on mythology, was the goddess of prosperity. The statue was about three feet high. The goddess' breasts were enormous, her nipples obvious.

"Who's that woman with your date?" Griffin asked Saif. "A bit older, I think."

"That's Bobby's date."

"Mine?" Bobby said, over Griffin's shoulder. "Who said I wanted a date?"

"Who said *I* wanted a date?"

"That, Saif," Griffin responded, "is a whole 'nother story."

This exchange took place out of the corner of their mouths, as the five of them lingered in the foyer before joining the party. The party was about to come to them.

Dr. and Mrs. Venkatesan approached. Seeing them together, it was hard to believe they'd met on the day of their arranged marriage in Calcutta. She walked a deferential three strides behind her husband, a slight man with a few wispy hairs on the crown of his otherwise bald head. He was an anesthesiologist at GBMC with an open, honest face patients took to immediately.

Mrs. Venkatesan was a tiny, very dark skinned woman, a homemaker and aspiring grandmother. When she smiled, which was frequently, her teeth flashed a brilliant white. She wore a lime green sari and thick, clunky glasses. Her only extravagance was a pair of open toed shoes, passionate red, poking out from under the hem of her sari.

Spotting Griffin she hurried over to give him a hug. While doing so she whispered, "You must help Saif tonight," nodding toward the fireplace as her son had done.

★

"I'm Griffin Gilmore," he introduced himself, looking at both women by the fireplace. Saif's chubby date met Griffin's glance only briefly before bestowing the meekest of nods and lowering her eyes once more. The older woman looked at Griffin very directly. Then she looked at Bobby and held her glance even longer. She extended a slender arm – which jangled softly from her many silver wrist bracelets – in Bobby's direction.

"I'm Shebana Mehta." She held the handshake a suggestively long time.

"I'm Bobby Lowell, Saif's friend since high school. Is that a Boston accent I'm hearing?"

"You've got a good ear there."

"I'm an actor," Bobby replied. After kissing her hand, in a French accent he said, "Such a pleasure, Madame Mehta."

"Bobby," Saif demanded, "the food table."

"What about it?"

"We need to go there."

"We do?"

"We do."

The five of them went to the food table, where Griffin speared and ingested a Bombay potato so spicy he felt beads of sweat form on his nose.

"You really should try your mother's cooking," Griffin said. "It's outstanding."

Saif refused to be distracted. "I want to switch."

As innocently as he could manage, Bobby asked, "Switch? Switch what?"

"You know switch what."

"Why are you venting, Saif? Ah. You want my date? Shabana-"

"Mehta. Yes."

"What do you know about Ms. Mehta? Age?"

"Thirty six."

"So, an older woman."

"She's divorced and as you can see, she's ah-"

"She's what exactly?" Bobby wondered.

"Well, she's ... she's killer. Just look at her."

They all scoped her out. Kit's jaw hung open. Shabana Mehta wore maroon colored slacks and a tight, midnight blue silk blouse. She sensed their glances and reacted by running a hand through her black hair, arching her chest in the process.

"And your date?" Griffin asked.

"Shantoo Joshi. Been in this country four years. Her spoken English is so-so. My Mom's told me several times she got a perfect 800 score on her med school achievement test."

"While you scored a mere 780 on the Graduate Record Exam, as I recall. Are you threatened by her perfection?"

"Griffin, she has a mustache."

Griffin looked in Miss Joshi's direction, who spotted him and resumed her downward glance.

"Well, yes, she does. But honestly, Saif, it's hardly visible from here across the room."

"I want to switch."

"Sure thing," Bobby said, waving to Mrs. Venkatesan, who looked on with concern from the other side of the living room. "You take the gay divorcee. I get the future doctor with a mustache. Go ahead, break your poor mother's heart." Bobby waved again at Mrs. Venkatesan. "Want me to call your Mom over here? Right now?"

"My date is not my style."

"No," Griffin said, taking over the lecture from Bobby. "I don't think she is either. But that's no reason you cannot march yourself back over there and talk to her. Make your mother smile. We'll be your wingmen. We'll keep Ms. Mehta occupied, give you the chance to move in for the kill."

"Okay, I'll talk to her. But there won't be any killing tonight. Any other words of Inspiration?"

Griffin speared another Bombay potato. "You really should try these."

Forty five minutes later Griffin told Saif they'd be leaving.

"Give me five minutes," he replied. "I'll meet you at your car."

Saif arrived carrying an envelope, which he handed to Griffin. "You asked me to find whatever scholarly articles I could on Alexandra Webb and Deborah Miller."

"She pronounces her name De-BOR-ah," Griffin corrected.

"There's a good bit by her in there. I couldn't find anything written by Alexandra Webb other than the expected stuff for

Future-Ride. Some of De-BOR-ah Miller's writing is pretty technical. Lots of equations and variables. She's smart, no denying that. But … Call me if you need anything explained."

★

June 12
9:15 am

"Couldn't sleep last night after Saif's party," Griffin told Kit, the next morning on the front porch. Griffin's voice had the rawness of exhaustion. After the Venkatesans' party, sometime around three in the morning, he gave up on sleep and hunkered down with his computer. "Since I couldn't sleep anyway, I went online to check out Future-Ride, Alexandra Webb, and De-BOR-ah Miller."

"Learn anything?"

"As I already knew, Future-Ride is clearly a bona fide company. It's listed in Dun & Bradstreet, Hoover's Online, Factiva, and elsewhere. Founded early Nineties. The company's fine, of that I'm sure, but what about the women who run it? Neither Alexandra Webb nor De-BOR-ah Miller turned up in the WATCH database for criminal records.

"From People Tracker I learned Alexandra Webb was born in Augusta, Georgia. Nothing phony about that lovely accent. She was educated at the Sorbonne. She's been with Future-Ride since finishing her graduate degree. I couldn't track down anything she's published.

"De-BOR-ah Miller was educated at Stanford and has been with Future-Ride two and a half years. She's authored a pair of articles for scholarly economics publications. Which I duly tracked down and read. I read the two articles Saif supplied as well. Tried to, at least. I'll admit that a good bit of her writing is statistical ebonics to me, but I figured enough out to know the woman is a total shark. Unburdened by a social conscience of any kind. She's obviously bright. But – BTW, do you know what a Dead Cat Bounce is?"

"No clue," Kit responded. "Should I?"

"It's a Wall Street expression. When a company tanks and its stock drops to near zero, venture capitalists buy up the stock. That gives the company a brief bounce, as if still alive. Happened to Enron. Investors make money, even though the company is now nothing more than a body laid out in the morgue of capitalism. De-BOR-ah Miller thinks that's fine. She worships the free market."

Griffin closed his eyes, felt the morning sun grab his face.

"You learn anything?" he asked Kit, in a croaky voice. "When you and Annie went to see the security guard at Oakecrest Village."

"We may have." Kit wore another Hawaiian shirt. This one showed five sea gulls landing on a beach. "Or maybe not. This comes from the guard who talked to the guy who may have stolen the car."

"The whiskey and Aqua Velva man."

"Him, yeah. The guard's name is Rockefeller. You don't expect a security guard to have that name, but he does. The guard told us a detail that didn't make it into the newspaper article."

Eyes still closed, Griffin asked. "And the other detail is?"

"Griffin, he said 'Crappola.'"

Griffin opened his eyes. "Crappola?" he repeated, laughing. "Who said crappola? The security guard named Rockefeller?"

Kit elaborated: "No, the guy who probably stole the car from Oakecrest. The guy you probably saw drive away from the museum? The security guard overheard him say, 'What is this crappola?' He was talking to the cab driver who dropped him off at Oakecrest. The driver couldn't change a twenty."

"Then he's got to be local talent hired for the job," Griffin concluded. "Not somebody the man in white sent over from Spain to steal a car and be his driver. You ever hear anyone outside of Baltimore say 'Crappola'?"

"Nope."

"Me neither," said Annie, pushing through the front screen door, carrying a tray with a pitcher of orange juice and three glasses. Her earrings shimmered in the morning sun.

She poured the orange juice into the glasses. Before Griffin took his first sip his attention was pulled to a car turning onto their street. It was a limo, so relentlessly polished the black gleamed in the sun. The three of them watched from the porch, orange juice unsipped, until the limo stopped in front of the house.

"Got to be the Duke," Griffin said.

"Did you ask him here?"

"Absolutely not, Annie. He has our address, but why is he here and not off doing whatever it is dukes do all day? I'm not sure I'm in the mood for his *ad nauseum* lectures on the ancestral wine today."

"Heavy on the *nauseum*," Annie said.

"Let me get something from inside the house to show the Duke." Griffin looked at Annie and Kit and told them, "Everybody grab their glasses, so they don't go flying."

★

Half a minute later Griffin was back on the porch. He held the picture Grace had sent him of the man in white making his way through Arazzo Castle. Griffin watched Duke Ferlinghetti climb out of the limo's back seat. He wore black slacks and shirt, the slacks the most heavily starched Griffin'd ever seen. Those slacks could have stood on their own and walked away if they wanted. In the seat vacated by the Duke, a pair of long, attractive woman's legs were visible.

"Kit," said Annie. "The chauffeur and whoever's in the limo are probably hot. Why don't I take a glass of orange juice to the chauffeur and you can-"

"Sweet!" Kit yelled, stumping down the steps, orange juice sloshing out his glass on his way to the woman in the limo.

"Sure you got game enough, Kit?" Griffin taunted from the porch.

To Griffin, Kit called back, "Watch and learn, my friend."

"Mr. Gilmore," the Duke said, from the street next to his limo. Shimmering waves of heat snaked skyward around him. "I believe someone in your government has stressed to you the importance in recovering my family's key?"

"She has," Griffin agreed.

As the Duke approached, he spoke with troubling softness. Was this the calm before the storm?

"She has explained that my consistent support of American policies in Europe might weaken if the key is not returned?"

"She has. She has also given me this. This is a picture of the man who stole your family's key. The picture's from a surveillance tape. The man also threatened to kill me, if that's of concern to you." Duke Ferlinghetti did not respond. Which told Griffin that, no, the Duke was not overly concerned with that possibility. "Do you recognize this man?"

Griffin walked down the steps at a somewhat slower pace than Kit had. He met the Duke on the sidewalk and handed Duke Ferlinghetti the picture of the man in white.

Griffin was surprised to see how old the Duke appeared in the morning light. He was 33, a year younger than Griffin, but seemed a decade older. The Duke's royal bald spot was grapefruit-sized and spreading.

"Do you know that man?"

The Duke took off his South American dictator shades. His brown eyes were surprisingly small and lifeless. He stared at the picture a long time. Griffin saw beads of sweat forming on the man's temples. Money out the ying yang, Griffin thought, and it doesn't prepare him for just another muggy Baltimore morning.

Griffin heard Annie speaking to the chauffeur about the weather. What Kit was chatting about to the blonde in the limo, Griffin could guess. The fact that she'd be eight-ten inches taller than Kit would not trouble him in the slightest. The Duke kept staring at the picture, a hardening look creeping into his eyes.

"No," he said at last. "I am quite certain. I have never seen this man before in my life."

"Based on his accent, I believe he is from your part of the world. Although Spanish, not Italian. Could he have some personal grudge against you?"

"No. I tell you I have never seen him before."

"Could his family have some sort of grudge against yours?"

"Not a chance," the Duke answered with certainty." I would recognize him in that case."

"He has some connection to a company in New York named Future-Ride. Future-Ride is an investment firm."

"I have never heard of them."

"So you have no idea what the connection between this man and Future-Ride could be."

Wearily, the Duke responded. "I have no idea whatsoever."

"Do you have any idea why he would take the least valuable of the twelve keys in the museum display?"

"That is a question for you to answer, Mr. Gilmore."

"He used the key to open the room at the back of the dungeon of your family's castle in Arazzo."

"Impossible!" came the reply. It was as if Griffin had suggested repealing the law of gravity. "I have known of that room all my life. The door has not been opened in my lifetime. I do not believe the door can be opened."

"Nevertheless, on Saturday it *was* opened, by this man." Griffin touched the picture. "With your family's key. The key he stole from me at the museum fundraiser. The key is everything to you, I understand that, but to this man the key was just a way to get into that room. The room turned out to be empty. This man," he touched the picture once more, "thought something would be there. Something worth an enormous amount of effort on his part. Have you any idea what that something could be?"

The Duke gave the question some thought. Griffin watched beads of sweat work their way down the sides of his face. Duke Ferlinghetti refused to acknowledge what must have been uncomfortable. It was a sort of aristocratic discipline that Griffin found unexpectedly sympathetic.

"I can't imagine what he thought could be in there," the Duke said at last. "The room has not been opened in my lifetime. What could he possibly have thought would be in that room?"

"I have no idea," Griffin admitted. He glanced around, looking for objects that might go airborne should the Duke's temper explode. That, Griffin saw, was not about to happen. Griffin understood the Duke had stopped by that morning with a believing in Santa Clause kind of hope the key might be miraculously recovered. But no miracles were on the morning's agenda.

95

The Duke turned dejectedly and headed back toward the limo in the slow shuffle of a child sent to bed without dessert.

It had never occurred to Griffin that he could feel sorry for Duke Ferlinghetti.

Griffin called out, "Hey, Larry!" Referring to the Duke by his first name was probably punishable by death or at least dismemberment, but Griffin did so again. "Larry?"

The Duke turned and slowly raised his head to meet Griffin's glance.

"We'll get your key back," Griffin promised.

Eleven

June 12
5:00 pm

At five that afternoon Griffin was awakened from a nap by Annie handing him his phone.

"It's Grace," she said.

Their bedroom was the only air conditioned room in the house. They had bought the AC unit used, and while it did its cooling job well enough, the unit gave off a steady series of *chunka, chunka, thunk, chunka, chunka, thunk* sounds. Griffin found the noise oddly relaxing.

Never one to bounce out of bed, he had some trouble waking from the nap.

"It's Grace on the phone," Annie elaborated, placing the phone against his right cheek.

"Yarp?" Griffin managed.

"Mr. Gilmore?"

"You're Grace."

"Yes. I am," she responded, with some patience. "I have information for you."

"Information?"

"Yes, Mr. Gilmore. We subpoenaed the phone records of the three lines at Future-Ride of interest to you – Alexandra Webb, Deborah Miller, and the line in a small alcove between their offices. I would have produced this earlier, but my boss had me deal with developments in the Middle East."
"Your boss?" Griffin said, almost awake now. "And how is Bernie? He remember me fondly from December?"

"He remembers you. Fondly is not the word I would use."

"Wait. You have phone records?" By now Griffin was completely awake.

"Yes."

"This means you know the phone number of the man in white when he called the alcove phone at Future-Ride. He called from Arazzo Castle on Saturday."

"We do."

"If you know his phone number, do you know his name? You know the man in white's name?"

"Unfortunately, no. We now know the phone was purchased in Madrid, Spain in March. Paid for in cash. Therefore, no record generated. I can't believe it would make any difference. He'd hardly sign his own name."

"Can you send me the phone records anyway?"

"They're on their way to your house by Fed Ex."

"The Fed Ex is due when?"

Annie held up a Fed Ex package. "Just arrived," she said.

Griffin gestured for her to open the package.

"There's something else in the package that may be of interest to you, Mr. Gilmore," Grace went on. "We arranged the phone numbers by frequency of calls made. The package has the complete list, all calls made on all three lines for the past three years. It's a lengthy list." That the anal retentive Grace had been so meticulous was no surprise to Griffin. She went on, "Just about all the calls by Alexandra Webb and Deborah Miller are to banks and mortgage lenders, investor clients. The kinds of calls you'd expect Future-Ride executives to make."

Griffin was awake enough to note a certain Here's-What-You-Don't Know tone working its way back into Grace's voice.

"But, Mr. Gilmore? That other line, the one not belonging to either woman, is of far more interest. What do you know about that third line?"

"It's in an alcove. Other than that, nothing at all."

"As you say, that third line is in an alcove. The blueprint for the Future-Ride offices is included in the Fed Ex package. Officially, this alcove phone is for the use of clients, who need privacy to make calls they don't want overheard by the folks at Future-Ride.

"Let's say somebody needs to check with a banker or fellow investors without prying ears overhearing. Just close the door to the alcove and you've got the privacy you desire. It's not unusual for law firms to have alcove phones like that. Investment firms like Future-Ride have them too."

"Sure," Griffin said, understanding the reason for the alcove phone. "Everything you say makes sense."

"I'm almost to the part that doesn't. There's one number called from this phone that's very unexpected."

"This number is for calls made *from* Future Ride? Not calls received?"

"Exactly. The calls were always made after seven at night, which is late for clients to be around and in need of a phone."

"Still, it could be a client, say in an earlier time zone."

"Except that the calls were made to a residence, not a business. And it's this time zone. The address is 5722 Gist Avenue. In your town."

"In Baltimore?"

"Yes. The home owner's name was Hans Baeder."

"Was? As in, Hans moved away or died?"

"He died last year. All the information we could compile on Mr. Baeder is in the package I sent you. One last thing, Mr. Gilmore. The calls stopped in June of last year. This could all be irrelevant. And what, if anything, it has to do with your man in white, I cannot say. But it's well worth your checking out. Of that, I am certain."

"Why are you so certain? Who was Hans Baeder?"

"Someone in the Nazi Party."

"You mean the American Nazi Party?" Griffin responded. "The white supremacists? The skin heads? Lots of tattoos? Those clowns?"

"No. I mean a German Nazi. Hans Baeder was one of the real Nazis, the ones who worked for Adolph Hitler. Call me when you've made some sense of that."

Reaching for the Fed Ex package, Griffin agreed he would.

★

Griffin dumped the contents of the Fed Ex package onto the bed. Annie went back downstairs, leaving Griffin to the materials Grace had sent.

Griffin looked first at the blueprint. The Future-Ride space was unexpectedly small, only eight rooms: Alexandra Webb had an office, as did De-BOR-ah Miller; there was a kitchen and the alcove with the phone; there was the conference room where Griffin and Bobby had met Alexandra and De-BOR-ah; and there were two other rooms, barely larger than cubicles, for analysts. The biggest room was Alexandra Webb's corner office.

Griffin heard banging noises coming up from the living room. The sound was barely audible over the *chunka, chunka, thunk* of the bedroom air conditioner. To Griffin the air conditioner and the banging combined to sound a little like a disco struggling to get airborne.

Next Griffin turned to the three lists of phone calls. Alongside each number called was information Grace had compiled: the frequency that number had been called; who the phone called was registered to; whether that location was a business or a residence; and the dates of the calls.

The lists for calls made by Alexandra Webb and De-BOR-ah were dozens of pages each. That, Griffin concluded, was to be expected. Busy executives would make many calls every work day over the course of three years.

The banging noises continued from the living room. What was Annie doing down there?

Griffin looked next at the calls made from the alcove phone. This third list was no more than a few pages. One number on the alcove phone list caught his attention, as it had caught Grace's. The number had been called 19 times over 19 months. The calls ended in June 2016 after starting in November 2014. The calls were always made after seven at night. To a residence in Baltimore. As Grace had said, the phone at that residence was registered to a man named Hans Baeder.

The noise continued to drift up from downstairs. The AC kept up its *chunka, chunka, thunk* refrain.

Next he picked up the information on Future-Ride personnel. The company had undergone heavy staff turnover. Perhaps it was the lingering recession. Perhaps, Griffin reflected, it was the unpleasantness of working with De-BOR-ah Miller.

He looked at the dates of employment for each individual. He compared these dates with the dates when the calls had been made to Hans Baeder. Only two people had been at Future-Ride the entire 19 months during which the calls to Hans Baeder were made: Alexandra Webb and De-BOR-ah Miller. One of the women kept calling Hans, though Griffin had no idea why.

Griffin picked up the last document Grace had sent. It was two pieces of paper, stapled. Who staples pages anymore, Griffin asked himself; Grace apparently. On the top of the first page, in sixteen font letters appeared:

BAEDER, HANS CHRISTIAN
The first line below that was:
BORN: Stuttgart, Germany, October 29, 1927
Then,
JOINED WEHRMACHT: September 1943
Poor soul, Griffin thought. Hans joined – *had* to join, Griffin assumed – the German Army at all of fifteen.
RANK ENTERING WEHRMACHT: Private
RANK AT TIME OF GERMANY'S SURRENDER: Private
JOINED NAZI PARTY: September 1943
From his reading Griffin knew that the vast majority of German soldiers were not Nazis, they were German soldiers. Why would the Nazi Party take or even want a fifteen year old? Especially one who never rose above the rank of private?
EMIGRATED TO UNITED STATES: September 4, 1954
PROFESSION: carpenter
A carpenter in Baltimore? What would someone at a Manhattan investment firm possibly want with a Baltimore carpenter, and an elderly one at that?
EMPLOYER: Bow Saw Construction Company/ Catonsville, Maryland

HOME ADDRESS: 5722 Gist Avenue/Baltimore, MD
DURATION OF RESIDENCE: 1964-2016

More than half a century in the same house! Griffin thought to himself. There'd been stretches of his life when Griffin lived three different places in the same year.

CITIIZENSHIP STATUS: Uncertain at this time; he may have been denied citizenship due to his Nazi Party membership

DIED: Baltimore, July 4, 2016
CAUSE OF DEATH: Pleurisy
PLACE OF BURIAL: Woodlawn Cemetery, Baltimore

Griffin smiled at the irony of the German immigrant who fought against the Unites States in the Second World War dying in America on the Fourth of July.

★

Griffin walked over to the air conditioning and switched it off. The silence was momentarily deafening, replaced by what he now recognized as hammering in the living room. Griffin walked downstairs, into the living room, and stopped at the source of the hammering. Annie was putting together a bookcase. He was still holding the pieces of paper with the skeleton of Hans Baeder's biography.

"Nice bookcase," he said to Annie, his mind very much elsewhere. "It'll be a nice addition."

"It's not just an addition, Griffin," Annie corrected him. "This will be the first bookcase for your books in our house together."

"Annie, I'm sorry, it's just that-"

"It's just that you won't really be able to enjoy the bookcase until this is over."

He did not bother to wiggle away from her observation. "Yes."

"Unless of course you want to finish this?"

Griffin's lack of skill with home repair was an ongoing joke between them.

"Uh, sure," he said. "Which end of the hammer do you hold again?"

By way of answer, Annie hammered in another nail with three quick, well placed strokes.

"Is Kit in his garage apartment?" Griffin asked, as Annie reached for the next nail.

"He stopped by when you were asleep." She started hammering again. Over the noise she said, "He said to tell you he's available if you need him. Until then, he's watching a M*A*S*H* marathon."

"I'll go get him. While I'm getting Kit? Can you do a MapQuest for me? 5722 Gist Avenue, in Baltimore. A man name of Hans Baeder lived there." He summarized for her the biographical details he'd learned about Hans Baeder. "Why was Hans of so much interest to someone at Future-Ride? Maybe seeing the house he lived in will give me some idea."

She pointed the hammer at him again, this time the business end. "Sure. I'll MapQuest."

"Thanks. You are aware you shouldn't use the hammer on the computer."

"I'll use it on your head if you don't clear out of here."

Twelve

June 12
6:27 pm

Kit, designated navigator, consulted the MapQuest directions
Annie had run off.

"Stay on this until we get to Park Heights. Couple more
miles. Then hang a right. If you'd of let me drive the Triumph
I'm leasing, we'd be there now. Now that is one sweet ride."

"Thanks," Griffin replied, shuddering at the thought of Kit
behind the wheel. "But we'll be there soon enough."

They crossed over I-83. The car radio played "Call Me
Maybe." For whatever reason, Griffin thought of the man in
white and knew he would wince with displeasure at the song.
They started up the long hill toward the Pimlico race track on
their left. A bit later they turned onto Park Heights.

"Quick left, first street you see," Kit ordered.

They made a few turns in a neighborhood of one way
streets and battered houses down on their luck for decades now.
They parked in front of 5722 Gist Avenue.

"Tell me again what we're doing here at Hans Baeder's
house?" Kit said. "What's Hans Baeder got to do with the man
in white?"

"Not sure."

"Then why are we here?"

"Because someone at Future-Ride phoned Hans Baeder, here, at his house. Called every month for 19 months. Remember the surveillance tape Grace sent? First thing the man in white did coming up from the Arazzo dungeon empty handed was call Future-Ride. Why would he do that? We know Hans Baeder is connected to Future-Ride, the calls every month show that. Is Hans connected to the man in white?"

"Is he?" Kit asked.

Getting out of the car, Griffin said, "Why don't we have a look around, maybe that will enlighten us."

★

He stood on the sidewalk to 5722 Gist waiting for Kit to catch up. Kit wore an Army green tee shirt and camo pants, attire inspired by the M*A*S*H* episodes he'd been watching. Griffin pulled out his phone.

"Who are you calling?"

Griffin pointed his phone at a FOR SALE OR RENT sign, with agent's name and number, attached to the front porch railing.

"Let's see if we can get inside Hans Baeder's old house."

The agent was in his office on Reisterstown Road. He promised to be by in fifteen minutes to show them the place.

"In the meantime," Griffin said, "let's have a look around out here. See what we can learn about Mr. Baeder."

5722 Gist Avenue was a brick duplex. Griffin guessed the house was two bedrooms and built in the late 1940s. The brick was an exhausted looking red. The three second story windows were the old style of 16 tiny panes of glass. The houses on both sides of 5722 had gotten their windows upgraded, but Hans Baeder had not.

Eyeing the tired house from the sidewalk, Griffin said, "Hans Baeder got 19 calls in 19 months from someone at Future-Ride. Why in the world would a New York investment company, with a minimum $750,000 investment, repeatedly call the carpenter who lived here? Kit, does this look like the residence of a man with that kind of money to invest?"

Kit agreed it didn't, not even close. They started across the uncut front yard, grass knee high in places. Kit was hurrying to keep pace with Griffin and tripped over something hidden in the grass.

"What'd you find?" Griffin asked.

"It found me," Kit replied. He pushed the grass to one side with an investigatory toe.

"Metal base of something."

Griffin looked as well. "From an old flagpole," he concluded.

"They really should cut this grass sometime this century," Kit complained.

The two men walked up a short flight of brick steps to a small, rectangular cement porch. Much of the porch was taken up by an old fashioned wooden glider, needing painting. Kit asked, "What's with the pillow on the glider? The glider's too small for me to lay down on. Had to be too small for Hans."

"Hans lived here well into his eighties, almost ninety. He may have needed the pillow for a bad back."

They stared through the picture window to the living room, empty except for a battered recliner. On the recliner rested another pillow.

Kit and Griffin walked around to the back of the house. They looked in through the back door at the tiny kitchen. A single frying pan with broken handle sat on the stove. The cabinet drawers had been left open and they could see the shelves were all empty.

They returned to the front yard to wait for the real estate agent.

Griffin and Kit killed time playing Give Me a Word. It was a game they'd started playing in first grade.

Griffin would say to Kit, "Give me a word," and Kit would write a word on a piece of paper. Kit would read the word aloud and Griffin, within seconds, would alphabetically arrange all the letters in that word.

Waiting for the real estate agent they went through *instantaneously* (a,a,e,i,l,n,n,n,o,s,s,t,t,u,y) and *stupefy* (e,f,s,t,u,y). Kit was about to read Griffin *foreshadow* (a,d,e,f,h,o,o,s,w) when the agent arrived.

★

The real estate agent turned out to be a tall, impeccably dressed – black slacks and dark purple shirt open at the collar that Kit noted approvingly – and constantly smiling black man named Charles Johnson. The man had rounded cheekbones and a wide, welcoming face. Shaking hands with Kit and Griffin, the agent insisted they call him CJ.

CJ apologized as he unlocked the front door.

"Sorry about the dust," he said. Griffin was reminded of the man in white trudging back through the dust of the Arazzo Castle dungeon, bitterly disappointed. Would this effort turn out the same?

"The place has been empty since the prior owner died last summer. As I understand it, his only surviving relative lives in Germany and it took time to track her down. Meanwhile, this place sat empty." CJ's smile never flagged. "This is the living room. Nice afternoon sun through the picture window here."

They moved into the dining room. A chair with three legs filled one corner. Along the wall were shards of glass, suggesting someone had swept up broken glass with less than a thorough broom.

"Who was the previous owner?" Griffin asked. He looked away from CJ as he did. Griffin knew he was not the actor Bobby was. Griffin could not look at someone as affable as CJ and lie.

"German gentleman, Mr. Baeder. He lived here *for-ever*. Kept to himself. Did you notice the porch glider outside? He sat on that for hours, I understand. He had a flagpole out there in the front yard. Love to sit here and watch the flag in the breeze. The flagpole came down in a storm. By then Mr. Baeder was too sick to put up another one.

"Neighbors say he didn't talk much. When he did, Mr. Baeder had a noticeable accent. Never lost it. I suppose some parts of your past are so strong you can't escape them. In his late eighties and he had a lady friend, believe it or not." The smile, if anything, brightened. "Slap a coat of fresh paint on these walls and this room would sparkle." They entered the kitchen. There was more broken glass in here. Griffin picked up the frying pan with the broken handle.

"CJ? Any idea why this pan was left behind? The living room recliner and chair in the dining room too."

"Left behind is right."

The smile kept going. Griffin was well aware the smile was a salesman's smile from a talented salesman in full sales mode, but, still, you couldn't help but feel good with CJ.

Who explained: "After the owner died – as I say his name was Baeder – his will said that his possessions should all be donated to charity. There was nothing else to worry about – no money in the estate. They left behind the stuff so old and beat up the charity couldn't sell it at auction."

They started up the stairs to the second floor. Their steps echoed loudly – and sadly, Griffin thought – throughout the empty house. Some broken furniture and a pan with the handle snapped off? Is that all that's left of a man living here more than 50 years?

"CJ, any idea which charity it was the Hans Baeder left his stuff to?"

CJ's smile slipped a little.

"How'd you know his name was Hans?"

"I didn't know," Griffin said, eyes downward in the general direction of the top step. "I just guessed. Hans is such a common German name."

The smile popped back onto CJ's face.

"Some charity that sponsors music for inner city children," he explained. "The charity operated through the Peabody Institute, you know the music school downtown? The furniture, pots and pans and whatever else he left behind was auctioned off to raise funds for instruments and lessons. What's still here today wasn't up to auction standards.

"As you can see, two bedrooms up here. The bathroom has all original fixtures. You could rehab if you're interested in buying. Some folks prefer the original."

They went into the smaller bedroom. It was empty except for a broken bookcase on its side.

They left that room and went into the other bedroom. "Here's the master bedroom."

Griffin's eyes went instantly to the far wall.

"Oh, that," said CJ. "Shown a lot of properties in my time, never seen anything like that."

Floor to ceiling, the far wall was musical notation, the lines and notes all done in pencil. The music started with a cleft in the upper left corner and covered the entire wall, a total of six lines of music. Griffin estimated there must have been a couple hundred notes in there.

"Incredible," Griffin said, without need of acting. "I've never seen anything like it either."

He pulled out his phone, which he pointed at the wall.

"CJ, any reason I can't snap some pictures of that wall?"

"Snap away."

Griffin took twelve pictures, making sure every note was captured.

Griffin knew only Hans Baeder could have done this. As surely as he knew that Kit would soon turn up in CJ-inspired black slacks and deep purple shirt open at the neck, Griffin knew this was Hans Baeder's doing.

Griffin could also tell that as Hans had worked his way across and down the wall his hand had gotten shakier. The precision of the carefully drawn ovals of the first notes steadily gave way to the sprawling, lopsided notes of the sixth line of music. Hans was probably dying by the time he finished this, Griffin realized.

"Either of you read music?" CJ asked, smile still securely in place.

"Nope, sorry," Kit answered. He stood to the left of the real estate agent.

"Neither do I," Griffin said. He stood to CJ's right. "But I can read English."

He pointed. There, in the lower right corner of the wall, written in a very shaky hand, appeared a single word:

MOZART

Thirteen

June 12
7:47 pm

Griffin drove home from Gist Avenue much faster than he'd driven out. He and Kit rode in silence. Griffin knew what he needed next, but wasn't sure how to get it.

Annie greeted them in the living room. She was freshly showered and wearing the baggy yellow tee shirt Griffin referred to as her Pokemon shirt. In the voice of a game show host, she announced, "What do we have for the contestants, Johnny?"

She sidestepped gracefully and with a flourish gestured to the completed bookcase.

"Thanks, Annie. It's really very nice."

"Have you thought about which book you'll shelve here first?"

Griffin indulged himself in a moment's daydream: *Gatsby* or Camus? Couldn't go wrong with early LeCarre…With some effort he yanked himself back into the present.

"I need to call Saif," Griffin said. "I have no idea if he can do what I need."

"Easy peasy," was Saif's reply. "Check your email in fifteen minutes. It'll be on your computer." Saif teased Griffin: "Griffin? Your computer's the TV-shaped object in your house."

"Saif said fifteen minutes," he told Annie and Kit, though neither had any idea what would be happening in that time. He started pacing.

"You're not going to pace for fifteen minutes, are you?" Annie asked.

Griffin thought for a moment. "That had been the plan, yeah."

"How much," Annie wanted to know, "how much shower tile grouting can you clean in fifteen minutes?"

Quite a lot, it turned out. Griffin had worked up a sweat, scrubbing away in the close, steamy confines of the shower, when Annie called to him, "Saif's email's here."

The email came with six attachments. The text of Saif's email read:

SOME ASSEMBLY WAS REQUIRED. HERE ARE SIX PICTURES, ONE FOR EACH LINE OF MUSIC. WHAZZUP?

Griffin typed: THANKS. NOT SURE WHAT"S UP. BACKATCHA.

Griffin spread six 8 by 11 inch pictures on the dining room table. He explained to Annie how he'd taken the twelve pictures with his phone camera in the master bedroom of Hans Baeder's house on Gist Avenue. Then Saif had worked his cutting and pasting magic, merging the twelve pictures into six, one picture for each line.

"Saif's work is seamless, isn't it?" Griffin said, looking at each picture in turn. "One picture, one line of music. The notes are completely legible. Now, what does this music tell us? I'm stumped. Kit? Annie?"

Kit shook his head. Annie said, "I don't know either, but I know who might. Miss Paulette."

"Our ninth grade music teacher?" Griffin responded, greatly surprised. "Miss Paulette? I haven't thought of her in years. What made you think of her now?"

"I've run into her a few times at Kenilworth Mall. On my trips to buy nails for the bookcases I'm building. Miss Paulette's retired now and is at the mall most nights, she told me. Why don't we see if she can help us with this. Unless you have another idea? Or maybe you'd like to finish cleaning the shower tile grouting?"

★

They met Bobby in the parking lot of the Kenilworth Mall. The four of them walked inside until they reached the railing overlooking the food court.

"There she is, by the fountain." Annie pointed. "Miss Paulette. Same table as the other times I was here."

She wasn't hard to spot. In the midst of tables full of sullen teenagers sprawling in chairs, there was Miss Paulette, sitting very upright and very much alone.

"Think Miss P will remember me?" Griffin asked.

She most certainly did.

"Ah, Mr. Gilmore," Miss Paulette said, as they approached. "Tell me, Mr. Gilmore, how did you manage it?"

"Beg pardon?"

"You cut half my classes and still managed to elude detention."

She seemed smaller than Griffin remembered; then again, teachers seen for the first time years after graduation inevitably did. She gave her head an exasperated shake. Griffin had forgotten how effectively she could do that.

"I've often wondered how you pulled it off, Mr. Gilmore. Cutting all those classes. Somehow you must have gotten into the Assistant Principal's office and rewritten the attendance reports. That much I can figure out. But how did you manage it? Could you enlighten your old teacher?"

"Couldn't it be my charm?" Griffin's suggested.

"You were a bright young man. Still are, I assume. Though you have a good bit more brains than charm."

"A backhanded compliment if I ever heard one, Miss P," was Griffin response.

Her hair was greyer than he recalled – it'd been 15 years since Griffin had seen her, so no surprise – and precisely brushed. Her half moon glasses hung on a silver chain around her neck. Her face was rescued from ordinariness by piercing blue eyes.

"Do you remember my cohorts?" Griffin said, waving a hand at Kit and Bobby flanking him.

"I'm a cohort now?" said Kit. "What exactly does a cohort do?"

Miss Paulette said, "Mr. Covington, I certainly recall you. And this would be Mr. Lowell, I presume."

Bobby bowed, taking an imaginary curtain call. "It would be," he said.

"Why don't you all pull up a chair," Miss Paulette offered. She sat in a stiff-backed style that made midshipmen look wimpy. "If you can spare your old teacher a few minutes on a Saturday night. Though I suspect this is not merely a social call."

"You suspect right," said Griffin.

★

As he put the pictures of Hans Baeder's wall on the table in front of Miss Paulette, Griffin explained the origin of the pictures, careful to give as few specifics as possible: "I took these pictures with my phone. They are from a wall in an empty house in west Baltimore. I believe this was done by the previous owner, who has died. He must have been a classical musician."

Miss Paulette slid her half moon glasses onto her nose. Eyes on the pictures, she replied, "A fair assumption."

"See at the bottom of this picture?"

"Mozart."

"Did he – Mozart – compose this music?"

Miss Paulette did not answer at first. Her head moved slightly from side to side. Griffin could tell she was hearing and enjoying the music in her mind. Her blue eyes sparkled with pleasure.

After looking at one picture then another, until she had studied all six, she finally said, "Some of it, Mr. Gilmore. Mozart composed some of it."

"I'm sorry," Griffin said. "I don't understand. Then again, I'm afraid I'm not very musical-"

"Oh, that I remember."

"I'm not musical and I'm not following. How could Mozart compose only *some* of this? Where there are musical notes and the name Mozart, one would think all the notes were composed by Mozart."

"In this case, one would be wrong. Mozart composed only some of this. Here, look at this picture." The four of them did as instructed. Miss Paulette had lost none of her front of the classroom command. "I recognize this. This entire line is from Mozart's *Eine Kleine Nachtmusik.*"

"*Night Music,*" Griffin promptly translated.

"That's correct. Even you would recognize the opening notes of *Night Music.* The start of this other line is from *Night Music* also. As is the last half of these two lines. The rest I don't recognize, so I assume someone composed it. Perhaps the owner of the house, as you have surmised. Your problem was never insufficient IQ, Mr. Gilmore. It's what you did with your considerable talents that's so troubling."

She concluded: "Taken as a whole, these six lines are a mixture of Mozart and someone else."

"What does that tell us?"

Miss Paulette looked up from the pictures. Her face was a blend of pleasure and puzzlement.

"What does what tell us about what or whom precisely?"

"What does the music tell us about the composer – the one who isn't Mozart?" Griffin asked, referring to Hans Baeder.

Miss Paulette took off her glasses and gave Griffin a direct glare. "You've always done this, Mr. Gilmore." Her voice as well as her face were rigid. "You make leaps of thinking without explaining exactly where you are."

"It's my superpower," Griffin said, a joke which yielded only a glare.

"Forgive me, Miss P. I'll go step by step. First of all, what instrument was the music composed for? Can you tell that?"

"Violin," Miss Paulette answered confidently.

"So the man who owned the house played the violin?"

"Almost certainly, yes."

"Can you tell where the composer – the one who wasn't named Amadeus Mozart – studied music?"

This caused Miss Paulette to think a few seconds. She held her glasses as she stared off somewhere in the mid-distance, thinking.

"Europe."

"Can you make a guess which part of Europe?"

"I'd say the continent." Some more thinking; more glasses holding and more staring. "But not the Mediterranean. They're too flashy. What he is showing us here is very much in the old school style. Likely German."

Griffin wondered, Did Hans Baeder study in Germany? Probably.

"Traditionally classical training," she added. Miss Paulette looked at Griffin, a smile tugging at the corners of her brightly lipsticked mouth. Matter of factly she told him, "You wouldn't last a week in the discipline of that schooling, Mr. Gilmore."

Griffin sat up straighter briefly, then abandoned the effort. "I don't doubt it. A few last questions."

Griffin wanted to learn whatever he could about why Hans Baeder – who was dying at the time – wrote the music on his bedroom wall.

"Did this man improve the Mozart?"

The sharp teaching tone returned. "Mr. Gilmore, no one but God could improve Mozart."

"Is it any good? What this guy added to the Mozart?"

"Yes, it's very good. But..." The half moon glasses went back on. She studied the pictures more intently. "But..."

The 'but" – repeated – surprised Griffin. Normally, Miss Paulette organized her thoughts before speaking and wasn't a "but" kind of person.

"But? But what, Miss P? You've got that but-I-can't-explain-it look on your face. The same one you had when talking about my cutting your classes. Which was nothing personal."

"But the notes that were added? They're a little off."

★

Off?" Griffin repeated, "What do you mean, off? Just a few minutes ago you seemed impressed by the skill of- "he checked himself from identifying Hans Baeder – "by the skill of the composer."

"Oh, I am impressed."

"Then what's going on?"

"It isn't easily explained."

"Could you try?"

Her forehead wrinkled with uncertainty. Griffin had forgotten how dramatically she could do that. She absolutely had that look of uncertainty dialed in. Deep ridges and furrows appeared on her forehead as she tried to unriddle the notes.

"I do know this composition is not the result of ignorance or an accident. It's skillful and deliberate."

She pointed to one of Saif's photographs.

"This line of music is entirely and accurately Mozart's."

She pointed to three other pictures.

"Parts of these lines are Mozart's as well. Parts aren't. The parts that aren't don't flow in the same way as Mozart's do. It's close, but not quite the same.

"For example, these two lines," she pointed to the last two photos, "are entirely someone else's, not Mozart's. The sequence of the notes is a bit off. The pace of the music: a half note where you'd expect a quarter; a note repeated which shouldn't have been. There's a lot of that. I can't imagine why. It is a little off and I cannot explain it."

"The man who wrote those lines of music was probably dying when he did so," Griffin observed. "Could that be the explanation?"

The schoolmarmish sting returned to Miss Paulette's voice.

"No. It could not. As I stated previously, Mr. Gilmore, this composition was skillful and deliberate. This scoring is not rushed and it is not the sloppy product of someone weakened by illness." She went on in her struggling to stay patient manner. "It's certainly not accidental. It's very well done.

"There is something else that puzzles me here, Mr. Gilmore. There are many repeated notes, a kind of stutter. Mozart would never do that; no competent composer would. It's impossible for anyone with any musical training not to notice the repetition. It's like the skip in a record." She smiled slightly. "Records are what we listened to music on before CDs or streaming."

A little off? A stutter? Repetition impossible to ignore? Why, Griffin asked himself. Why was it done? Why did a dying Hans – who was getting a monthly phone call from Future-Ride at the time – go to this much effort to rewrite Mozart in this strange manner?

"Thanks, Miss P," Griffin said.

"I'm guessing you'll be back," she said.

"I'm guessing we will, too."

Fourteen

June 15
9:45 am

Monday morning rain clouds rolled in, angry grey and moving fast, with a chilling breeze. Griffin, Annie, Kit, Bobby and Saif were meeting on the patio outside the Panera at nine. The sky reminded Griffin of the tornado at the beginning of *The Wizard of Oz*. He checked the sky without spotting an old biddy on a bike.

For a long moment Griffin listened to the swishing sound of traffic passing on York Road. He swirled his cappuccino, sipped, and said, "You know, for a while I thought this thing with the Duke and his key and the man in white and Hans Baeder was all tangled like a hairball some cat coughed up. I don't think that anymore. I now think there's a symmetry, a kind of elegance even, to all this."

"An elegant hairball?" Kit asked.

Griffin swirled his cappuccino again. This time he did not sip. "Here's where I think we are. Let's review the tape."

He put a pad of paper on the table and withdrew a pen from his shirt pocket. The others leaned closer to watch. Griffin drew a box on the left side of the page.

"This box," he explained, "represents the man in white. "We know next to nothing about him. Other than: probably Spanish, certainly refined, knowledgeable about the history of European nobility, extremely well prepared, good marksman.

"He desperately wanted a key – he was willing to kill me for it, if necessary. Using the information he got from the Duke's blondes, he did what was necessary to get the key. Which opened a room at the back of the Arazzo Castle dungeon. But the room turned out to be empty, much to his disappointment. What does he want that key for? What did he expect to find in that room at the back of the dungeon? We'd love to know.

"Down here," Griffin drew another box, at the bottom of the page, "is Hans Baeder. We don't know much about him either. We do know he was a classical musician, a violinist, probably studied in Germany. He survived World War Two as a German soldier, never rising above private. He came to this country, worked as a carpenter. Lived modestly in a west Baltimore duplex for half a century.

"For reasons I cannot begin to fathom, Hans, a man with very little money, was called 19 times by someone in Future-Ride, a Manhattan investment company. Nor can I explain why Hans went to the considerable effort of filling his bedroom wall with notes that are a combination of Mozart and his own musical composition. A composition which our old music teacher Miss Paulette described as 'a little off.' A knowledgeable musician and his work is a little off? Any reason for that?

"And, perhaps most strangely, he was a Nazi. Probably ninety percent of all the Germans in the military during the war were *not* Nazis. Why was Hans? Our cup runneth over with questions."

Griffin drew a box on the right side of the page.

"This third box is Future-Ride. We know a bit about the company and some about Alexandria Webb and De-BOR-ah Miller. Future-Ride is a Manhattan investment company and these are the ladies who run it. One of those ladies called Hans Baeder once a month for 19 months. Kit and I checked out Hans' house. What a Manhattan investment company could possibly want with the man who lived there, I cannot begin to guess.

"At the top here," Griffin drew a circle at the top of the page, "is Duke Ferlinghetti. It was his request to recover the key that started all this. He felt his family honor was at stake. But all the Duke is interested in is a key and this has advanced well past that key."

Griffin put an X through the Duke's box.

"I think we can comfortably remove the Duke. For all his royal turdishness, he plays no role in our quest, other than awaiting the return of his family's key."

Griffin stared at the remaining two boxes he had drawn. He started to sip his cappuccino, then abandoned the effort, lost in thought. At last he said, "Here are the most intriguing facts about the connections between these two boxes."

★

Griffin drew one line between the Future-Ride and Hans Baeder boxes and another line between the Future-Ride and man in white boxes.

"See this link between the man in white and Future-Ride?" With his pen Griffin retraced the line linking the boxes on the left and right sides of the page. "We know he called Future-Ride at least once, from Arazzo Castle. Did he call only that one time? One hundred times? We can't tell. On that phone he made only that one call to Future-Ride. That's all we can be certain of.

"But that's not the link we're interested in today. Here is the line we are focusing on today."

Griffin darkened the line connecting Future-Ride and Hans Baeder.

"We don't know which of our two ladies made those 19 calls from Manhattan to Hans Baeder, but there is undeniably a connection here. What is that connection? Any thoughts?"

Griffin sipped his cappuccino as he waited.

"Money?" suggested Bobby. The word came out unevenly. Mornings were not Bobby's best time. He gulped his black coffee.

"I don't think so," Griffin answered quickly. "Kit and I saw Hans Baeder's house. A duplex, ragged around the edges. In a neighborhood that was working middle class in its best days. Which were long ago. The real estate agent told us there was no money in the estate, only the house. For Hans Baeder, at least, those calls can't be about money."

"Something illegal?" Kit offered. He wore black slacks and a dark purple shirt open at the collar, a la CJ, the rental agent. Griffin had to admit it looked good on Kit. "Money laundering, drugs, whatever? Didn't you say the calls were made after seven at night, nobody else around to overhear? And from an alcove phone, where no one else could listen in?"

Through a long sip Griffin weighed Kit's points.

"Possibly," he said at last. "But it's hard to see a former German violinist who's working as a carpenter laundering money. Drugs? You were there, Kit. Did that weary, old house on Gist Avenue strike you as the palace of a drug kingpin?"

"Sex," proposed Saif. He was so embarrassed by the word he looked away from everyone, as if suddenly enthralled by the grill of the SUV parked in front of them.

"Hans is — was – 30 years older than Alexandria Webb and 50 years older than De-BOR-ah Miller. A vastly older man with a bad back pursued by a high powered Manhattan investment executive? Besides, the rental agent, CJ, said Hans had a lady squeeze of his own. No, we can safely delete sex here."

"So? Griffin?" Annie tapped the lid of her cup of green tea. She was wearing tomato red capri slacks that had never quite fit; Griffin thought she looked fabulous in them. "What do you think is the connection between Hans and Future-Ride is?"

"Annie, I have absolutely no idea. And that's what we need to find out."

"Here are our assignments for today," Griffin said.

★

He turned first to Bobby. "I'm giving you a long shot, Bobby.

"Call the Spanish embassy in Washington. Tell them you want to track down somebody who saved your life. Tell them you were at the Baltimore Museum of Art fundraiser and a man pulled you out of the path of a truck. The truck would have killed you otherwise. Gush as much as you can manage. You want to thank this unknown hero, but you never got his name. All you know is he's tall, 6'5", limps, has a Spanish accent, dresses in white. Was anyone matching that description in Baltimore on the date of the fundraiser?"

"That *is* a long shot."

"Good actors transcend bad scripts."

"Who said that?"

"I just did. Saif?"

★

Griffin looked at Saif, surprised again to see how young he seemed for someone about to be awarded his doctorate. In fact, Griffin knew that Saif would have had his doctorate four years earlier, except he had stayed home to help his father recover from a heart attack.

"Yes, boss?"

"Go online, if you would. Can you read German?"

"*Nein.*"

"But there must be translation software. Use that if need be. Check out Hans Baeder's role in the war. The Germans, Nazis in particular, were legendary for their precise record keeping. Then again, this was decades before computerization and the war may have destroyed the records. Still, find out whatever you can about what young Hans did in the war."

"What unit did Hans serve in?"

"Couldn't say." Griffin handed Saif the two pages of biographical information he'd gotten from Grace. There was a soft rumble of distant thunder. "That's the sum of what we know about Hans Baeder during the war. He was a musician and after the war he worked as a carpenter. Those are starting points. Learn what you can. Around teaching classes and preparing for your doctoral defense coming up."

"Annie and Kit?"

★

Griffin handed Kit and Annie the materials he'd been given in the Future-Ride conference room.

"Go through this. Try to find a link between Future-Ride and Hans Baeder. Or between Hans and Alexandra Webb or De-BOR-ah Miller. Anything in the annual report imply a connection? I scanned the report and saw some German companies. Look into them. Any musical connections? Or – I can't imagine how – any Nazi connection? There's a company brochure with brief bios of Alexandra and De-BOR-ah.

Could they have a personal connection to Hans? Try to find the link."

Annie and Kit agreed they'd do that.

"I'll visit Bow Saw Construction Company in Catonsville, where Grace learned that Hans worked all those years. What can they tell me about him? I'll pose as a representative of the estate, wrapping up a few details. I printed up some cards yesterday. That'll give me the excuse to ask questions. My hope is to learn whatever I can about that wall of music on Hans' bedroom. And why in the world was Hans Baeder a Nazi?

"Meet back at the house at six. We've done pizza and Chinese. Everybody up for Caribbean tonight?"

Bobby answered, "Sure, mon."

Five minutes later Annie, Kit, Saif and Bobby had gone. Griffin stayed on the patio, as the breeze picked up, the sky grew grayer and the thunder pounded more loudly.

He watched a red haired man smiling as he walked to his car with his two daughters and their beagle. For a moment Griffin envied the man his obvious, ordinary happiness. He knew he wouldn't smile like that again until this was over.

He stared at the boxes and lines he'd drawn on the page. For a while he looked at the line between the man in white and Future-Ride. For a full minute he studied the line between Hans Baeder and Future Ride. Then he drew a dotted line between the boxes for the man in white and Hans Baeder, making a triangle. Inside the triangle he put an enormous question mark.

Fifteen

June 15
10:48 am

By the time Griffin reached Bow Saw Construction Company off Rolling Road in Catonsville, the rain had started. The dash from his Malibu to the construction company offices left his thin cotton shirt soaked through. Griffin was directed to the office of Tom Morton, company president. The air conditioning in Mr. Morton's office was fired up so high Griffin felt his shoulders twitch in a kind of shiver.

Tom Morton was sitting at his desk, staring in the general direction of nothing in particular. He had a wide, fleshy, indulged face, mid-forties. For the head of a construction company, Tom Morton spent little time in the sun. His skin was pasty white. The man's cologne was almost overpowering. Griffin had no eye for toupees, but wondered if he was seeing one now. The hair seemed inhumanly black.

Griffin approached, business card at the ready. He placed the card on the desk. He got out, "I'm with Estate Eval-"

The man held up an annoyed hand, in a don't bother me yet gesture. The hand, Griffin noted, was perfectly manicured, shining like a new car's bumper. There were none of the cuts or calluses of a man who worked with his hands.

"I'm expecting a call," Griffin was told. Tom Morton continued to stare at nothing. "You'll have to wait."

Griffin waited a minute or so before approaching again. Another business card went on the desk. The annoyed hand shot up once more. Griffin was gaining a far deeper appreciation of the term "self-centered" than he'd ever wanted. He waited some more. The phone rang. Tom Morton listened no more than a few seconds.

"I knew you'd screw this up," he yelled into the phone. If Tom Morton ever had any self-restraint, he'd outsourced it long ago. "I want *two* pair of the suede boots and *three* pair of the calf high. No, I don't need any work boots. Think you can manage to keep all that straight?"

He absolutely radiated anger. It came off him the way heat rises from just-poured asphalt. All for someone mixing up an order for boots. He put down the phone with a flourish of disgust.

During this rant Griffin was looking at a silver framed diploma on the wall. Did they offer a course in condescension at Hampden-Sydney College? If so, Tom Morton had aced the class.

"Yeah?" he said to Griffin.

A third business card joined the others.

"I'm with Estate Evaluators," Griffin said, speedily. "Here to ask some questions."

"About?"

"About Hans Baeder."

"Hans Baeder?" He could have said "Daffy Duck?" for the tone he took. He asked Griffin, "What do you want to know about that old guy?"

"When did Mr. Baeder start working for your company?"

"So long ago I wasn't alive. My Dad hired him."

"What kind of work did he do for your company? Mr. Baeder?"

"Carpenter," Tom Morton replied, with a hint of impatience.

"What kind of carpentry did he do?"

"The everyday kind of carpentry. Those guys are a dime a dozen."

"Was Mr. Baeder married?"

"I couldn't possibly remember," Tom Morton said, his impatience with Griffin's Q and A more than hinted at now. He did not glance at his Rolex, but his hurry-this-along tone was the equivalent.

"Could I look through Mr. Baeder's personnel file?"

"Long since tossed in the trash."

Tom Morton's secretary entered the office. Her perfume joined his cologne and the combination left Griffin close to gagging. She placed a hand on his left shoulder as she said, "You've got lunch with the bankers in half an hour, Mr. Morton."

"And how could Hans Baeder possibly compete with your bankers," Griffin muttered.

She glared at Griffin, frowning. Her frown moved from Griffin to the door then back to Griffin, an unsubtle hint. He noticed her hand slide inside the presidential shirt as she spoke. He guessed the woman had not been hired for her typing speed.

"I'm cutting this short," Tom Morton announced, dismissing Griffin with the jab of a stubby finger. If finger points could kill, Griffin would have been dead by disembowelment.

Griffin was back at the front door of the company offices, preparing himself to sprint to his car through the rain, when someone called to him from down the hall.

"I couldn't help but overhear," someone said. "You want to know about Hans Baeder?"

Sixteen

Whoever had called Griffin was in no hurry to be found.
The first room down the hall Griffin looked into was filled
with boxes of copier paper and office supplies. The room next
to that contained rolled up blueprints, most piled on the floor.
Awaiting him in the third room was an elderly gentleman, a
good bit north of 80, Griffin figured.

"You wanted to know about Hans Baeder," the man stated.

Griffin acknowledged he did. There was no place in the
small room – it wasn't really an office – for him to sit.

"Would you like to hear about the day I met Hans Baeder?"

Yes, please.

The man was completely bald. His skin had a parchmentish
tinge to it. Griffin had never seen anyone who seemed so ancient. Still, he carried himself with a certain dignified bearing, a
man proud of what he accomplished in a lifetime of hard work.

"This was 1955, when I met Hans. And no, I'm not going
to think about how long ago that was. Do the math yourself.

"We had a customer, home owner on Ken Oak Road, I
still remember that. He was a very persistent fellow." Griffin

gave the man a go ahead nod. "One day the owner called me to complain. That morning the bottom step on his porch stairs snapped when he went for his *Baltimore News-Post*. Had it been the top step he said he might of blown out his knee, which was prob'ly right.

"'Your guys didn't get it right the first time. Send somebody out here. Fix it,' the fellow tells me.

"So I send out a crew of two guys. Two hours later, phone rings again.

"'Your crew showed up, all right,' says the fellow, this home owner. 'But your guys must of had a liquid lunch. They smelt of malt liquor. They slap a step down, hammer in a couple nails, and call it a day. They don't even bother hauling away the rotted-out step. Plus which, they left a hammer. You gotta get out here yourself. Fix it,' he tells me again.

"So out I go, try to take care of this myself. You know, Mr.-"

"Gilmore. Griffin Gilmore." Too late, Griffin realized he'd given his real name. He just wasn't as good at role playing as Bobby. If this man asked for a business card, Griffin had no idea how he'd explain away the name on the card, Jay Gatz.

The man never asked for a card. Instead he leaned across a rickety desk to shake hands. His hand was calloused and his handshake, despite his age, was very strong.

"I'm Mel Morton."

"And Tom Morton is-"

"My son. He runs the shop now. I started Bow Saw Construction the month I returned from the war. Where was I?"

"The day you met Hans Baeder."

"You got t'understand one thing, Griffin. The week before I met Hans, I'd been on a site and a half-built partition fell on me. Missed a couple days work, and for a while walked around with my back bent, 'cause I couldn't straighten it.

"There I am. Bent halfway down, staring at the mess with the steps these two clowns have left me, and wishing I could send them packing. But where do I find anyone to take their place? Where was I?"

"The day you met Hans Baeder."

"So there I'm standing, back bent like I'm giving a permanent bow. Got no idea how I can fix this. And the home owner is giving me an earful. Can't say's I blame him. Their work really wasn't good enough.

"That's when this man I later learn is Hans Baeder walks up. He's carrying his carpenter's tools. He's coming back from a job interview on a site someplace. Didn't get hired. Hans doesn't say, but I've always figured it was because of his German accent. Afterward he tells me he's walking home from the bus stop. Hans never did get his driver's license. Used to come in here every day by bus, carrying his tools. Where was I?"

"You just met Hans Baeder."

"So's this man I do not know picks up the hammer those bozos left on site. He coulda used his own hammer, but he was making a point. Even I'm smart enough to figure out what he was telling me. He can do their job.

"With a single, soft stroke he hits the underside of the step they just put down. The step goes flying up, that's how poorly it'd been installed. He does the same to the other four steps. One hammer swing placed exactly right. Never says a word. He hands me each of the old steps and I can see the termite damage. My guys were supposed to fix that, and they hadn't. It was just a question of time before they rotted out too. This guy, who still hasn't said anything, just saved me a boatload of problems. Maybe spared me a lawsuit too.

"'I fix,' he says. He obviously had an accent, which I knew was German.

"He goes to my truck. Brings back a piece of lumber. He struggles a bit, he's so frail. Still, he gets the lumber to the steps. Measures. Measures again. That's when I started paying real close attention, since every good carpenter measures twice and cuts once. Which is just what he does. Only needs to cut each board the one time. Does this for all five steps. Never says another word. I hire him on the spot. Told those two other guys I'd mail them their last check.

"That's the day I met Hans."

★

For a moment Griffin listened to the rain rushing through the downspout by the window. The rain gave off a busy, headlong noise which Griffin, who never cared for sitting still, enjoyed. He began with an easy question, before working toward why Hans was a Nazi.

"Mr. Morton, did Hans ever marry?'"

"No."

"Long time girlfriend?"

"Yes. Gal named Miriam."

"You know her last name?"

Mr. Morton narrowed his eyes in concentration. The man's struggle to recall was painful to watch. Griffin flashed what he hoped was an encouraging smile. After a full minute, Mel Morton said, "No. Sorry. I almost had her name there. Hans mentioned her a few times, but he kept his private life pretty much private."

"Mr. Morton? Hans was a musician? Played the violin?"

"He did."

"You ever hear him play?"

"He couldn't play. Not anymore. Hans was wounded in the war."

"Did he have a favorite composer, Mr. Morton?" Griffin asked, working his way toward asking about the wall of musical notes in Hans' bedroom.

"Couldn't say one way or the other. I never heard him mention anyone."

"Mr. Morton, did you ever go to Hans' house?"

"To it, sure. I dropped Hans off many an afternoon."

"You ever go inside?"

"Come to think of it, I never did. I knew I'd be intruding. He kept to himself."

Regretfully, Griffin concluded he was not going to learn anything about Hans' wall of music from Mel Morton.

"Mr. Morton-"

"Mel."

Griffin remembered that in their brief conversation, Mel's son had not asked to be called by his first name. Griffin was certain the briefness of the conversation had nothing to do with it; they could talk until the Apocalypse and Tom Morton would never make that request.

"Mel, do you know how or where during the war Hans was wounded?" Griffin's default plan was to at least learn what he could about Hans' unit. That, he sensed, might explain why the teenaged Hans was a member of the Nazi party. "Do you know which unit he served in? Did he ever say?"

"Hans lost all of his little finger and half the ring finger of his left hand. He never talked about getting wounded, but I couldn't exactly miss that."

"His unit, Mel?"

"He didn't say and I didn't ask. You got t'understand, Griffin. The war was a huge unspoken between us. I joined up in 1944. Lied and said I was 18; I was 16. I got to Europe in time to be in the battle for Hurtgen Forest." His voice took on a sudden, unexpected ferocity. "My Christ, it was awful. The cold. The killing."

More softly, he went on. "I didn't want to know what Hans'd done in the war. He didn't want to know what I'd done. Easier for both of us that way. So, no. I couldn't tell you what unit of the German army Hans served in."

The rain pounded more quickly through the downspout. Griffin knew he was not going to learn from Mel anything about Hans and Mozart or why Hans Baeder joined the Nazis. Griffin knew he shouldn't even ask about the Nazis. Mel wouldn't know and the question would unnecessarily hurt him, who so clearly respected Hans.

★

"Help me up, Griffin."

Griffin did. There was a hollowed out feel to the man. It occurred to Griffin that Mel Morton was quite possibly dying. Did Mel know? If so, he wasn't especially troubled by the fact.

"Where was I?"

"I'm not sure."

A half minute of silence followed. The rain continued to push noisily through the downspout.

"There's a picture on the shelf behind the desk, Griffin. Would you bring that over?"

Griffin did and handed to picture to Mel. Mel brought the picture very close to his eyes. A smile filled his face and left him looking much younger.

"This picture was taken late fifties. See those two men standing close together?"

Griffin saw a pair of black men, broad shouldered and wearing overalls.

"Joe and Tom Robinson. Cousins. Great workers. You could not wear those guys out. That's me next to them."

Griffin could tell it was Mel Morton, the better part of a lifetime ago. Looking first at the man in the picture and then at the man holding that picture, Griffin had never felt the briefness of life so sharply.

"And that's Hans to my right."

Hans Baeder would have been early thirties when this picture was taken. Griffin thought Hans looked much older. He was so sickly thin he made Mel Morton and the Robinson cousins look as wide as linebackers.

"Hans had pleurisy," Mel said. "That's why he's so skinny."

"Pleurisy is an inflammation of the lungs," Griffin stated. "Pleurisy typically leaves its victims with a chronic, painful cough."

"Which Hans had. He contracted pleurisy at age ten. While he worked here, and after he retired, I drove him to the doctor's four times a year. Codeine helped some. Some days the coughing was so bad he'd ask me to wrap his ribs in adhesive tape. That helped some too. He never complained and he never stopped working. But the cough was always there.

"Hans liked to work alone. He preferred the solitude. He was a wonderfully skilled carpenter. Tommy is wrong about that – carpenters like Hans are *not* a dime a dozen."

"Why did Hans prefer to work alone, Mel? His cough?"

"More than that, Griffin. He escaped into the quiet. But Hans didn't always work by himself. I loved working alongside Hans. Hours would pass without the need for either of us to say anything. We knew what we were doing and we knew each other that well. It was a true pleasure working with Hans."

"I'm sure it was."

"Let me tell you. During the war Tom Robinson had served on a destroyer sunk by a kamikaze off Okinawa. Joe

Robinson was in the Coast Guard, making the run to Murmansk through the U-boats and the Arctic cold. None of us minded silence."

Griffin looked again at the photograph. It was not a posed photo, with smiles encouraged for the camera. The men had been captured on film while loading lumber into a truck. It's a sunny morning. There is an almost tangible sense of the men looking forward to the workday.

"They're all gone," Mel said. The youth-inducing smile had left his face completely. "Nate, Joe, Hans. My wife took this picture and she's gone too." He shivered. "Won't be all that long til I'm gone as well."

"Mel, by any chance do you remember Hans mentioning a New York company named Future-Ride?"

"New York? I don't think Hans went to New York in his life. Was Future-Ride a construction company?"

"No. An investment firm."

"An investment company!" The surprise in Mel Morton's voice led to a brief coughing fit. Once he recovered, he told Griffin, "I can't picture Hans having anything to do with an investment firm. What would he have to invest?"

Neither man spoke for a while. The silence was so sharp Griffin nearly jumped when it thundered outside. For a while he stared at a file cabinet, dented and, he was willing to bet, empty. He walked over to Mel's desk. He picked up the pad of paper there. Other than an old rotary phone, which Griffin figured was disconnected, the pad was the only item on the desk. On each page appeared, in oversized letters: THINGS TO DO TODAY. Every page was completely blank.

On the top page Griffin wrote his name and home phone number. "If you remember Miriam's last name – Hans' girlfriend - call me, please."

Griffin had not learned anything about Hans Baeder and the wall of music. Nor had he learned anything about Hans and the Nazis. Still, he felt his time well invested. He was starting to get a sense of Hans Baeder as a person, and to like the man.

"I spend my day here, Griffin. Maybe someone from the old days will stop by. It happens. Not as often as it used to, but it happens."

"Mel, I hope it happens today," Griffin told him and two minutes later was back outside in the rain.

★

No sense in running to the car, Griffin decided. After 50 rain-thick feet Griffin felt like a load of wash in the rinse cycle. He stopped running. At some point you just can't get any wetter; might as well walk.

He mentally replayed the conversation with Mel Morton. Not only hadn't Griffin learned why Hans Baeder was a Nazi, the fact seemed more improbable than before. A fifteen year old, even one weakened by pleurisy, serving in the German army, that Griffin could understand. The demand for man-power in those times must have been desperate. But why would the Nazi Party want Hans?

Griffin's phone rang as he was reaching for his car keys.

"Mr. Gilmore? This is Sergeant Ahearn, Baltimore County PD. Our mutual friend Grace asked that I give you a call."

"A pleasure to hear from you, Sergeant," Griffin truthfully said.

"May I inquire? Were the results of my tutoring on picking locks worthwhile? I realize you can't get into specifics. Was your evening – some sort of fundraiser, I believe you said it was – a success?"

"You're a skilled teacher, Sergeant. That part of the evening went fine," replied Griffin, referring to his breaking into the display case of keys at the Baltimore Museum of Art fundraiser. "Unfortunately, the same cannot be said of the entire night."

"This may or may not be connected. There has been a development Grace said would be of interest to you. Can you stop by the Towson station right away, if you're not too busy, sir? Should be entertaining. If you're available."

"I am available, Sergeant. But do I have time to change out of wet clothes?"

Seventeen

June 15
12:27 pm

"Mr. Gilmore," Sergeant Ahearn said, "I want you to meet a young woman with all the makings of a fine cop. Not even twenty weeks out of the academy and she's got the instincts of someone on the streets for twenty years. Officer Felice Fernandez, this is Griffin Gilmore."

Griffin had read someplace that you can tell you're getting older when the cops start looking younger than you are. Shaking hands with Officer Fernandez, Griffin thought she looked to be in middle school.

Speaking to the other cop, Sergeant Ahearn explained. "First time I worked with Mr. Gilmore, it was right before this past Christmas and snowing. He went into a residence at night, unarmed and alone, to help us capture an armed felon – who had killed someone only hours before."

"I'm impressed," said Officer Fernandez, and Griffin could tell she was.

"No need for that," he corrected her. "I was hardly selfless. For doing what I did the charges against me were dropped. What have you got for me, Sergeant?"

"Officer Fernandez, why don't you tell us about your morning?"

She was short and stocky, with the blocky upper body of someone who enjoyed her time in a weight room. Her black hair was kept bristling short. Her cop shoes were brightly polished.

"This happened just after eight this morning. I was in my cruiser on Perring Parkway. No rain yet and rush hour traffic heating up.

"Everybody else is barreling down Perring Parkway, usually over the speed limit, hurrying to get into work. I notice this one car is keeping precisely to the posted limit. The car stops at a light that just turned yellow, when everybody else plows through. Nobody drives that defensively, not without a reason. I'm thinking, this is the behavior of somebody with reason to be cautious."

"Who was the driver?" Griffin asked, wondering why he'd been called here to the police station for this.

"The driver is a Caucasian male, early twenties. Blond, well dressed. I'm two lanes over and I can see this guy's head swiveling every which way, looking around. Nervous, drugged up, or both. No passengers.

"I notice a rear light is out. That's reason enough for a stop. When the light changes I put on the cherries and siren, pull the car over. My partner stays in the cruiser, calling it in. I approach the vehicle, ask for license and registration, all very standard procedure. When the driver reaches for the registra-tion, the glove compartment slides open up wide enough I spot a handgun in there, a Glock.

"He knows I've seen the gun. He hops out of the car and dashes off into traffic. I arrest him, probably saving his life in the process, by yanking him out of the path of an oncoming eighteen wheeler. Haven't gotten a thank you note yet."

"You might be waiting a while for that," Sergeant Ahearn warned. "Don't let it keep you up nights."

Office Fernandez continued. "On the floor of the back seat of the car, in gloriously plain view, is a shoe box. The box is filled, not with shoes, but with cocaine. A righteous bust," she concluded.

"A truly righteous bust," Sergeant Ahearn agreed. His sleepy-eyed look never changed, but Griffin could tell he was delighted with Officer Fernandez's performance. She, Griffin could also tell, was thrilled with her sergeant's praise.

"While I'm seizing the Glock I have me a look around in the glove compartment. I find a whiskey bottle. A receipt from 1996, believe it or not. I find road maps, precisely folded. Can't remember the last time I saw road maps."

Why am I hearing this, Griffin asked himself.

"Also in the glove compartment, I find this."

Officer Fernandez handed Griffin a business card.

"I've got one of those," Griffin said, surprised.

It was a business card from Future-Ride.

"Does yours smell like this? Take a sniff," Sergeant Ahearn invited.

Griffin did. "Whisky."

"Not the expensive stuff, either. I'm getting another smell in there, but I can't place it."

Griffin sniffed again. "That's Aqua Velva, Sergeant."

"My God, you're right," Sergeant Ahearn almost shouted. To Officer Fernandez he said, "Told you this guy was good."

"Not good enough to understand what's going on or why I'm here."

"Maybe this'll help you. Turn over the card," Sergeant Ahearn ordered.

Griffin flipped the business card over and read what was printed on the back in blue ink: 5722 GIST AVENUE

★

"Wait a minute," Griffin said. He was disappointed in himself for not realizing this earlier. "This car you stopped, Officer? Was it a 1996 Buick Riviera? Registered to a Miss Andrea Platts, deceased, formerly of Oakecrest Village retirement community?"

"All correct. How did you know?"

"Lucky guesses," Griffin told them. Obviously neither cop was fooled. "License plate, Maryland tags DNR 187?"

"No, different plates. The perp admitted in my earlier questioning the plates had been switched," Officer Fernandez informed Griffin. "He says he didn't do it, switching the plates."

"He say who did switch the plates?"

"Not yet."

"That 5722 Gist Avenue address," Sergeant Ahearn broke in, "is presently unoccupied. It used to belong to someone named-"

"Hans Baeder. He died last summer."

"5722 Gist Avenue is in the city, Mr. Gilmore. I contacted some folks I know in the Baltimore PD. That house had been burglarized. I spoke to the cop who investigated the burglary. I wasn't sure he'd remember it, but he did. As best he can tell, the burglary occurred during Hans Baeder's funeral last July. That is the sort of detail a cop is likely to recall."

"Did the Baltimore City cop say what was stolen? Is it possible to tell?"

"Usually you can tell, sure. This cop, name of Bob Brown, says he's pretty certain nothing was taken. There was something somebody was after, definitely, but they didn't find it."

"What makes him say that? How can he tell they didn't find it? Whatever it was someone wanted to find."

"The house wasn't just tossed – thoroughly searched – it was absolutely trashed. Cabinets left open. Drawers scattered on the floors. Bookcases thrown to the floor so hard they broke; chairs broken, too. Glass shattered all over the place. Someone was good and mad. Bob Brown guesses the burglar was paid to find something and got enraged when he couldn't. Folks in the duplex next door probably would have called the cops for all the noise, but they were at Hans Baeder's funeral.

"Grace sent me a request to keep an eye out for anything we came across involving 5722 Gist Avenue. She seems to view me as your guardian angel. Based on your performance in December, I am more than willing to oblige. She did not explain why I should watch out for that address. She doesn't even seem terribly upset that the address is in Baltimore City and I'm a County cop. Grace never was a stickler for jurisdiction. When Officer Fernandez showed me the business card – with the address on the back – from the glove compartment, I called you. Thought you might like to watch Felice question the driver about the card."

"Who's the driver?"

"The perp's name is Timothy Dean," Sergeant Ahearn answered. "Twenty two. From Worthington Valley. Father a surgeon, mother a banker. They have a condo in Ocean City and one in Colorado for the skiing, with a sauna for the après-skiing. A cabin on the coast of Maine. Ocean City isn't good enough for the family, of course. He attended private high school. Dropped out of Princeton. Pushed out is more accurate.

"That's the great thing about this country, isn't it?" Sergeant Ahearn kept on, his voice rising with the sarcasm. "Even those born to every advantage in the world can throw it all away to drugs."

"About the Glock you seized from the glove compart-ment?" Griffin asked.

"Ballistics tells us the gun has never been fired at all. We've traced it. The Glock was stolen from a Harford Road gun shop last year. No way of knowing how many times the gun has been sold and resold on the street. Glocks are popular with bangers and thugs. Those guys don't give receipts. The Glock's a dead end, I'm afraid."

"How about the business card? Fingerprints?'

"It's been dusted for fingerprints. Yielded nothing. Judging by your face, that doesn't surprise you."

"It doesn't," Griffin replied, reminded of the man in white slipping on surgical gloves in the museum and later in the Arazzo Castle surveillance tape.

"Can you ask Mr. Dean if he knows who wrote on the back of the card? How'd it get into the glove compartment? Whatever you can learn about that card, I'd appreciate."

There was some link between Timothy Dean and Fu-ture-Ride; the business card proved that. And there was a link between Timothy Dean and Hans Baeder; the Gist Avenue address on the back of the business card showed that. Did that mean there was a link between Timothy Dean and the man in white? If so, what was at the center of these links?

"We know one thing about the card already," Sergeant Ahearn said.

"We do?"

"Look at the seven in the address."

Griffin caught his point immediately. "The seven has a horizontal line through it," he observed. "That's the European style, not American."

Did that, Griffin asked himself, mean the man in white had written the address? Could the man in white have an in-terest in Hans Baeder?

Officer Fernandez started walking toward the interrogation room.

"And, Officer?" Griffin called after her. "Can you find out if he got this card from a Spaniard?"

★

Griffin looked again at Sergeant Ahearn. He hadn't noticed the cop's effort at growing a mustache since their last meeting in December.

"Nice 'stache," Griffin told him. "You going to keep it?"

"My wife hasn't decided yet," Sergeant Ahearn replied.

"Your wife makes the decisions on your facial hair?"

"You married, Mr. Gilmore?"

"Not yet."

"When you are married, remember this conversation."

They both looked through a window into the interrogation room. Timothy Dean was looking away, struggling to appear unconcerned, as the policewoman approached.

Sergeant Ahearn said, "You never know how these things'll turn out." Take that kid in there," the cop said of Timothy Dean. "Spoiled rich kid, right? You think guys like that will fold with the first nasty glance, and some do. Others turn out to be as hard as the hardest gangbanger. You just don't know."

Griffin turned to watch the interrogation through the one way window into the room next door.

"Mr. Dean," Officer Fernandez began.

"I'm not answering any questions until my lawyer gets here," Timothy Dean informed Officer Fernandez. He flashed a smile of sarcastic superiority. "I don't want the public defender you offered. My mother called a law firm downtown she deals with. A lawyer named Cam MacManus will be here soon. Until then, I don't have to answer any of your questions."

"You understand your rights. That's good. You don't have to say anything at all. Still, I think you should answer my questions."

"Why is that?" he challenged.

Timothy Dean leaned back in his chair, his legs crossed casually at the ankles. In his shirt pocket rested sunglasses Griffin assumed were Cartier. He seemed so young to Griffin he might have been in his prep school, chatting with his buddies in the cafeteria about this weekend's party. His khaki slacks and blue button down shirt contributed to the private high school air.

"I have it within my power to make recommendations to the prosecutor, a woman named Jennifer Fletcher. If you cooperate here, I will speak to her about the charges to be filed against you. I will not at this time ask you about the gun or the cocaine, the crimes you have been charged with."

"I told you, the gun isn't mine," he replied in a borderline whine. "I never saw it before. I had no idea it was in the glove compartment. That's why I took off." He descended into full whining mode. "As for the cocaine-"

"I'm telling you I'm not asking about the gun or the cocaine."

Timothy Dean flicked a lock of dirty blond hair from his forehead. It was a gesture Griffin suspected went over well with the private school girls. Officer Fernandez was duly unimpressed.

"What do you want to ask me about?"

Officer Hernandez got right to the meat of it. She lifted her hands, revealing the Future-Ride business card beneath. "We wanted to ask you about this."

Eighteen

June 15
12:34 pm

"We found this business card in the glove compartment of the car you were driving."

"Never seen it before."

"Mr. Dean, if you want me to talk to the prosecutor on your—"

"But I've never seen that card before," he insisted shrilly. All the confidence had bled from his voice. "I never looked in the glove compartment. All I did was drive the car."

Officer Fernandez pushed the business card across the table.

Timothy Dean wrinkled his nose at the smell. He tried but failed to pick up the card, which fluttered back to the table. Griffin at first assumed that was due to the handcuffs. Then he realized the prisoner's hands were shaking. He was coming down from whatever drug high he'd been on.

Officer Fernandez slid the card between two of the fingers of his right hand. He raised his hands to his nose.

"That's him. Mr. Whisky and Aqua Velva."

"That's who?"

"I don't know his name." The prisoner raised his manacled hands to his face, as if warding off the verbal explosion he expected to follow. "I swear I don't know his name."

She told him, "Why don't we start with where you met this guy whose name you don't know."

"Substance advice counseling. Court-ordered group therapy sessions. Those things are a total waste of time and he was a total blowhard."

"Blowhard?"

"He couldn't shut up about all the women he'd scored, all the drugs he did. How he could slug back a pint of whisky faster than any man alive. I had sixty days of the court-ordered counseling. Don't know how long he was there for or why exactly, but he stopped while I was still going. Nobody missed him."

"Did you catch his name?"

"Never asked him for it. Trust me, no one did."

"What did he look like?"

"My height. Skinny, but a pot belly. Dark hair, ponytail. Faded blue eyes. Said 'crappola' a lot. I'd never heard the word before."

Griffin had and recently, from Kit, by way of the Oakecrest security guard. It was the guard who'd heard the car thief at Oakecrest say 'crappola.' No question: the man Timothy Dean was describing had stolen the car from the deceased Andrea Platts; the man Timothy Dean was describing had been the driver for the man in white at the museum fundraiser.

The prisoner went on, "He had tattoos everywhere you could see."

"Where was this?"

"Where were the tattoos?"

"No, Mr. Dean. Where was the court-appointed therapist?"

"The therapist was in Perry Hall. Belair Road."

"When?"

"September."

Griffin saw that Timothy Dean was blinking with un-natural frequency. Beneath the table his legs were pumping as if sprinting. That, Griffin supposed, was some sort of drug withdrawal symptom.

"September was nine months ago, Mr. Dean. You've seen him since then, haven't you?"

"Last night. Bar in Essex, Eastern Avenue. No, I don't know the name. Biker bar, mostly. I was into the second day of my binge by then."

"That what took you to Essex, Mr. Dean? Scoring drugs?"

He did not bother to reply. Griffin understood the subtext of the exchange. What else would take the Worthington Valley son of a surgeon and a banker to a biker bar in Essex? Other-wise, it was like a Fortune 500 CEO dining at a soup kitchen.

"I've got a monkey on my back. You know the origin of that phrase? Learning it was the only thing of value I got out of that therapy."

"Why don't you tell me about that."

★

"As the therapist explained it, monkeys run wild in different parts of the world. Some tourists – not knowing any better – let the monkeys climb on their backs. The monkeys seem so entertaining and playful, right? Once they're on your back, though, it's close to impossible to get them off. Try, and they start choking you. That's where I am right now. I can feel the hands of a monkey, and they're tightening round my throat."

Timothy Dean fell silent. He stared straight ahead. For the first time Griffin saw the man's pupils. They were enormous.

You could have driven a garbage truck through those pupils. Griffin watched tears welling up.

Eventually, gently, Officer Fernandez prompted, "You were in a biker bar in Essex last night."

"Yes. I was. That's where I see this guy I know from counseling. The one I described before. This wasn't someone I normally would look at twice. Lord knows I wouldn't approach him. But he was always boasting about all the drugs he scored, so maybe he can help me out here. When I see him in the bar I act like he's my oldest, best bud. I knew it was pathetic, playing at being his friend for the drugs. My God, when we heard a police siren he actually called it a *si-reen*. It was all so pathetic. Even at the time, I knew.

"I buy him some shots. Whiskey. We go outside to his car, parked behind the bar. Do some coke and other pharmaceuticals. I was blasted out of my mind, but even then I could tell this guy smelled awful. He was not overusing a shower. And whiskey and Aqua Velva do not mix."

"What was his name?"

"If I knew it then, I don't know it now. Sorry. I probably called him 'Dude.' He was the kind of guy who actually liked getting called Dude."

"Can you describe Dude's car?"

"I don't have to describe it. You have it."

"What's that?"

Griffin understood what Timothy Dean was telling Officer Fernandez, though she did not yet.

The prisoner explained: "That's the car I was driving this morning when you stopped me."

"How did you get-"

For the first time Timothy Dean talked across Officer Fernandez.

"My Dad used to get a new car every year. About this time of year. Still does, but now without me." Timothy Dean was crying. "It was such a big deal for me. I'd bug him for weeks to take me to the car dealership. Finally, the day would arrive. My Dad would say, 'Which color should it be, Timmy?'"

Timothy Dean was weeping openly now. His voice wobbled – it reminded Griffin of a car tire with a blowout limping toward the shoulder of the road – but the man pressed on.

"He knew the car he wanted, usually a Lexus. I'd tell him, 'Lemon yellow' or 'Apple green' or 'The color of blueberries.' Whatever color I wanted, that's what he'd buy. I don't know what color he's driving this year. He won't see me until I'm straight."

"You'll be placed in a rehab program," Officer Fernandez promised him. "Of course, that will only work if you take the program seriously. As you are smart enough to understand."

Timothy Dean nodded, composing himself.

"You were talking about the car," Officer Fernandez said, after a bit.

"The car I remember very clearly. I'd never been in a car so old and huge. I told him I liked it. Maybe the only truthful thing I said to him all night.

"We head back into the bar. He picks up a woman. I couldn't get wasted enough to go anywhere near someone like this. Fat, bleached out blonde hair. Tube top that didn't cover her rolls of fat. Her tube top says YOU CAN'T TELL ME YOU DON'T WANT THIS. In fact, I could say that. Easily.

"She's in shorts she's got pulled down low so nobody misses her butt crack. A plumber would be embarrassed to have that much butt crack flashing. You have sex with this woman? You're asking for diseases the doctors haven't identified yet, let alone found cures for."

Griffin would not have predicted it, but he found himself rooting for Timothy Dean in his rehab.

"All I know is, I'm down in Essex, not certain where. The guy I drove down with has slipped off sometime in the action. How am I going to get back to my apartment in Hunt Valley? Then Dude – can I just call him that? Dude tosses me the car keys. 'All yours,' he says.

"He pulls me against a wall. Leans in close – I stifle a gag – like he's whispering a great secret. Except, his voice never drops below the decibel level of a jet engine. I doubt there was anyone in the place who did *not* hear him."

★

Timothy Dean started blinking even more rapidly. His voice was speeding up as well.

"'The old woman who owned the car doesn't need it anymore,' Dude tells me. He giggles, like he's gotten off the greatest joke ever delivered. I sure don't get it. I think I'm just staring at him, unsure exactly what is happening here. I'm holding onto the car keys the whole time.

"'A guy paid me to get the car in April,' he tells me next. 'Paid well too. This is a big guy, but not an American. Wears nothing but white. Can't walk without limping.' Dude loves to boast, but I'm getting the vibe this part is all true."

"What did your associate from the bar think of this guy who hired him?"

It was, Griffin felt, the exact question to ask. Officer Fernandez really was good at her job.

Timothy Dean paused, struggling to think, then said, "Didn't like him. That much I could tell."

"What else did Dude tell you about the car and this guy who hired him? What exactly was Dude hired to do?"

"Dude had to get the car. Then he had to put the car someplace safe for a while. Then he used the car to pick up the big guy in white who limps."

"Pick him up where?"

"Didn't say."

At the Baltimore Museum of Art fundraiser, Griffin was willing to bet.

"What else did Dude tell you, Mr. Dean?"

"Dude said, 'He told me to just leave the car in a parking lot someplace. After I dropped him at the airport one night."

Officer Fernandez sought to clarify what Timothy Dean had just said. "The he you're talking about here? The guy who hired Dude. He's the guy who's not an American and who wears only white? Big guy, limps?"

"That's what Dude said."

"When did Dude take this guy to the airport, did he tell you?"

"He did. It was a week and a half ago. A Thursday night."

The night of the museum fundraiser, Griffin thought. And it was definitely the man in white Dude was driving. Two days later the man in white would be in Arazzo Castle. What Griffin couldn't work out yet was whether it was the man in white who gave Dude his orders or someone at Future-Ride. Or both, possibly.

Timothy Dean went on, "'But,' Dude tells me, 'I needed the wheels, so instead I got some other license plates and switched the plates. I held onto the car. This guy's out of the country. He'll never know I kept the car. What's it to him?'"

Officer Hernandez asked a quick question: "Do you believe that car was stolen?"

Timothy Dean gave a quicker answer: "Don't you?"

He was blinking and speaking more hurriedly.

"'There's a box on the floor of the back seat,' Dude is telling me and the rest of the bar. 'The address where you got to deliver the box tomorrow is right on the box.' Even with my brain cells mostly fried, I know why the address is written on the box. Someone knows Dude can't be relied on to find the place and deliver the box any other way.

"'Take the box there tomorrow morning,' he says. 'And the car is yours.'

"The address turns out to be on Belvedere Avenue, where it hits Perring Parkway. That's where I was going when you stopped me."

"Do you know what's in the box?"

"Never looked."

"Could you guess?"

"That's why I was making the delivery. Instead of just dumping the box in the trash someplace. I knew the delivery had to be made. I didn't want someone coming after me."

By this point his words were tumbling out like a child running downhill. He was smacking his wrist against the table's edge. He had closed his eyes, apparently unable to control their blinking.

"The first few days of rehab will be difficult for you," Officer Fernandez said. "But you can get rid of the monkey, if you really want to."

Timothy Dean did not answer. Griffin got the sense the man was making up his mind about what Officer Fernandez had said.

"You never looked in the glove compartment, you said."

"No, I didn't."

"So you never saw the business card or know anything about it."

"No, I don't."

There was a knock at the door of the interrogation room. It was Timothy Dean's lawyer, announcing the questioning would have to stop.

★

"That's it," Griffin said to Sergeant Ahearn, shaking hands. "Thanks."

"We'll do our best to find out who Dude really is, Mr. Gilmore. We'll track down the Perry Hall therapist," the Sergeant promised. "Though I'm guessing Dean's lawyer will fight us, claim doctor-patient privilege. And I'll ask the lab to do a handwriting analysis of the printing on the back of the card. Though I can predict what I'll hear."

"Which Is?"

Sergeant Ahearn delivered a surprisingly funny imitation of a whiny bureaucrat: "The sample's too *small* to make a judgment. It's printed and that's *different* from handwriting. The 5722 is a number, which is *different* from writing. Mr. Gilmore, I'll ask, but don't get your hopes up on that."

"I appreciate it. All of it," Griffin said.

His hope was that the handwriting analysis would establish whether someone at Future-Ride or the man in white had written the Gist Avenue address on the back of the business card. Whoever wrote the address gave Dude the assignment. What that someone was after, Griffin could not guess. Certainly it was more than a key.

"Mr. Gilmore, that rich clown talking to his lawyer in there right now? We both know he got the car he was driving from the man who broke into the house at 5722 Gist Avenue, owned by Mr. Baeder. The break in that took place during Mr. Baeder's funeral."

"Yes."

"Do you think this lowlife who Dean calls Dude is capable of that kind of planning?"

"Not even remotely capable," Griffin answered. "Somebody wrote on the business card the address Dude was supposed to break into – since he's too stupid to remember the address without help. Timothy Dean has got to be right about that. Dude announces what he's done loudly enough everyone in the bar can hear. Planning does not seem to be in his skill set."

Sergeant Ahearn gave Griffin another look. That look could strip paint from a wall, reveal what the wall looked like beneath.

"That's why you're here isn't it? You want to know why this braindead lowlife with the tattoos and drugs, this 'Dude,' broke into 5722 Gist Avenue. He was after something and you'd like to know what that something is."

"Yes," Griffin answered. "And I'd like to know who sent him to get it."

Nineteen

June 15
6:06 pm

A bit after six that evening, Griffin arrived home, lugging a bagful of five Caribbean dinners. The rain had stopped hours earlier. The oppressive heat slammed back in. Except for a few damp patches beneath the trees, there was no sign it had rained at all.

From the sidewalk he heard Saif describing his most recent mother-driven date:

"She was as wide as she was tall."

Bobby's response was, "But isn't it the inner beauty that counts?" to which Saif replied, "Not exclusively."

Griffin joined them on the porch.

"Since nobody placed a specific order," he began, reaching into the bag, "I ordered dinners I thought matched that person's personality."

"Why is that a bit scary?" Kit asked.

"Let us see. Here's rice and dhal with okra, for Annie. Who made a New Year's resolution to eat more vegetables."

"Griffin, it's June," she pointed out.

"Better late than never."

He reached into the bag for a second dinner.

"Some Mahi-Mahi for Saif-Saif."

"Thank you, thank you."

"For Kit." Out came a third dinner. "Pulled pork sliders. I have no idea why I picked that, except it sounds like something you could say suggestively to a woman.

"For Bobby, coo-coo and dumplings."

"Coo-coo to you, too."

"And, for me, baked goat cheese. Since I'm the goat dragging you through this chase for the key, which is leading us to we have no idea where."

Half hour later, the Caribbean dinners done, Griffin announced, "Everyone? Let's go inside, see where we are."

★

Once they settled into the living room, Griffin said, "Bobby? I choose you."

From the couch Bobby said, "You asked me to call the Spanish embassy in Washington."

"And?"

"And, amigo, my phone performance today took even *my* breath away. I gushed. And gushed some more. I begged. Pleaded. I cried. I kept this poor woman, her name was Ms. Iglesias, at the Spanish embassy on the phone for the better part of an hour. She tried to track down the brave, selfless, gallant – did I mention brave? – Spaniard who supposedly saved my life at the museum fundraiser. I had Ms. Iglesias in tears. No luck. *Nada*. Total washout."

"No surprise. As we agreed, it was a long shot, maybe a no shot. At least we can be fairly certain the man in white's not a diplomat or a dignitary visiting from Spain. But thanks for trying."

Griffin stifled, though not completely, a belch. The goat cheese promised an active digestive evening.

"Annie and Kit? You looked at the Future-Ride financial information. Anything?"

"Quite possibly. For this, we need to go into the dining room."

As they went there, Annie continued speaking. "Saif was good enough to help us with this on the computer."

Saif took a seat in front of his laptop resting on the dining room table.

"First," he cautioned, "Annie and Kit need to explain what they found."

"Griffin?" This was Kit. Griffin noticed how red-rimmed and tired Kit's eyes were. He'd worked hard today, clearly. Griffin felt a burst of gratitude for his oldest friend. "We looked into the German companies Future-Ride worked with, like you suggested. Future-Ride worked with eleven companies in Germany. We found they clustered."

"Clustered?"

"Best way to explain this is to see what the eleven German companies Future-Ride worked with over the past three years do *not* have in common."

"Okay, Kit. What don't they have in common?"

"They aren't near Berlin or Frankfurt, the political and financial capitals of Germany. They're not in the same industries – one company manufactures pajamas and another provides tax advice. One makes computer software; one provides domestics to clean houses. Some are large corporations, some fairly smallish firms. Some are publicly traded on their stock exchange, others are not. There are no individuals in common in any of the companies' executives or their boards of directors."

"What do they have in common, then?" Griffin wondered.

"Saif?" Annie said.

Saif crossed his arms like a genie. Then, in a quick move he tapped the Enter key on the keyboard. He did so with a bit of Watch this! flair. Griffin could tell Saif was enjoying his role.

"What they have in common," Kit concluded, "is geography."

Saif pointed at the computer screen. The others had seen this already; Griffin was playing catch up.

On the computer screen was a map of Germany. There were two clusters – that was indeed the right word – of red circles. One cluster was in the north and the other in the south of the country, toward the border with Austria.

"Each red circle on the screen represents one German company Future-Ride worked with. Let me enlarge and split the screen so you can see where the clusters are."

Saif made a few more taps on the keyboard. The pattern was now obvious, undeniable. In the north were five red circles in and around the city of Hamburg. In the south were six circles outside the smaller city of Ulm.

"Well played, everyone," Griffin said, staring at the screen. He began pacing. "This outcome cannot possibly be a random result. It has got to be unrandom. Is unrandom a word? Whatever. This is a definite pattern, all the companies Future-Ride acquired clustering in two places. Now, for the question all this is leading up to: What do these two places have in common?"

"We were discussing that very question while waiting for you to show up with dinner," Kit said.

"Well?" Griffin said. "Might as well tell me."

"Well," Annie said. "We're hoping *you* might know."

Griffin stared at the screen a long while. He stifled a small belch. He stopped pacing long enough to touch the screen with a tentative fingertip.

"Well," he said at last. "I have no idea."

★

The goat cheese complained to Griffin again. This belch he tried to disguise behind a cough. He managed a passable imitation, though he suspected Annie was not fooled.

Post-belch/cough, Griffin said to Saif, "Did you get the chance to look into Hans Baeder's war record online? Do we know anything more about Hans than we did this morning?"

"A bit more. Did you know Hans Baeder was wounded in the war?"

"I did," Griffin replied. "Hans lost his pinkie finger and half his ring finger of his left hand." Griffin recounted the rest of his conversation with Mel Morton at Bow Saw Construction that morning. "But Mel had no idea where or when Hans was wounded."

"That I can tell you. It was in Bavaria. And I can tell you when. The morning of August 17, 1944. In an Allied bombing raid on a German railroad line. He – Hans Baeder – was awarded their equivalent of the Purple Heart. And can you guess where in Germany Hans was wounded?"

"Where?"

"Ulm," Saif answered. "Hans Baeder was wounded outside the town of Ulm. Which more tightly ties him to Future-Ride. They have worked with six different companies in Ulm, which is a fairly small place. Though of course Future-Ride worked with these companies decades after Hans was wounded.

"But, Griffin? I couldn't find out what unit he was with. Or why Hans joined the Nazi Party. The two questions you asked me to answer I couldn't answer. I tried, believe me, I tried."

Saif slapped the table with both palms. It wasn't a loud or notably angry slap. But by the standard of Saif's always mannerly behavior – in high school everyone's parents wanted to know why their child couldn't be as well behaved as Saif Venkatesan – Saif's slap was the attention-grabbing equivalent of a shotgun blast.

"Simmadown, Saif. What you got today paints in the background some."

Saif seemed as surprised by his outburst as everyone else. After tucking his hands in his lap, he resumed. "I did learn one detail about the young Hans today. It's not too surprising, considering what you and Kit saw on the bedroom wall of the house on Gist Avenue. You sent me the pictures you took."

"Speaking of that house," Griffin said. He started pacing. "I found out today that 5722 Gist was burglarized during Hans' funeral last summer." Griffin summarized the questioning of Timothy Dean by Officer Fernandez. "The as-yet unidentified Dude was looking for something in Hans' house. He was furious when he didn't find it and wrecked the place. But I interrupted you, Saif. What did you learn about the young Hans today?"

"Hans Baeder was a child prodigy."

Griffin began pacing faster. "Violin?"

"Yes. Studied at a conservatory in Dresden, Germany. The school and all its records were destroyed in the Allied fire-bombing of Dresden at the end of the war. I did find online an article in Hans' hometown newspaper from 1935 when he won a scholarship to the conservatory at age eight. The article includes a quote from the conservatory's headmaster, a man named Shurzdach, about Hans' gifts as a young violinist."

Abruptly Griffin stopped pacing, muttered, "Our problem is…" and everyone leaned forward to hear what their problem was.

But Griffin said nothing more and everyone leaned back again.

The pacing resumed, and Griffin mumbled "What we don't know yet is ..." and everyone leaned forward once more to find out what it was they didn't yet know.

Finally, Griffin said, "What?"

"What what?" Bobby said back.

"What did they want?"

"What did who want?" This was Annie. She instructed Griffin, "Stop pacing. Take a deep breath." He did so. "Good. Now, going step by step and speaking slowly, tell us what you're thinking."

★

"Hans Baeder's house was burglarized during his funeral. That we know from today's interrogation of Timothy Dean by a Baltimore County policewoman. The man Timothy Dean knew as Dude likely did the breaking in of Hans' house. What was he after? Dude? That's the question at the core of all this. He wasn't after money; couldn't be. Hans Baeder was a carpenter. He never made much money. Kit and I have seen his house at 5722 Gist. This isn't about money." Without meaning to, Griffin quoted the man in white. "So what was Dude after?"

"Something to do with Hans' music," Saif suggested.

"Must be," Griffin agreed. "But what?"

No one said anything. Without the clomping of Griffin's pacing, the silence sounded preposterously loud. He looked out the dining room window directly into the setting sun. He couldn't see anything of the world outside, which seemed appropriate. The goat cheese acted up again, but this time he made no effort to hide the belch.

"Here's another question floating around in all this. Why is Hans Baeder, a former child prodigy on the violin, weakened terribly from pleurisy, made a member of the Nazi Party at the ripe old age of 15? As I understand it, very few real soldiers joined the Nazis. They were just soldiers. Why force some 15 year old violinist – a sickly one at that – who never rose about private to join the Party?"

Griffin closed his eyes. The warmth of the sun was surprisingly pleasing.

"One last question. Who ordered the break in of Hans Baeder's house? A Future-Ride business card was found in the glove compartment of the car Timothy Dean was driving. Was it one of the Future-Ride women who ordered the break in? Why in the world would an investment company executive do that? And, as Saif, Kit and Annie have so convincingly demonstrated tonight, Future-Ride has some unrandom and unexplained interest in two places – and nowhere else - in Germany. Hamburg and Ulm. Why?"

"That's a lot more than one question," Annie pointed out.

Griffin turned to look at the others in the dining room. Then he talked on.

"Or did the man in white order the break in? The 5722 Gist Avenue address was written on the back of the card in the European style. Could well be from a Spaniard. Maybe the Baltimore County PD handwriting analysis will tell us whether the writing on the back of the business card is by a woman or a man. That should resolve the issue.

"I will boldly say it all comes back to: What did someone want from Hans Baeder? Of all the questions, that for me is *the* question. We can't very well ask Andrea Webb or De-BOR-ah Miller. We have no idea where the man in white is or even who he is. Only way we can find out what someone wanted from poor Hans is to find out more about him. Poor Hans is right. Mel Morton, his old boss, clearly thinks the world of him. I'm starting to like him too. How could he be a Nazi? How do we find out more about Hans? Maybe learning about that Ulm air raid might help. Any ideas?"

It was Saif, still apologetic about his outburst a few minutes before, who spoke:

"Can I help with that?"

Twenty

June 17
9:09 am

"This is Billy Williams? Who you?"

"Mr. Williams, this is Griffin Gilmore. I'm calling from Baltimore. Mr. Williams, I have a friend named Saif Vankatesan. He's a statistics professor at Johns Hopkins University here in Baltimore. One of the professors on his doctoral defense panel is an historian, who recommended I call you. The Air Force Historical Agency agreed you're the man to call. I understand you might be able to help me."

"Depends on what you want help with," Billy Williams announced, in a voice loud enough the telephone seemed superfluous.

Griffin feared that the man, whose age he knew to be 93, might be hard of hearing. Accordingly, he shouted into the phone.

"Mr. Williams! I need to ask you a couple of questions! About an Air Force raid in Germany!"

"Son, you don't have to shout. My hearing is still fine. My hip's been replaced once and my right knee twice. I assume you don't care to hear about problems in my sex life."

"No, sir," Griffin replied, quietly but quickly, before Billy Williams could change his mind about sharing his sex life. "Mr. Williams, I need to find out whatever you can tell me about an Air Force raid during the last year of the Second World War. I understand you're the expert."

"That's what I figured you were calling about when I saw an area code I didn't recognize on the caller ID. Not too many folks call me about my 35 years selling compressors. My territory was the whole Midwest. Retired to Tampa 30 years ago. I'm still here! Who'd a thunk it? But you didn't call long distance to hear any of that, did you?"

Griffin jumped into the sliver of silence before the freight train that was Billy Williams' voice started rolling again.

"About the raid, Mr. Williams?"

"You got a place and date, son?"

"Yes, sir. Ulm, Germany. August 17, 1944. The planes hit a railroad line."

"Let me go on my computer here. That surprise you? A man born when Calvin Coolidge was President using a computer?"

"Never gave it much thought," Griffin answered honestly. It wasn't hard to see why Billy Williams had been so good at selling compressors, Griffin decided. The man must have verbally bludgeoned prospective buyers into sales.

"I do appreciate your time, Mr. Williams."

"Thing of it is, Griffin? If I didn't have calls like yours from time to time, I do believe I'd be in Peaceful Rest Cemetery at the end of my street long ago. But death isn't a club I'm ready to join just yet. And call me Billy," he insisted.

Had they been together, Griffin knew they'd be shaking hands at this moment. Billy Williams's handshake, he was certain, would be enthusiastic to the point of bone-crushing.

Having this conversation several states apart struck Griffin as a wise precaution.

"There's someplace I got to be in a few minutes, Griffin. Until then, I'll do what I can for you."

"Appreciate it, sir."

"Billy! Go ahead, call me Billy! Won't kill you."

"Thanks, Billy."

Griffin listened to the tapping of keystrokes.

"Just so you know, Griffin. I've worked with the Air Force to put together my database. A lot of the squadrons have their own websites; I have that information as well." He continued to type. "I can get you the basic information on most Air Force missions in the European Theater during the war. Can I ask why you're interested?"

He didn't even consider lying to Billy.

"I know someone – of him at least – who was wounded in the raid."

"Here we go." The typing stopped. When Billy spoke again it was in an uncharacteristically subdued voice. "If you're telling me the truth about knowing someone wounded in the raid-"

"I am, Billy."

"That someone you know who was wounded in the raid was German. There were no American casualties."

"That's right, Billy," Griffin said, wondering if his admission would cause Billy to slam down the phone. "The person I'm calling about was German. His name was Hans."

★

To Griffin's gratitude Billy did not slam down the phone. Instead, still speaking in a subdued voice, Billy Williams told him, "The older I get, the more time I spend thinking about those folks on the ground. Back then, they were the enemy. I can't quite see them that way anymore.

"Here we go. August 17, 1944. Our planes took off for Ulm at 5:45 in the morning. From Pianosa Airfield on an island near Sicily. Visibility is listed as excellent. Weather conditions also excellent. Twelve planes participated in the raid. This was a planned raid. By that I mean they hit the target which had been identified before takeoff. The railroad line in Ulm was the target, which you knew. The raid is described as 'partially successful'"

"Which means what?"

"Which means the target was struck and maybe destroyed and maybe not."

"Is there is no way of knowing now, Billy?"

"None."

Griffin exhaled, and said, "But I interrupted you."

"All planes returned from the raid safely. No flak. That's anti-aircraft fire. No German fighter planes. By this point in the war there weren't many left." Billy Williams' voice had none of its former salesman's bluster. Replacing it was a voice unexpectedly youthful, but softer, a voice still a bit surprised by its survival. "The planes on the raid were B-24s, Liberators. The B-24 was twin engine, carried a crew of six. I was bombardier on a B-24 myself, Griffin. Sat by myself in the glass nose of the plane. Any mission without anti-aircraft or fighters, we called that a milk run. Course it wasn't a milk run until you touched down back at base.

"You could look me up online, if you had a mind to and knew where to look. Williams, comma, William C. I was a sergeant. And I was a member of the Lucky Bastards Club."

"The what, Billy?"

"Anyone who got through 35 missions was in the Lucky Bastards Club. It wasn't any kind of a club set up by the Air

Force. It was just a kind of recognition. The only rule in the club is that when you joined, you were expected to buy everyone drinks the day you got back from your thirty fifth mission. I will always consider the money I spent buying those drinks the best money I ever spent in my life. Might sound funny to you, but I never washed my flight suit that whole time. Why wash away the luck?

"After 35 missions they rotated you back to the States. Even then I knew it was just luck I got home and so many others didn't. Their number was up. Mine wasn't; that's all." Then Billy said, "There's a note here that the planes hit a target of opportunity as well as the rail line at Ulm."

"Which means?"

"The planes bombed something they unexpectedly found at the target that was worth bombing."

"Which could be?"

"Could be anything, Griffin. Maybe tanks or trucks were there. Maybe train cars. The pilots had a standing order to go after any train cars they saw. Could be almost anything." Billy's typing resumed. "For the luvva Mike," he said.

For the love of Mike? Griffin thought. Last time I heard that expression was from my grandfather, dead now twenty years.

"What is it, Billy?"

"Here's something I can't explain, Griffin. There is a space on the form that details how the information necessitating the raid was obtained. I've seen 'Reconnaissance' written in that space and I've seen 'Intelligence.' Here, the explanation is 'Classified.'"

"Seventy years later, it's still classified?"

"There was a war on, you know. This record reflects events at the time."

"Can you tell me why it's classified?"

"I can't, no. I have records from the war only. You'd need to contact someone who has access to more current information." That somebody, Griffin knew, would be Grace.

"Griffin, I'm sorry but I've got to go. I'm due at the church in fifteen minutes. A buddy of mine is getting married."

The boisterous salesman's voice returned. In fact, the voice sounded jacked up louder than before.

"My buddy's my age! Sandy Heaps, his name is! Walking down the aisle at age 93! Marrying Mrs. Greenblatt, a widow! What can I tell you! He's robbing the cradle! The bride's only 77!"

Within seconds of thanking Billy Williams and saying goodbye, Griffin was calling Grace.

★

June 17
7:02 pm

Grace returned his call a little after seven that night. Griffin was edging a sidewalk that didn't really need edging, but he couldn't sit still.

"You really are a bright fellow," she began.

This from a woman who didn't part easily with compliments?

"That goes without saying," responded Griffin. "So why are you saying it now?"

"You asked about the raid on the Ulm rail line, August 17, 1944."

"Yes."

"You want to know why the source of information on the raid's purpose was listed as Classified."

"I do. Do you know?"

"The information was listed as classified, not to protect the identity of the source – as was usually the case – but to protect the identity of the target."

"The rail line at Ulm?"

Waiting for her reply, Griffin banged the metal edger against the curb. A chunk of dirt dislodged.

"Not the rail line; that was hardly a secret. But what was on the rail line that March morning was very secret."

"What was on the rail line?"

"A train."

"What's so secret about a train?"

"This train was used by the Special Task Force for Music. That was a unit in the German army composed entirely of Nazis. Have you heard of the fine folks in the Special Task Force?"

"Never," Griffin admitted. He banged the edger against the curb again. The last piece of dirt dropped off. "Should I know about them?"

"Few people do. I didn't either."

A louder, faster bang of the edger.

"What can you tell me about them, Grace?"

"I could tell you amazing things. But I won't. I know you well enough, Mr. Gilmore, to know that you will want to discover this for yourself. As you research, you'll be planning your next steps.

"I'll get you going. I'll give you the best sources to check. I'm certain the theft of the Duke's key is explained by this. I don't know what else and who else you've been looking into, but the Special Task Force has got to be at the starting point for everything that follows, including Future-Ride and your man in white. Somehow. Of that, I am certain. You have stumbled into an extraordinary, hellishly disgraceful, almost unbeliev-able corner of history."

"But you won't tell me anything now?" Griffin asked. "About this Special Task Force For Music?" When Grace said she wouldn't he banged the edger against the curb so hard sparks flew.

Twenty One

June 17
10:10 pm

Griffin researched the Special Task Force for Music through dinner, which turned out to be macaroni with jalapeno cheese. He ate two helpings and remembered neither. Afterward, he was surprised to learn he'd polished off half a pitcher of lemonade during dinner, which he did not recall either. Griffin stayed at the computer – not counting an astonishing number of bathroom breaks – until midnight. He was back there at six the next morning.

Kit stopped by at eight o'clock that morning with a "Whattayasay" sent Griffin's way. Griffin looked up from the computer to find him standing there; for how long, Griffin had no idea.

"Kit, can you research something for me?"

"I was planning to go to the Mercedes dealership this morning. See about leasing a car. I stopped by to see if you wanted to join me.

"Last time I took a test drive at that dealership'" Kit explained, "I got stopped for speeding. The salesman said something about next time bringing a responsible adult with me. Since I don't know any, I thought I'd bring you."

"Why don't we give the driving citizenry of Baltimore a break this morning, Kit. I want you to look into a charming character, a Nazi named Alfred Rosenberg. Go online, library, whatever works for you. Put together a couple paragraphs on him, if you would. Rosenberg organized something called the Special Task Force For Music. That's what we're interested in. We'll meet tonight here at six. Can you be ready by then?"

"Don't see why not."

"And can you call Bobby? He's got an audition this afternoon, a production at a local college. Can you tell him to meet us here at six?"

"I'm on it."

"Thanks," Griffin said, and turned back toward his computer and the growing stack of pages he'd printed out. He'd already exhausted the sources Grace recommended and was following trails of his own.

Kit started to leave the dining room, then stopped.

"Give Me A Word," Kit said. "Oblivious."

Griffin answered, "b,i,i,l,o,o,s,u," without looking up.

★

Forty five minutes later, Sergeant Ahearn called. Annie took the call and handed the phone to Griffin, who hadn't heard it ring.

"No ID on 'Dude' yet, Mr. Gilmore. And Timothy Dean's lawyer is fighting us for his client's counseling records, like I predicted. Doctor-patient privilege, don't you know. Those counseling records are the only way to get Dude's real name."

"Didn't Dean say it was court-ordered counseling? Doesn't that force the doctor to release the records?"

"You might think so, but no. Our lawyers will fight it out with his lawyer. You and I stay out of the way. I'll let you know the outcome.

"Our hand writing analyst wimped out, as I also predicted. She won't say if the writing is by a man or a woman. She won't say if the writing is European or American. She is pretty sure the ink used is blue," he went on sarcastically. "Past that, she's not willing to go. I'll stay in touch."

★

Griffin resumed his research. At 10:30, Mel Morton called.

"Her name was Miriam Freitag."

"Whose name, Mel?" Griffin replied, his attention very much elsewhere.

"Hans' Baeder's girlfriend. Her name was Miriam Freitag. I should have remembered when you were here. I used to call her his Gal Friday. Freitag means-"

"Friday in German. Thanks, Mel."

Griffin was about to hang up when he remembered the blank pad of paper with THINGS TO DO TODAY on Mel's desk. Griffin forced himself to chat a while.

An hour or so later, Annie served him chocolate milk and a peanut butter and jelly sandwich, with the crusts cut away, exactly how Griffin liked it.

"I'll be at the mall," she informed him, soundlessly placing the plate on the table. "I need some nails for the new bookcase. And I'll hang with Miss P if she's there."

Distractedly, Griffin replied, "Thanks. Everyone will be here at six."

At ten after one Griffin called Saif in his office.

"Professor, two items. First is easy- peasy, as you say. Can you get me the phone number and address of a woman named Miriam Freitag? She was Hans Baeder's girlfriend. She's probably local." Griffin hesitated, before admitting, "A terrible thought just hit me."

"You're worried if Miriam is still alive?"

"I am."

"If she is, boss, I promise I'll get you her name and address. What else?"

Griffin could hear Saif typing, already at work on the Miriam Freitag assignment.

"Find out whatever you can about the violin section of the Special Task Force for Music, during the Second World War."

"Special Task Force For Music? Never heard of them."

"I hadn't either until last night. I've been reading up on them for hours. Can you meet here at six?"

"It won't be Caribbean food again, will it? That was a bit spicy for my tastes."

"Too spicy! Your parents are from India. Can food be too spicy for someone with your gene pool? Subs and sodas work for you? " Saif told him that would be fine. Griffin said, "Can you email me Miriam Freitag's phone number as soon as you get it?"

Saif promised he would and Griffin returned to his research.

★

Just after three o'clock Griffin, with the phone number Saif provided, called Miriam Freitag. As expected she proved to be local, and, as it turned out, very much alive.

In the phone conversation Griffin reprised his role as a representative for Estate Evaluators, in need of firming up "just a few details" about the estate of Hans Baeder. Miriam Freitag said she was leaving for her cousin's house in Philadelphia that night, but would be willing to meet him to discuss Hans when she returned.

When would that be Griffin asked, unable to dampen the urgency in his voice.

"I'll be back Friday, late afternoon," Miriam Freitag told him.

Miriam was pleasant and polite, speaking in a grandmother's voice, Griffin thought. But there was an unmistakable undercoating of steel to that voice.

★

Soon after, Griffin emailed Grace. He asked her for the exact dimensions of the room at the back of the Arazzo Castle – the room which caused the man in white to be so disappointed.

Grace quickly emailed back:
8 FEET DEEP, FIVE FEET WIDE, 7 1/2 FEET HIGH. Griffin did the math in his head: 300 cubic feet. I KNOW BETTER THAN ASK WHY YOU ARE ASKING.

Griffin emailed his reply:
YES, YOU DO. BTW – CAN YOU DO A PASSPORT CHECK ON ALEXANDRA WEBB AND DEBORAH MILLER? HAS EITHER BEEN TO GERMANY IN RECENT YEARS? THX.

★

Not long after Griffin's email exchange with Grace, Annie returned. She was carrying a small brown bag.

"Nails from the mall?" Griffin asked, nodding at the bag. He was stretching in the living room, feeling tight and stale from too many hours blurred together in front of the computer.

A fan was going; Annie must have switched it on at some point during the day. His shorts and tee shirt looked slept in. After a moment's recollection, he realized they *had* been slept in.

Sometime later Annie stuck her hand in front of the computer screen, blocking Griffin's vision and getting his attention that way.

"It's after five o'clock," she cautioned him. "You should go pick up dinner."

Annie pushed the button to shut down the computer. Griffin did not complain.

"You're right. I'll get the subs and soda. I'm ready for tonight."

★

They ate dinner in the screened back porch. The porch had no chairs yet, so Griffin carried in the two dining room chairs and three from the front porch.

"It seems," Griffin said, placing the subs and sodas on a folding card table. "It seems there has been some grumbling amongst us about my international choice of cuisine last time. Tonight? I'm going as American as possible. Subs for all!" He looked at Annie. "And you, Ms. Knaack, will be happy to note I remembered to bring sodas. We have Italian cold cut, we have ham and cheese, we have tuna fish. We have sundry other choices. Let the feeding frenzy begin!"

Five minutes later – just before Griffin started his second sub; Kit was on his third – Griffin remarked, "We'll get down to business later. But, for now, and I'm sure I speak for all of us, Saif. Inquiring minds have got to know: How's your love life? Any blind dates lately?"

"Whoa, Griffin," Saif begged. "Not while I'm eating."

"That bad?"

"Worse. Last date we spent the entire meal discussing the china patterns she wanted once we got married. She actually brought pictures to the restaurant. Keep in mind this is a blind date I met minutes before."

Twenty minutes after that Griffin cleared away the plates and trash.

He wanted to sum up all those hours on the computer with a single sentence. He began, "Now we know why Hans Baeder was a Nazi."

Twenty Two

June 18
6:36 pm

"Now we know why Hans Baeder was a Nazi," Griffin said again, more loudly. Finally he could put a mental check mark through that item on his Questions To Be Answered list. He felt his adrenaline pumping. "It made no sense before. Hans was as far from the Aryan ideal as it was possible for a male to be. He was a sickly fifteen year old, a child prodigy on the violin, in love with Mozart. Why was he a Nazi?

"Saif and Kit, you two could probably guess about Hans, at least a little. Annie and Bobby, I'll fill you in.

"It was Hans' knowledge of violins that made him a Nazi." Griffin massaged his eyes. He was suddenly exhausted, totally blasted from the hours of research. "For what it's worth, I'm glad it was violins that put Hans in the Nazi Party. And not any of the other hideous qualifications the Nazis insisted on for membership. I won't deny knowing that relieves me greatly."

"So why was Hans a Nazi, Griffin?"

"Kit, Hans was a member of the Nazis' Special Task Force For Music. I assume everyone in the Special Task Force had to join the Nazi Party. To insure their silence, I suppose.

"We know Hans Baeder was a member of the Special Task Force For Music because he was wounded in an American bombing raid. Saif got the date of the raid: August 17, 1944. I called an older gentleman in Florida, Billy Williams, about the raid. Billy told me the American planes hit a rail line outside Ulm, Germany. On the railroad tracks that day more than 70 years ago was a train commandeered by the Special Task Force."

"What did they do?" Bobby asked, rattling the remaining ice cubes in his cup. "This Special Task Force."

"They looted, Bobby. They stole. They plundered. They seized whatever they wanted. They helped themselves to the spoils of war. Adolph Hitler fancied himself an artist and ordered the artistic treasures of conquered Europe – paintings, sculptures, and musical scores and instruments – stolen. The best was brought back to the Music Office in Berlin.

"We're concerned with the stolen musical instruments. No one today will ever know how many musical instruments the Special Task Force For Music grabbed. The loot must have been enormous. Staggering. Simply transporting it must have been a challenge. They were bringing in 200 pianos *a week* from France alone. Hitler ordered this to happen, but the nuts and bolts of the Special Task Force was the brainchild of a truly twisted character named Alfred Rosenberg. Kit will now tell us about him."

★

Kit jawed down the last of his American cold cut sub, extra hots. He pureed the sub's contents with a swig of lime aid. He reached into the pocket of his blue blazer, which he wore with navy blue chino shorts, for his notes. When he spoke, Kit's usual joking tone was nowhere present.

"The Special Task Force For Music was the evil spawn of a real charmer named Alfred Rosenberg. Rosenberg was one of the original Nazis. He actually joined the Nazi Party months before Adolph Hitler, which I didn't think was possible. He was the Party leader before Hitler. Rosenberg is the one who selected the swastika as the symbol for the Nazis.

"Rosenberg was in charge of the" – Kit consulted his notes, written in his usual rune-like penmanship – 'the spiritual and philosophical education of the Nazi Party.' In that role he drafted for Hitler's signature a proclamation establishing the Special Task Force For Music. He viewed all of human history as a battle between the forces of light, the Aryans, and the forces of darkness, the Jews. On that last point, Jesus gave him some trouble since Jesus was, after all, a Jew. Rosenberg cranked up some crackpot scholarship revealing that, in fact, Jesus was part of an Aryan tribe living in Israel at the time. It'd be funny, if it wasn't so awful."

Somewhere a neighbor struggled to start a lawn mower. A dog barked two doors down, a golden retriever who flopped on his back to get his belly rubbed at the slightest sign of affection. The contrast between the everyday noises of a summer night and the horrors they were discussing was so unnerving that for a few seconds Griffin was unable to speak.

★

"Saif," he managed eventually, "what did you find out about the Special Task Force and violins specifically?"

"Not all that much, Griffin. So many of the records must have been destroyed in the war. I am sorry."

"Don't be," Griffin reassured him. "With all the fighting and the firebombing, the near-total devastation of Germany, most of the records must have been destroyed."

"The information is very limited," Saif agreed.

"I'm certain you did as well as anyone could. Besides, I'm becoming convinced there's another reason the record is so thin, which I'll get to in a while. Just tell us what you can."

"The few records that do exist illustrate the legendary German precision – date, time, and place of acquisitions all specified."

"What they stole and when they stole it," Griffin summarized. "And who they stole the instrument from?"

"And whom they stole the instrument from. Many of the violins were taken from victims of the Holocaust, who were hardly in any position to stop them." Saif's voice had a kind of sour taint to it, which Griffin figured was caused by the distaste Saif felt for the unpleasant subject. "The Special Task Force For Music was plundering so many musical instruments they couldn't keep them all. They sent out squads of specialists. The specialist's job was to decide which were the most valuable instruments. The specialist had to determine what was worth sending back to the Music Office in Berlin and what wasn't."

"Saif? By a specialist you mean a musician knowledgeable about the instrument he was examining? For example, a pianist would examine the pianos. A flutist examines the flutes, and so on."

"Presumably, yes."

"A child prodigy on the violin would examine violins."

Saif caught the implication, as Griffin knew he would. "Whoa. Hans Baeder."

"Do you think Hans Baeder, former child prodigy, might have been a violin specialist?"

Saif hesitated before answering. He was not, Griffin knew, comfortable with speculating. Still, he concluded, "That's likely."

"How big was the Special Task Force?"

"More than 300 people at its peak, Griffin. Far less by the war's end. It's safe to suppose many of them were killed in the bombing and the fighting. One last thing."

"Which is?"

"Which is, Griffin, that the Special Task Force was in Italy. That much is known and no surprise at all. Think of all the loot awaiting them in Naples and Milan, and Florence and Rome."

"I've got to ask. Did they get to Arazzo?"

"They did, Griffin. And only a few days after the Ulm air raid. They may have gone to Arazzo to recuperate. That's it."

The lawn mower finally coughed to life. Griffin listened for a few seconds to the oddly reassuring sound.

"Here's the question," he began. "Here's the question that I think ties together Duke Ferlinghetti's key and the man in white and Future-Ride – either Alexandra Webb or De-BOR-ah Miller – and Hans Baeder."

Bobby crumpled his cup. The sound wasn't loud, but was so well-timed he grabbed everyone's attention. He had that skill for taking center stage.

In a British accent, imitating Sherlock Holmes, he said, "That's elementary, Dr. Watson."

Twenty Three

June 18
6:47 pm

Speaking now in his own voice, Bobby said, "The question is: Where did all that loot go?"

"Exactly, Bobby. That, as you Shakespearean actors say, is the question. Where did it all go? The thousands of instruments stolen by the Special Task Force For Music? There isn't much of an historical record," Griffin conceded. "But there is some. There are a few facts, but other than that we have to connect some widely scattered dots. What do we know for sure?

"We know, as Saif just told us, the best of the stolen musical instruments were brought back to the Music Office in Berlin. We know the Music Office, like so much of Berlin, was turned to rubble in the Allied bombing. Those are historical facts, as is the fact that the Music Office warehouses were virtually empty by the time the American and British troops from the west and the Soviet troops from the east captured Berlin.

"No doubt many, many instruments were destroyed in the bombing of Germany, which was ferocious. But we are talking about a spectacular haul here. Keep in mind the legendary

German efficiency – and the limitless Nazi greed. They stole the best instruments that European culture has produced over centuries. Violins by Stradivarius and who knows what else. Where did it all go?

"The historical record tells us that in late 1944 and the opening months of 1945 the Special Task Force shipped their take to safer locations in Germany. But the Allies kept pressing into Germany and no place was safe for long. At this point, in the fog of war and the collapse of the Third Reich, the record shifts from the historical into almost mythical lore. The question we need answered is: Where did all those instruments go?"

"Where did they go, Griffin?" asked Kit.

"Some believe the loot went into mine shafts; others say massive underground bunkers whose locations were known only to the Nazis. The most frequently listed places for these mine shafts and bunkers are Hamburg in the north and Ulm in the south."

Annie pointed out, "Those are the two places where Future-Ride did so much business, Hamburg and Ulm. What's the word you used for the pattern we came up with, Griffin? Unrandom?"

"Whether it's a word or not, I'm not sure."

"But it can't be random," Annie persisted. "Future-Ride does all that work in Hamburg and Ulm and nowhere else in Germany."

"No," Griffin agreed. "It's not random. Now we know what one of the ladies at Future-Ride is after. She's after something stolen by the Special Task Force. Something that might have been hidden in the areas of Hamburg or Ulm. But we don't know exactly what that something could be. It's a safe bet whatever's being sought could fit into the fairly small room at the back of the dungeon in Arazzo Castle. Since that's where the man in white thought he'd find it. That's what the key was for. Whatever *it* is.

"There's a reason Future-Ride did business with those eleven companies in Hamburg and Ulm and nowhere else in Germany. Doing business with companies in those two places almost certainly gave one of our Future-Ride ladies the excuse to go to those places. She could look around, do some on the ground investigating. Her cover story for all those trips to Hamburg and Ulm is legitimate business. Not only would Future-Ride pick up the tab for the trip, but she has an airtight alibi."

"Which of the Future-Ride ladies do you think made those European trips?" Bobby wondered. "I know you expect Grace to tell us."

"She will. I've asked her for a passport check. That will let us know how many trips abroad Alexandra Webb and De-BOR-ah Miller have made. Then we'll know which woman it is."

Bobby persisted. "But which of the women do *you* think it is, Griffin? Is it Alexandra Webb or De-BOR-ah Miller? I couldn't tell when I was Dr. Briggs and I can't tell now."

"I couldn't say yet," Griffin admitted. "But here is what I can tell you now."

★

"There are two documented attempts to hide the Special Task Force's stash," Griffin resumed. His throat hurt from all this talking. "The destination for one attempt was a monastery in Bavaria. There is a bill of lading for shipment by rail."

"A bill of lading would have a date and list of contents shipped," Saif stated. As always, he was quick to the point.

"Unfortunately, this one doesn't," Griffin said, with obvious frustration. "The document was found in a burned out basement in Hamburg. That part of the bill of lading with the date as well as identification of the contents to be shipped was burned and unreadable. This much is known about that shipment – When British troops reached the Bavarian monastery in May 1945, they found nothing of value. Did the shipment reach its destination? Was it stopped before it got to the monastery? The historical record won't ever tell us.

"But here is a detail I learned today in my research – the rail line in Ulm, where Hans Baeder was wounded, is on the way to the monastery. The shipment might have been the one hit by the American bombers in the raid Billy Williams told me about. We may never know for certain. But I believe that is exactly what happened."

Griffin sipped his root beer. Not only was his throat gravelly from so much talking, he needed to collect his thoughts before moving into the next part. After draining his drink, he said, "Putting the Bavarian monastery to the side for a moment, there is just one other identified effort to ship musical instruments.

"In Silesia, five boxcars were left on the train tracks, when the Russian Red Army showed up earlier than expected and the Germans fled. The Russians appropriated the five boxcars of instruments. Whatever was in those boxcars has not been heard of since. What the Russians took and where it went remains unknown. And will likely stay unknown.

"This, I think, is why the raid in which Hans Baeder was wounded was listed as classified. The Americans and British wanted very much to limit criticism of our Russian Allies. The Russians had, after all, helped themselves to the spoils of war, stealing back from the Germans what the Special Task Force had stolen. Consequently, anything about the Special Task Force For Music was deemed classified information. That's part of why the surviving record is so sparse.

"Now," Griffin tried to say, but his throat gave out.

★

Annie handed him her Styrofoam cup. He slugged back the last inch of orange soda, feeling like a marathoner tossing back Gatorade on the run.

"Now, I know via my phone conversation with Billy Williams, and this was confirmed today on a web site Grace recommended, that the August 17, 1944 raid on the Ulm rail line was partially successful."

"What's that mean?" Kit wanted to know. "Partially successful?"

"A good question," Griffin said. "I asked Billy Williams that. Billy's the expert on air raids during the war. He's in his Nineties and retired to Florida. And still quite the character."

"What did the expert say?" Bobby followed up. "What does partially successful mean?"

"The target was hit. But was it destroyed? Maybe yes, maybe no. We already knew the target was hit – Hans was wounded in the raid."

"If this bombing expert can't say," Bobby wanted to know, "who can?"

"Miriam," Annie said, a heartbeat before Griffin could answer. "You told me Miriam is the name of Hans Baeder's girlfriend. He might have said something to her about it."

"Miriam Freitag, the girlfriend's name is. Mel Morton called today to give me her last name," Griffin explained. "And, yes, maybe Hans told Miriam something. Annie and I will see

Miriam Saturday after she's back from going out of town. Saif got her address. According to Mel, normally Hans was close to totally silent. If Hans talked to anybody about the raid where he was wounded, it would have been Miriam Freitag. Miriam is our next step.

"Here's what we want to learn from her: Does she know what was on that Special Task Force train? And did anything survive the partially successful air raid?" He stopped speaking, his throat sandpapery again. Annie held up her hand for him to pause. She went into the kitchen and returned with a pitcher of lemonade. He poured some lemonade into his cup, sipped – it didn't really mix well with the dregs of orange soda – then resumed.

"We can safely conclude that one of the ladies at Future-Ride or the man in white or both believe something survived the Ulm air raid. Whatever survived the raid is what they're after.

"The ladies at Future-Ride? Clearly one of them believes something survived the Ulm raid. That's why those 19 calls were made from the Future-Ride alcove phone to Hans Baeder. Hans survived the raid. He was wounded in the raid, but survived. Why else would they call him, other than to find out which violins survived with him? It certainly could not be about a carpenter making a $750,000 investment, minimum.

"The man in white? I think that's what the man in white was expecting to find in the room at the back of the Arazzo Castle dungeon. He's after whatever violins survived the air raid at Ulm when Hans was wounded.

"That's got to be why Hans Baeder's house was burglarized during his funeral. Dude, the druggie Timothy Dean talked about during his interrogation, broke in, looking for something. Which he did not find. Who ordered him to break in?

Someone at Future Ride or the man in white? Or are they working together?"

Griffin pressed on. "I found out today from Grace the dimensions of that room at the back of the Arazzo Castle dungeon: five feet deep, five feet wide, seven and a half feet high. That is just about the size of a storage facility cubicle, the kind you rent for a month at a time. Annie, remember when we moved your friend Katie Mac's stuff into the storage place by I-83?"

"Katie Mac is not exactly my friend."

"I understand. But remember how many boxes we got into that storage cubicle? Must have been twenty, more. You'd cram another box in there and think, that's it, this has got to be full. Then you could cram in a few boxes more.

"Point is, even that small room at the back of the dungeon could have held quite a few instruments. Violins, probably, since that was Hans' specialty. Think how much a floor to ceiling room full of Stradivariuses would be worth. Or is it Stradavarii? Whichever. Either way, nothing was there in that room at the back of the dungeon. But now we know, though still not specifically, what the man in white was expecting to find. What would it be worth, a roomful of the most valuable musical instruments the Nazis could steal?"

"Billions and billions," answered Bobby, in his impression of Carl Sagan.

Out of the corner of his eye, Griffin spotted a look of confusion crease Annie's face.

"What ? What is it?" he asked her.

"Griffin? That doesn't-" she hesitated.

"Go ahead, Annie. You think I've got something wrong. No need to be so defensive. What do you think I missed?"

Twenty Four

June 18
7:00 pm

"Let's say you're right," Annie replied. "Let's say that room at the back of the dungeon in Arazzo Castle is filled – filled floor to ceiling with violins stolen by the Special Task Force For Music. The ones that survived the air raid. At least, that's what you think the man in white believed."

"I do, Annie. What else would explain how much effort he put into getting the key for that room? The Special Task Force stole so much from all over Europe. Some of it, the very best of it was supposed to be in that room. For whatever reason, the room was empty. But that's what the man in white expected to find – a roomful of looted violins."

"Then how did he plan to get all those instruments out of the room, up the stairs from the dungeon, and out of the castle?"

"How?" Griffin thought for a bit, coming up with, "Return when the castle was closed to the public. He could hire some help, a van…" Griffin drifted into silence, sensing where Annie was heading.

"He'd be on camera the entire time, wouldn't he?" Griffin said. "The surveillance camera film Grace sent us shows that. There are cameras all over Arazzo Castle. That's how we saw the number he called at Future-Ride. He didn't know the exact range of every camera, but, sure, he knew about the cameras. He and the crew he'd have to hire to carry everything out would be caught on film. There is simply no way to avoid that, is there?"

The more Griffin thought about it, the worse his theory became.

"And what about the security guards?" he offered next. "Grace said there are guards on duty in the castle at all times. There are guards around when Arazzo Castle is open to the public and there are guards around when it isn't. The guards would stop him, wouldn't they? And..."

"And what, Griffin?"

"And the man in white told me: This isn't about money." Griffin exhaled heavily. He gave Annie a weak smile. "Sorry. I don't know how the man in white planned to take whatever it was he expected to find in that room." He recovered slightly: "I don't know *yet.*"

Annie softly touched his forearm twice.

"You will."

★

No one said anything for a while. Griffin was thinking about his next step, a visit to Hans' girlfriend Miriam Frietag. The silence was broken by the ringing of the front doorbell.

"You expecting anyone?" Griffin asked Annie.

Annie said she wasn't.

"Anyone expecting anyone?"

196

No one said yes.

"It's too late for the Fed Ex guy," Griffin said. "I'll go see who it is."

He walked to the front door, figuring he'd open it on a couple of Jehovah's Witnesses or a neighbor.

On the porch stood a very attractive woman in her mid-to-late twenties, wearing pale blue medical scrubs. She had the dark skin of an Asian Indian, but by her confident manner Griffin could tell she'd been raised in this country. There was absolutely nothing submissive about her. He had never seen her before.

"Can I help you?" he asked.

"Have I got the right place?" She glanced at a piece of paper in her hand. "Dr. Venkatesan's handwriting isn't the best."

"If you said Venkatesan, then you're in the right place," Griffin answered. "You here to meet Saif?"

She nodded, embarrassed.

"Did his father send you or his mother?"

"He did. He's one of the docs I work with."

"You're at GBMC then."

"For my residency. Dr. Venkatesan gave me this address, but I think his wife put him up to it. I met her once. She was definitely checking me out."

"Ever had her samosas?" Griffin inquired. "Simply killer."

"You didn't think they were too spicy?"

"Is it possible for food to be too spicy? I'll get Saif."

"Wait." For the first time uncertainty crept into her voice. "I've got all of twenty five minutes more for my dinner break. I'm just doing this as a favor. I don't want to waste my time or Saif's. He's probably busy."

"He is busy. But, no, I don't think this will be a waste of time. In fact, I know it won't be. Let me go get him."

Griffin hurried through the house to the back porch.

"Someone here to see you," he told Saif.

"Here? To see me here?"

"Yes."

"Who?"

"Didn't catch her name. But you'll want to see her."

"What about-"

"Just go, would you? She's on the front porch, waiting for you."

Saif gave Griffin a puzzled look, but got up from his chair.

Less than two minutes later, he was back. Griffin had suspected that might happen, so he stood in the kitchen blocking the doorway to the back porch.

Saif tried to step around him. "I need to get something on the back porch. I left my laptop-"

"No you don't," Griffin said. He crossed his arms and continued to block Saif's path. "You're looking for a chance to back out. What's her name?"

"Janice Singh."

"And that's as far as you got, I bet."

"Didn't you see her, Griffin? She's gorgeous."

"I noticed. And what did you tell the gorgeous Janice?"

"I told her I'd be right back."

Everyone edged into the dining room to look through the bay window at the woman on the porch. She was checking her watch.

"You're being rude, Saif," Annie told him. "Get back out there."

Saif looked Griffin full in the face and his panic was nearing melt down. "What do I say to her?"

"Thank her for coming by."

"Right."

"And whatever you do, don't forget to tell her you'll see her again."

"Right."

"And, Saif?"

"What? What?"

"Try not to let her see you drool."

Twenty Five

June 20
4:00 pm

Miriam Freitag lived on the fourth floor of a Tudor-ish apartment building on Park Heights Avenue, just outside the Baltimore City line. Griffin and Annie knocked on Miriam's door on a humid Saturday afternoon precisely at four o'clock. Griffin's sense of Miriam was that she was a woman who expected punctuality.

She must have been lurking behind the door because she answered the knock immediately, letting loose a demanding, "Who is it?" There was nothing frail or demure about Miriam Freitag's voice.

"It's me, Ms. Freitag. Griffin Gilmore," he called back. "You remember, Ms. Freitag? You and I spoke on the phone. I'm with Estate Evaluators. I want to ask you some questions about the estate of Hans Baeder. Can we come in?"

What if Miriam changed her mind about seeing him? Griffin had no idea what he'd do if she kept the door closed. She didn't; the door slid open. But she kept the chain latched.

"Who's this then?" she asked, waving a thumb in Annie's direction.

"This is my associate, Ms. Anne Knaack." Griffin had requested Annie wear an outfit designed to put an elderly woman at ease. Everything Annie had on was varying shades of beige and brown. Griffin thought there was absolutely nothing dowdy about the way she looked. "Can we come in, please?"

Miriam unlatched the door and Griffin and Annie started into the apartment. She asked to see Griffin's license, which he provided. Without warning, Miriam then grabbed a chunk of Griffin's hair and tugged his face down close to hers. Since Griffin was about a foot taller, this required a serious tug. She compared the face on the license with the one yelping with pain in her foyer. Annie coughed into her palm to hide her giggle.

After ten seconds, which seemed much longer to Griffin, she released him. Without apology she said, "You'll have tea with me? Mr. Gilmore? Ms. Knaack? Tea? On the porch? Both of you? Please?"

Miriam Freitag was tiny and grey haired. She stood with her back bent slightly forward, as though carrying a great weight.

Annie and Griffin agreed tea would be delightful. They followed Miriam as she stepped briskly through the living and dining rooms and onto the glassed-in porch, hands out as she went. She's nearly blind, Griffin realized. Only years of familiarity with the apartment allowed her this mobility. Griffin assumed she seldom if ever left this place. The apartment had the claustrophobically stale smell of the elderly.

"Lovely music," Griffin said, to make conversation as they walked. A classical music CD was playing in the living room. He guessed, "Is that Mozart?"

"*Eine Kleine Nacht Musik*," she answered.

Griffin and Annie exchanged a glance. That was the music Hans Baeder had scored on his bedroom wall – with changes of his own.

As the three of them settled into chairs, Miriam said, "This silver tea set is my grandmother's from Dresden. It's my last connection left to that time and place."

She poured the three cups of tea without spilling any. The tea pot gleamed in the afternoon sun. Griffin had a very precise mental image of Miriam sitting alone of an afternoon, polishing the tea service, impatient for the day to end.

They sipped in uncomfortable silence, uncomfortable for Griffin at least, until Miriam spoke. "You want to ask me about the estate of Hans Baeder? You're just following up today? That's what you said on the phone. These are just routine questions about Hans for your company?"

"Estate Evaluators. Yes, ma'am."

She sipped her tea while considering what Griffin had said. Griffin got the clear sense she wasn't taken in.

"You want to ask about Hans?" she asked him.

"Yes."

"But first," Annie slipped in, "we'd like to know about you."

★

Annie and Griffin had prepped their questions but Annie's question was one they hadn't planned. He worried it might prove a tactical mistake until Miriam replied, pleased to be asked, "Me? Very different and very much the same as Hans.

"I was born in Dresden, March 18, 1932. My father was an economics professor at university there. As the Nazis gained power his position became less secure. He was not only Jewish but a socialist. Two of his faculty colleagues, men he'd invited to our apartment for schnapps, informed on him to the Nazis. We left Germany in the middle of the night, 1936. All I remember of the world outside our apartment was a cherry tree I liked to climb."

She smiled at the memory. As Griffin watched the smile dissolved.

"We escaped to America. My father taught at Columbia and Chicago and Carnegie-Mellon. He became progressively disillusioned with the socialists and by his death had become a Reagan Republican."

The look on her face remained distant and impassive. She stopped speaking, sipped some tea, continued.

"I did not marry until I was 38. An old maid, I was called, after I left the room. Then I met a doctor who stunned everybody by asking me to marry him. I wasn't convinced. My friends thought me a fool for hesitating. This was my last chance to grab the gold ring. Did I want to spend my life as 'Aunt Miriam' to everyone else's children?

"So, foolishly, I agreed. He drank most nights, my husband the doctor. And most nights when he drank, he beat me. Once again, I escaped in the middle of the night. This time from Scarsdale. This time with my husband passed out on the bathroom floor. I chose Baltimore because it was the one place my husband announced he had no desire to visit. His grandmother had cut him out of her will and he was angry at her. Good for her. She lived in Baltimore.

"I wound up as an office manager for a firm of architects downtown. That's how I met Hans."

"Hans Baeder?" Griffin burst out. His interruption seemed to hang in the air, the way a car door slamming in the night lingers. He knew he needed to throttle back a bit. More normally, he said, "That's the Hans you're referring to."

He doubted Miriam noticed. She held her tea cup airborne, forgotten, a foot above the table as she began her story of meeting Hans Baeder. They met at a dinner where Bow Saw

Construction was given an award for renovating an old Quaker meeting house on Charles Street.

Griffin was grateful Annie was along because Miriam was facing her, offering Annie the story. Miriam likely would not have been as talkative with Griffin alone.

To keep the words flowing, Annie asked, "So Hans was a carpenter?"

"Hans was a first rate carpenter. Beautiful craftsmanship. He had great patience and a gentle touch."

"Not all carpenters do," Annie offered. The comment pleased Miriam greatly. "Miriam, weren't you and Hans a couple for many years?"

At first Griffin feared his question had offended her. Rather than answer it, she ordered him, "Step over to the porch railing, Mr. Gilmore. Tell me what you see."

★

"Miriam, starting from your apartment building, looking out I see a parking lot and pine trees nearly as high as the building."

"Past the trees, Mr. Gilmore. Can you read the name on the building on the far side of Park Heights?"

"Temple Oheb Shalom."

"And you can't see it from here, but the building to our right is the Baltimore Hebrew Congregation. Now, it's a little after four on a Saturday afternoon. Are there any people on the sidewalks?"

"Quite a few." Griffin went on to describe the people he was seeing, since that seemed to be her point. "The men are all wearing skull caps. Black slacks, sports coats, all black. The clothes look thick and woolen-y. They can't be all that comfortable in this heat. There's some fringe sticking out from underneath their suit coats."

"That's the prayer tallis."

"Some of the men are wearing those wide brim hats. The men are all bearded."

"And the women?"

"White jackets, black skirts, many ankle length. Hair pulled back. Shoes that would be called sensible, though perhaps not stylish."

"See any children?"

"Lots of kids. Large families. All the kids are dressed in black and white like their parents. Walking along like miniature adults."

"This, Mr. Gilmore," Miriam explained, "is the place I have lived since escaping to Baltimore all those years ago. When I met Hans my friends were…"

"Disappointed?" Annie suggested.

"Disgusted. 'How can you date a Nazi?' they accused me."

"How did they know Hans had been in the Nazi Party?"

"They didn't know, Mr. Gilmore. He'd been in the *Wehrmacht*. That they knew. For them, that made Hans a Nazi. Hans never denied serving in the army. He was just a child! That was bad enough for them. If they'd known he actually *was* in the Nazi Party, I can't imagine how they would have reacted. Just being with Hans was such a *shonda* – such a scandal.

"I had a friend, died last year, wonderful woman. She'd been in the concentration camp at Treblinka. She would touch the number tattooed on her forearm whenever she heard I'd been spending time with Hans. She was too decent to say anything, but that touch was a knife to my heart."

"How long were you and Hans together?" Annie asked.

"Forever, Ms. Knaack. Forever and no more than an instant, it seems now. Then Hans got sick. Sicker, I should say."

"He had pleurisy," Griffin said, still standing by the porch railing.

"Over the years it got worse. When he got so very sick I moved him here."

"Forgive me, Miriam. When did you move Hans here?'

"June of last year."

"Did you happen to check his phone messages after he was gone from his house?"

"There were no phone messages, Mr. Gilmore. Hans never wanted an answering machine."

Griffin now had the answer to why the phone calls from Future-Ride to Hans Baeder's house stopped. Hans had moved in with Miriam and was not there to pick up the phone. Without an answering machine, no more calls could have been completed. Why the calls were made and who was making them remained unanswered questions.

"Hans died here. In my bedroom down the hall. He never expected to survive the war. He told me that many times. He told me that during the war his dream was to die in a warm bed. Hans may have survived the war, but he never escaped it. At least he died in a warm bed. Mine.

"The afternoon of Hans' funeral I went to his house. He wanted me to have a few items. The house had been broken into. I called the police. Furniture was moved, chests searched, cabinets opened, glass broken and bookcases smashed. The policeman figured the thief was looking for money. Brown, the officer's name was. If the thief was looking for money, he was wasting his time. There was none to take."

It wasn't money Dude was looking for, Griffin had known that for a while. Dude was after something else. For what and who sent him there to look, Griffin still couldn't say.

"After the policeman left, I couldn't stop crying. I cleaned up his house a little, in tears the entire time. Poor Hans, even in death he found no peace."

★

Griffin returned to his seat and pretended to take a sip of tea. Now was the time to ask the questions no one but Miriam Freitag could answer.

"Miriam? Miriam, do you know why Hans joined the Nazi Party?"

"He was forced to. He'd have been shot if he didn't."

Griffin's assumption — his hope, truly — about Hans being forced to join the Nazis had been confirmed. In his relief Griffin brought his cup down too quickly, banging it with a *thonk* against the table.

"Hans was the quietest man I ever met," she replied, in unstated rebuke to Griffin's clumsiness. "He preferred carpentry projects where he could work alone hours at a stretch. No memories to chase him. The war was awful for Hans. Surely you can understand. His dream growing up was to play the violin. As a child he was a prodigy. But after the war he could not play the violin or even bear to listen to music like this."

She waved a hand in the air to indicate the CD playing.

"Mozart. Growing up, Mozart was his idol. This joy was taken from him. He even refused to speak German."

The Mozart suddenly seemed very loud. Griffin thought of the wall in Hans' bedroom, covered with a mixture of Mozart and his own composition.

"Are you sure, Miriam?" Griffin insisted, he hoped not too aggressively. "About Hans not listening to Mozart? Say, at his house."

"Usually we met here, Mr. Gilmore. But I know Hans never owned records or CDs or even a radio. When he wasn't working he liked to swing on his porch glider. He enjoyed the peace. Hans was entitled to that peace. I hope I brought him some in our years together."

"I'm sure you did," Annie reassured her.

"Thank you, dear. After my disastrous marriage I wasn't merely happy with Hans, I was grateful for him. You know, he seldom spoke of the war."

For the first time Miriam hesitated and Griffin and Annie could tell that what was to follow was painful for her to admit.

★

"One night I asked him about it. The war. This was the first night we slept together. Do I shock you, Mr. Gilmore? A divorced woman in her sixties having sex?"

"I, uh, well-"

"Good for you, Miriam," Annie said, speaking over Griffin's stumbling.

"When I asked, Hans tried not to answer. Oh, why wouldn't I leave him alone?"

The anguish in her voice was so shattering Annie gasped.

"I wish so desperately now I had. He was entitled to his peace. But I persisted. Eventually he talked about his work in the war, the trips he took to Amsterdam. To Leipzig. To Brussels, to Belgrade. Paris and Italy-"

"Where in Italy?" Griffin interrupted. Annie sent him a *slow down, Griffin* glance. "Did Hans say?"

"Rome and Florence, of course. He stayed a few days in a town called Arazzo. The castle there. Arazzo was not long after he was wounded."

Griffin and Annie shared a glance. Miriam never noticed. She resumed her story.

"They traveled always at night, for fear of the American and British planes. Always back to Berlin to the Music Office. At least at first. Later, when the bombing became too great, the stolen instruments were taken to Bavaria. That's where Hans was wounded, when his train was attacked by the planes one morning. This was outside Ulm, August 1944, the last summer of the war.

"Hans told me the trains he was on had nothing to do with the fighting. And thank God they had nothing to do with the camps. The Nazis were hoarding musical instruments looted from music schools and orchestras. Some were stolen from Jews sent to the camps. That's why Hans had to take an oath of loyalty to the Nazis. They needed his silence. For decades they got it.

"Hans was with the *Sonderstabe* of violinists, Mr. Gilmore. Their job was to evaluate and catalog and transport the violins the Nazis had stolen. That's where Hans first learned his carpentry skills. Carefully building crates to transport the violins.

"Before shipping, the *Sonderstabe* of violinists had to determine which violins were worth shipping immediately. They had to separate the gold from the *trayf*. And there was plenty of gold. Several violins by Stradivarius. One more valuable even than any Stradivarius. Hans made a box solely for this one violin, it was so remarkable. He never did that for any of the other violins, which were packed into larger crates.

"When the planes first struck that morning, he ran into the train car for this violin. That was the violin Hans was carrying when he was wounded. Parts of his left hand were blown off. You see, Mr. Gilmore, Hans was part of the Special Task Force For Music. Hitler himself ordered it. Hans felt terrible about being part of stealing musical instruments. Absolutely ashamed. I don't know that he ever forgave himself for his part in the thefts.

"Hans had a classmate at the Dresden conservatory where he studied violin before the war. The classmate was a French Jew who had to leave the school. He lived in Paris, had a music shop there. Hans would help the classmate deal with the Nazis when he could. Hans did feel good about that.

"It was Hans' old violin teacher at the conservatory who made him part of the Special Task Force. Otherwise, he would have been sent to the front as a soldier. He would not have lasted a month there. Later his teacher sponsored Hans coming to this country. He helped Hans settle in Baltimore. The teacher was here because he was a violin instructor at the Peabody Institute downtown."

"Miriam?" Griffin said. "You told us the raid where Hans was wounded took place in the morning."

"It did."

"But you also told us the Special Task Force trains always traveled at night. To avoid the Allied planes."

"They did. I asked Hans about that. He said a train of wounded soldiers needed to get through on the Ulm railroad line. So many of the other rail lines had been destroyed in the bombing.

"The Special Task Force train was sitting outside Ulm for hours, waiting on a railroad siding for the long train of wounded soldiers to pass. Hans said he'd never forget how beautiful and blue the sky was that day. Not a cloud to be seen. The American planes came out of that blue and hit them while they were waiting."

"The American planes were after the rail line," Griffin told Miriam, remembering his phone conversation with Billy

Williams. "They did not even know the Special Task Force train would be there. The train cars loaded with stolen instruments were an unexpected target of opportunity for the bombers. Hans and the Special Task Force were in the wrong place at the wrong time."

"Millions of us alive then could say the same, Mr. Gilmore."

"I'm sure, Miriam," Griffin said quietly.

"It's gone, all of it, gone. Both sides of my family burned in the ovens of Auschwitz. The city of Dresden incinerated by Allied bombers. The cherry tree I climbed, the men who informed on my father, all gone. Everything turned to ashes. Most days, I'm grateful I'm blind. Some days I play this music and pretend the war never happened. I pretend Hans is sitting here with me. Sometimes I'll hear myself call his name. Hans."

The longing in her voice was so overwhelming Griffin grabbed Annie's hand to keep her from crying.

Miriam addressed him directly. "Mr. Gilmore, don't think I believed for one moment your claim that you are just checking on the estate of Hans Baeder. There was no estate. Don't ever try to make a living where you are required to lie. Your heart isn't in it. I have no idea why you wanted to see me. I don't much care. You're here because I wanted to talk about Hans. Let yourselves out.

"Ms. Knaack, on your way could you bring me the picture you see on the bookcase in the foyer? The one by the clock that's stopped working."

She did as asked. She showed the picture to Griffin on her way back to the porch.

The picture was of a couple in their sixties sitting on a bench in the Inner Harbor. Miriam looks much as she did on her porch, wearing a similar grey pants suit. Next to her with his arm looped around Miriam's shoulder is Hans Baeder. He is pitifully thin. His blond hair is brushed straight back in the old style. He wears a tired-looking suit coat and tie. Neither Hans nor Miriam is smiling broadly, but it is clear they are comfortable with each other.

"Miriam," Griffin said. "I'm not lying when I tell you this. You need to leave this apartment. You said you have a cousin in Philadelphia?"

"Yes. I have an open invitation to visit as often as I want and for as long as I want."

"I suggest you take your cousin up on the offer as soon as possible. You may not be safe here. It's my belief events are about to start moving quickly and not always exactly as we'd like. And Miriam? We'll do right by Hans."

Twenty Six

June 20
5:07 pm

"You feel like driving around?" Griffin asked Annie, unlocking the car door on her side. He glanced back at Miriam Frietag's apartment and shivered slightly. "After that conversation I could use some aimless cruising."

They drove in silence for a while. The houses were getting noticeably poorer, many of them with shingles fallen off like scales from dead fish.

"That was so depressing," Griffin blurted out finally. "That entire conversation with Miriam. And I know I could have done a better job of restraining myself. I should have dialed back. And, you know, this neighborhood does not help me feel more cheerful at all."

Griffin was turning onto Paton Avenue when he made the admission. Paton was a single curving block. Griffin counted six boarded up houses with "No Trespassing Private Property" stenciled in big black letters on plywood filling the holes where windows and doors used to be.

As he looked out at the passing bleakness, Griffin said, "Annie, you have convinced me of one thing. You and Miriam."

Annie asked what that was.

"The room at the back of the Arazzo Castle dungeon? No way was it ever filled with loot from the Special Task Force. As you explained before, how would the man in white move all that out of the castle without the surveillance cameras catching every move?"

"Miriam said Hans was especially concerned with one violin."

"So concerned," Griffin agreed, "that rather than run for cover when the American planes attacked at Ulm, Hans ran back into the train car for this violin."

"Hans risked his life for this one violin."

"He did, Annie. Miriam also told us said it was this violin he was carrying when he was wounded. This was the only violin he built a separate crate for."

"Which violin was it, do you think?"

Griffin had to wait before answering. They were stopped at a light on Reisterstown Road. The radio of the car next to them was so loud Griffin could feel the rap as well as hear it. He let the car pull ahead. In the blissful silence he told Annie, "I wish I could say which violin Hans had. There is one thing we learned today. More accurately, something was confirmed."

"Arazzo Castle."

"Yes, the Special Task Force For Music stayed in Arazzo Castle. That's why the man in white went there. That's why he took the key from me." Griffin nodded as he worked out his reasoning. "It was logical for him to conclude the instrument – whatever it is – was in the room at the back of the Arazzo Castle dungeon. It's the most secure part of the castle. Grace talked about that. The Ferlinghetti family used it to shelter in the dungeon during World War Two air raids. The dungeon walls are three feet thick and the walls around that room thicker still. If you're Hans Baeder and you have in your possession a violin so precious you risked your life to protect it – What safer place is there than the room in the dungeon at Arazzo Castle?"

"How long has the man in white thought the violin might be in that room?" Annie wondered.

"With online research we found out the Special Task Force was in Italy. He may have found that out as well. Maybe he learned that just months ago. Maybe it was years ago. Whenever it was, there wasn't anything he could do without the key. Once he got the key—from me at the museum – two days later he tried to obtain the violin by himself. When that didn't work, first thing he did was call Future-Ride. We watched him do that on the surveillance tape Grace sent."

Annie said, "I understand why Hans Baeder would risk his life for one remarkable violin. He was devoted to violins. But why would he leave the violin in the castle? Why leave it anywhere?" she asked. "Why not just take it back to the Music Office in Berlin, with the rest on the Special Task Force's loot?"

Griffin felt a smile grab his face and not let go.

"Hans wanted to keep it away from the Nazis."

That pleased Annie as well, who said soon after, "It's a love story, isn't it."

For a few streets Griffin could not think of a response to that. Eventually he managed, "How's that?"

"At the heart of all this is a love story," Annie insisted

"Hans and Miriam."

"Miriam and Hans," she agreed.

They drove a few miles in a silence broken by Annie asking, with clear reluctance: "Griffin? Back there with Miriam? You meant it when you said things were about to heat up, didn't you? This might get dangerous?"

Griffin saw the worry on Annie's face.

"I'm afraid that's true."

"Miriam could be in danger? That's why you suggested she should leave town?"

"If someone connected her to Hans Baeder, she could be in danger, yes."

"What about the Duke?"

"What about him, Annie?"

"Isn't he in danger too? The man in white knows about him. Shouldn't he be warned also?"

Griffin smirked. "Aw, Annie, do I have to?"

"Griffin?" she warned.

"Okay. I'll suggest this would be a good time to take his blondes and clear out of Dodge. Revisit the ancestral estates in Italy. I'll contact Mel Morton as well. His son is obnoxious, but I assume he'd keep an eye out for his father. Billy Williams, Miss Paulette, and Professor Silverman have no connection to Hans Baeder. They're completely safe."

"So everyone's taken care of."

"Except us."

★

Saif arrived at Annie and Griffin's house just after ten Monday morning. As he stepped inside he apologized, "Sorry I can't stay for the brunch." From the dining room Annie waved with a pitcher of apple juice. Kit and Bobby were in the dining room, brunching away. "I'm teaching a class in ninety minutes. Then I have to get back to prepping for my doctoral defense."

"This shouldn't take too long," Griffin replied. They started toward the dining room. "Last night I spent some time on the computer. I reviewed the surveillance film Grace sent us a couple times. I came up with a theory I want to run past everybody. Saif, I'm hoping you can help me with something. Two somethings."

"If I can, sure thing. Things."

"Saif," Griffin began, "here's the first something.

"While you were on your way here this morning, I emailed you the surveillance film Grace sent. You remember the film?"

Saif, studying the tray of pastries Kit was holding, said, sure, I remember the tape.

"You brought your laptop with you?"

Saif did; he apparently did not leave home without it. Saif placed his laptop on the dining room table. He selected a strawberry pastry from the tray. This was done only with some deliberation. Saif Venkatesan did not make even minor decisions casually.

"That day when Grace sent the film, Saif, you saved it to my hard drive. You thought we might need to look at the tape again. Turns out, we do."

As Griffin was speaking Saif was booting up, which he did with remarkable speed and while holding the strawberry pastry between two slender fingers.

"Have you accessed the film yet?" Griffin asked and Saif said he had. "Can you go to the eleven minute, twenty three second mark on the film?"

In a few keystrokes Saif was there.

"As we can all see," Griffin explained, "by this point in the Arazzo castle tour, our man in white, name still unknown, has entered the gallery. In this gallery are floor to ceiling paintings, two harpsichords and three musicians preparing to play a private party. The party starts once the castle closes to the public in a few minutes.

"Here's why I think this part of the film is vital.

"Everyone remember that room in the back of the dungeon?" Nods all around. "The room for which the man in

217

white needed the key – the key we all worked so hard for me to steal. That room? I used to think that room was filled with loot stolen by the Special Task Force For Music.

"Annie and Miriam Frietag have convinced me that's wrong. How would the man in white have gotten out of the castle with all that loot? The logistics of moving all that stuff out of there into vans or whatnot are insurmountable. Security cameras, guards – we saw them on the film – around at all times. How would he get away with it? He couldn't."

"So you believe he's after just one musical instrument?" Bobby asked. "One violin?"

"Got to be."

"But, Griffin? Doesn't that present the same problem?" Kit objected. "The security guards, the cameras. If he's spotted," Kit pushed on, "wouldn't walking around the castle holding one musical instrument – a violin, we're all assuming – wouldn't that attract attention he doesn't want? And it's not like he can just pop the violin into a backpack." Kit pointed at the screen. "He's not wearing a backpack."

Griffin said, "Kit and everybody, here's what I think the man in white had planned."

Griffin turned to Saif. "Can you remove the greenish tint from the film? Kind of leach it out?"

"It can be done, Griffin. At about the eighty percent level. It won't quite be like we're there in the room with him, but the film clarity should improve noticeably."

In a few more keystrokes the gallery, the paintings, the musicians all suddenly acquired a clarity and sharpness previously missing. It was as though a green fog had lifted.

"His suit," Kit noticed immediately. "His suit isn't quite right. You couldn't tell before."

"That's because I don't think it's a suit. Saif, here's the tricky part. Can you show us what the man in white would look like without that tailor made Italian suitcoat he's wearing?"

"Sure," Saif replied. "The app for that sort of thing is not unlike Photoshop."

Saif placed the pastry on the back of his left hand as he typed. The pastry wobbled but stayed in place. The man in white's suitcoat disappeared.

"This is virtual reality, you understand," Saif cautioned. "It's the computer's projection of what the film would show with the suitcoat removed. It's accurate at perhaps the level of-"

"It's accurate enough," Griffin announced. "Look at the three musicians." Everyone did. "Now look at the man in white."

★

Bobby reacted first.

"They're all wearing the same shirt and slacks. The musicians and the man in white."

Griffin agreed. "They are. And that, of course, is not co-incidental."

Griffin extended his arms, palms up, in a Where's My Applause? gesture.

"Getting rid of the suit coat? You're saying it's just a kind of wardrobe change, Griffin? That's what you're saying?" Bobby was unconvinced. "That's why our guy here is wearing the same slacks and shirt as the musicians? It couldn't be just co-incidence? Or just some European clothing style?"

Griffin explained: "Here's what I think was his plan, Bobby. Or at least the man in white's hope.

"He goes into the Arazzo dungeon and then to the room at the back of the dungeon. He unlocks the door with the key he got from me. There's a violin in there. Just one violin. At least he thought there would be a violin there. Remember how disappointed he was when he came back up the steps."

"Okay. What if he's got the violin, as he hoped? What then, Griffin?" Bobby remained unpersuaded. "How does he explain to a security guard why he's carrying this violin? And he's got to be carrying it. As Kit says, he can't just pop it into a backpack he doesn't have.

"We're looking at virtual reality, remember," Bobby persisted. He had the unpleased facial expression of someone being urged to finish his vegetables. "In *real* reality he's wearing his suit coat."

"Saif," Griffin said, "if you would. Fast forward to the 18 minute, 16 second mark of the tape." Saif did. "Everyone, see the man in white pulling on that handle sticking out of the hallway wall?" Griffin pointed to the screen. "We – me at least – thought pulling the handle was just a nervous gesture on his part. I should have known better. The man in white is not one to get nervous. That handle is for a chute which goes to the incinerator in the basement. Grace told us about the incinerator chute. He was double checking to make sure the chute was open for him."

"He was going to drop the suit coat in the chute, wasn't he?" Bobby said, understanding Griffin now. "Then he looks just like the musicians. But he didn't toss the suit coat in the chute-"

"Because he never got a violin from the room in the dungeon," Annie finished for him.

"Exactly," Bobby agreed. "There was no need for his wardrobe change."

Bobby was now convinced about the suit coat. Annie and Saif were as well.

"Without the suit coat," Griffin plunged on, "even if someone in the castle spots him – say, a security guard walking around, as they do—he tells them, 'I'm playing the private party in the gallery in a few minutes. Where's the men's room?' Or whatever pretext he's planned to explain away why he's wandering around a part of the castle he has no business being in. He's dressed like the other musicians. He can come up with something plausible and persuasive.

"Then – this was his plan, at least – while carrying the violin he goes to the musicians in the gallery-"

"Who won't recognize him." It was Kit's turn to object. "This guy they've never seen before, carrying a violin. Wouldn't they report that?"

"They wouldn't expect to know him," Griffin answered. "I've looked into the various musicians who have performed at these private parties in Arazzo Castle. Grace sent me the information this morning before everyone arrived. Some weeks the performers are a group of musicians who regularly play together. But not usually. Most Saturday afternoons – and this was one – it's just a collection of performers hired individually. Apparently, because of Italian tax law it is actually cheaper to hire four musicians separately than as a quartet.

"So he goes to the gallery. He tells the musicians who don't know him, 'I left my bow in the car.' Or whatever. Off he goes, out of the castle. With the violin he wants so desperately. Even assuming a guard notices the door left open in the dungeon, the man in white's got enough of a head start to get away. He got from the Baltimore Museum of Art to Arazzo Castle in Italy in two days. He's good at moving quickly.

"Of course, none of that happens since the room in the back of the dungeon was empty. And thanks, Saif."

"Anytime," he replied. "I've got time for this pastry. Then I really have to get back to Hopkins."

"Not just yet. That's Something Number One. Here's Something Number Two."

Twenty Seven

June 22
10:35 am

"Saif, while researching and writing your dissertation, I assume you've spent time with foreign sources. Documents written in languages other than English?"

"Frequently. I've used a number of European sources. Asian, too," he went on. "The original language is no problem. Translation capability has improved to where I make a couple keystrokes and Shazzam! – the document I want is in English."

"Saif, here's one question we haven't been able to answer: Who at Future-Ride is working with the man in white, is it De-BOR-ah Miller or Alexandra Webb? You tracked down two scholarly articles by De-BOR-ah Miller. You and I read them. Not exactly beach reading, but I got enough to understand the woman is a corporate shark. But we don't have anything by Alexandra Webb. We know she got her doctorate from the Sorbonne. For her doctorate she'd have to write a dissertation, wouldn't she?"

"Of course."

Saif raised the pastry to take a bite.

"Aren't dissertations available online, even foreign ones written in another language? Say, French?"

"Sometimes." The pastry continued its upward arc toward Saif's mouth. "The more prestigious universities abroad almost always make their dissertations available online."

"Isn't the Sorbonne in Paris prestigious?"

"The Sorbonne? Prestigious? Of course it's-"

Saif was so surprised by the implication of his back and forth with Griffin that the pastry slipped from his fingers. It end over ended toward the table. Kit, displaying remarkable reflexes, snagged the pastry in mid-flight. In a single fluid motion, he popped the pastry into his mouth.

With soft-spoken regret Saif said, "I should have seen it before this."

"Me too," Griffin said.

Those were the last words spoken until after Saif tapped keys with stunning speed, shook his head once, tapped some more keys, shook his head again, then finished his typing. The translation from French to English was nearly instantaneous.

Saif was the one to break the silence. Pointing to the screen he stated, "That's the title page of Alexandra Webb's dissertation."

On the screen appeared:

ESTABLISHING THE VALUE OF VIOLINS STOLEN
BY THE SPECIAL TASK FORCE FOR MUSIC

by

ALEXANDRA WEBB

Griffin became aware everyone was awaiting his reaction. He said, "Looks like we owe De-BOR-ah Miller an apology."

★

An hour later the others had long since left the dining room: Saif, after grabbing another pastry for the road, to teach; Annie to the mall for bookcase nails and perhaps a chat with Miss P; Kit to his garage apartment; Bobby to wherever he went on his audition-free days. Griffin remained in the dining room, holding the copy of Alexandra Webb's dissertation which Saif had run off for him.

Griffin held but did not read the dissertation. He needed time to adjust to the news that it was Alexandra Webb, not the eminently dislikeable De-BOR-ah Miller, who had been the one to call Hans Baeder all those times from the alcove phone at Future-Ride. And it was Alexandra the man in white had called from Arazzo Castle when the dungeon proved to be empty, to his crushing disappointment.

Alexandra Webb and the man in white were after the same musical instrument, a violin almost certainly. Which one? Alexandra Webb's dissertation might tell him. Griffin settled in to read.

★

June 24
4:25 pm

From well down the hall Griffin could tell the man on the phone was in full verbal retreat. It was two days later and Griffin was walking the halls of the basement of the Peabody Institute in Baltimore. He was seeking the office of a violin professor who might be the son of a man described at some length in Alexandra Webb's dissertation.

"But, Mrs. Chen…" the man was saying into the phone, clearly backpedalling. "Of course I take my judging responsibility seriously…"

The man stood behind his desk, back turned, so he could not see Griffin's approach. Griffin watched as the man did something unexpected. He flicked off the lights in his office, plunging the basement office into twilighty gloom. The man sighed loudly.

"I've been full professor here at the Peabody for…Yes, Mrs. Chen… Yes, I know which end of the violin to hold…"

The violin professor began turning in Griffin's direction. Griffin ducked out of the doorway and leaned against a bulletin board announcing work opportunities at symphonies and orchestras around the country. He felt like a cowboy in a western gunfight sheltering behind a rock for cover.

The telephone onslaught continued a few seconds more, then stopped abruptly. Griffin felt certain Mrs. Chen had hung up. There was another loud sigh.

"Is someone there in the hall?" the professor called.

"Is it safe to come out?" replied Griffin.

The professor flicked the office lights back on.

"Mrs. Chen did not sound happy," Griffin offered, entering the office.

"She's quite the tiger mom." From behind his desk the professor told Griffin, "I'm sorry, but the decisions in this afternoon's violin competition cannot be changed."

"I beg your pardon?"

"You're not a parent here to complain about the results of today's violin competition?"

"I'm afraid not."

"Then don't be afraid. And please, come into my office."

★

Bearded and balding, the violin professor wore blue jeans and a blue button down shirt rolled up above the elbows. On the basis of little more than the man's easy manner Griffin guessed he was popular with his students here at the Peabody Institute. "Now, how can I help you, Mr.-"

"I'm Griffin Gilmore." They shook hands across a paper-strewn desk. The professor pointed at a chair. Before Griffin could sit he had to move stacks of music scores from the chair. Griffin glanced around the disheveled office. "Ah, professor, where should I put this?"

Griffin pointed to a box of thick cardboard perhaps three feet long leaning against the chair leg.

"That's a box to ship violins. For repair, typically. Why don't you just hand me the box."

As he did, Griffin asked, "Do people really complain about decisions in violin competitions?"

"Did you play Little League or rec league soccer growing up?"

"Not well."

"Take the worst sports parent you can remember and multiply that exponentially. That's what some music parents are like. But you didn't come here to endure my complaints. How can I help you?"

"Am I in the right place? I'm directionally challenged sometimes. Are you Dr. Mike MacGregor?"

Smiling broadly, the man behind the desk replied, "I am. I'm Mike MacGregor."

"Are you Dr. Mike S. MacGregor?" Griffin asked, stressing the middle initial.

Still smiling: "Yes."

"Is the 'S' is for Shurzdach?"

"Why, yes, it is," Professor MacGregor replied. His voice lost none of its friendliness, but his blue eyes, relaxed to that point, took on an unblinking wariness. "No one has ever come here and known that. How can I help you, Mr. Gilmore?"

Griffin pushed a bit further. "Are you related to Captain Wilhelm Shurzdach, who served in the German Special Task Force for Music during the Second World War?"

The smile was now wafer thin.

"Why do you ask that?"

The wariness in his eyes had darkened to distrust. Griffin got the very definite sense that if his answer was not to the professor's liking, Griffin would be told to leave. He'd be told graciously, that was the man's nature, but Griffin would be gone, without learning what he came here to learn.

"Two days ago," Griffin responded, "a friend of mine found online the dissertation of a woman who attended the Sorbonne. This woman's research for her dissertation was very thorough. She listed nearly 300 men who served in the Special Task Force For Music during the Second World War. The name Captain Wilhelm Shurzdach appears among them."

Griffin paused; hesitated really. The hesitation was not for dramatic effect, but because so much hinged on what was to follow. He said, "I believe William Shurzdach was your father."

"He was my father," Professor MacGregor acknowledged, his voice barely an exhale. Recovering, he continued, "Until this moment I could have counted on my fingers the number of people in all the world who knew William Shurzdach was my father and that he was part of the Special Task Force For Music. And – with the exception of my life partner – they were all relatives. How is it *you* know, Mr. Gilmore?"

"As I was reading this woman's dissertation on the Special Task Force For Music-"

"Let me stop you there, Mr. Gilmore. Is this woman who wrote the dissertation –this woman you haven't named – an historian?"

"Her name is Alexandra Webb. And, no, she's not an historian. She runs an investment firm in Manhattan."

The answer caused Professor MacGregor to raise a puzzled blond eyebrow, but he pressed on. "Whatever her profession, seems this woman has written with some thoroughness about the Special Task Force For Music. That was an ugly corner of an awful time in 20th Century history. Is that why you're here? Are you a historian of some sort?"

He studied Griffin for a while, before answering his own question.

"I don't think you're a scholar," he spoke kindly, almost smiling again. "You're an articulate man, but I've spent a good bit of my life in academia. You don't have the angels-dancing-on-the-head-of-a-pin air about you. This isn't some scholarly dispute, is it? I can't see you caring about publish or perish."

"I can't see me caring about that either," replied Griffin.

Professor MacGregor said, "This dissertation is obviously crucial here. Tell me more about that, why don't you."

"In the dissertation, each of the officers in the Special Task Force has a paragraph or so of biography. That's how I know that before the war Wilhelm Shurzdach taught at the music conservatory in Dresden. One of his star students at the conservatory was a young man named Hans Baeder.

"After the war he – your father – emigrated, from Germany to Baltimore, to teach violin at the Peabody Institute here. Hans Baeder settled in Baltimore as well. By all the accounts I came up with in my research yesterday, your father was a much-beloved teacher for many years.

"I checked the Peabody website for violin teachers," continued Griffin. "I saw the name Michael MacGregor, with middle initial S, as a violin professor. Might the son, who grew up in Baltimore, be teaching the same instrument at the same school in Baltimore as the father had? Could the S stand for Shurzdach? It seemed worth the drive downtown."

"You're bright and persistent, Mr. Gilmore. But my father died in 1964," Dr. MacGregor said. "More than fifty years ago. So I'll ask again. If you're not some historian-"

"I'm not."

"What are you then, Griffin? What do you want – judging by your face, I'd say need is more accurate – to know about my Dad?"

"I need to know whatever you can tell me about the unit your father served in, the Special Task Force For Music. And there's one man your father commanded in the Special Task Force – Hans Baeder. I'd like to learn anything at all you can tell me about him. And there's a question suggested by the dissertation I want ask you."

"Close the door," Professor MacGregor told Griffin.

Twenty Eight

June 24
5:25 pm

While Griffin was closing the door, Professor MacGregor went charging over to a closet. He began rummaging around in the closet. Papers tumbled off shelves and a book thumped to the floor.

"Here it is," he said.

He placed a shoe box on the desk.

"My mother gave me this for my eighteenth birthday. You need to understand. My father, Wilhelm Shurzdach, my birth father, died when I was two, in 1964. About the only memory I have of him is sitting on his lap while he guided my fingers over the strings of a violin. He couldn't play anymore due to a wound he suffered in the war.

"My mother remarried when I was seven. My partner is a psychologist who has got to be the last Freudian left in the world. He insists I must resent my stepfather for stealing my mother. But I don't; not one bit. My stepfather was wonderful to me and Mom. Talking to you now I have to consciously say 'stepfather' since I consider him my Dad. His name was MacGregor. He died two years ago. My Mom died last year. I still miss them both. When I was growing up Mom suggested I keep Shurzdach as a middle name. Here let me show you. This is a picture of the Special Task Force For Music."

From the shoe box he withdrew a rolled up black and white photo. He and Griffin placed a pile of books on each end of the two foot long picture to keep it flat. In the picture about 200 men stood along railroad tracks. Twin plumes of black smoke rose from a burned out shed in the background.

"The picture was taken somewhere outside Berlin, October 1944. That's my father," he said, pointing to the right side of the picture. "The tall man with his right hand on his hip. All the men around him were violinists also. He was in charge of their section of violinists. Their *Sonderstabe* it was called."

Griffin started looking where Dr. MacGregor pointed, but his eyes were quickly pulled away to someone else in the picture. This soldier was standing a few feet to the side of Captain Shurzdach. It was Hans Baeder. Griffin had no doubt whatsoever. It was Hans. Griffin was seeing a younger version of the Hans Baeder he had seen in the pictures Miriam Freitag and Mel Morton showed him.

In this picture Hans was a tragically thin teenager, a fifteen year old with the face of a twelve year old boy. He wore a Wehrmacht uniform so oversized for his tiny frame it hung on him like a bed sheet. He looked like a stiff wind would have knocked him down. Hans made the men around him look incredibly healthy.

"You recognized somebody, didn't you, Griffin?" Dr. MacGregor said. "You have one of the most expressive faces I've ever seen. My students, for all their considerable talent, sometimes I'm not certain they're hearing me. It's like their lights are on but nobody's home. You're completely different. You recognize someone in the picture and it's someone you think highly of. It's so obvious from your face. Who do you recognize?"

Griffin pointed to Hans. "This man. This is Hans Baeder."

"Is Hans Baeder in the dissertation that brings you here today?"

"He is. As you say, he was part of the *Sonderstabe* of violinists serving with your father. Hans is described in the dissertation as being particularly perceptive in evaluating the violins the Special Task Force obtained. Can you tell me anything about Hans Baeder?"

★

"I have a list of the men in the Special Task Force. Hans Baeder is the one you need to know about?" Dr. MacGregor reached into the shoe box for some typewritten pages. In the process he dislodged something metallic, which flashed in the overhead light.

"Professor?" Griffin asked, pointing inside the shoe box.

"This?" Professor MacGregor said, placing the papers on his desk and pulling from the box an oval signet ring. "Is that what you're pointing to?" Griffin nodded. "This was my father's ring. It is the ring awarded to members of the Order of Maximilian the Younger."

"I've seen one before," Griffin said, thinking of the signet ring worn by the man in white in the museum and again on the surveillance tape Grace had sent. "I'm fairly certain I've seen this ring before."

"Then you have seen something rather rare," the professor told Griffin. "Do you know about Maximilian the Younger of Bavaria? Is he in the dissertation which brought you here?"

"No," Griffin answered, realizing he was about to hear something unknown to Alexandra Webb, despite her extensive research. Eyes on the ring, Griffin said, "For all its thoroughness, the dissertation says nothing about rings or Maximilian of Bavaria. Who was he?"

Professor MacGregor also kept his eyes on the ring, which covered much of his palm, as he spoke.

"After Maximilian the Younger's death on February 23, 1821, an order named in his honor was inaugurated, celebrating his aid to violinists. In the nearly two centuries since, individuals have been inducted into the order. Each receives a ring like the one you see. They are inducted into the Order of Maximilian the Younger for their advancement of violins – composing, performing, or teaching. Teaching is why my father was awarded the ring in 1938, for his teaching at the Dresden Conservatory.

"Understand Mr. Gilmore," Dr. MacGregor went on, suddenly shifting into a sharp tone. The tone left Griffin no doubt that what was to follow mattered greatly to the professor. "My father was given this ring for reasons completely unrelated to the Special Task Force For Music."

"The ring is very big. Oversized," Griffin commented.

"King Maximilian ordered the ring oversized, a royal gesture to demonstrate his oversized appreciation. By tradition, recipients are not measured for the ring. They receive an exact duplicate of the first ring."

Griffin slipped the ring onto his finger; it was several sizes too large. He realized that even the 6'5" man in white, who probably had well above average sized hands, would find this ring too big to wear comfortably. Yet he wore it. The ring meant that much to him.

"Is someone inducted into the Order of Maximilian the Younger every year?" Griffin asked. He slipped the ring from his finger.

"By no means," was the reply. "Most years no one is inducted. No one has received a ring for more than a decade. The Order is highly selective. If you saw a ring like this elsewhere, Mr. Gilmore, you saw something quite rare."

Rare enough the ring can be traced, Griffin said to himself. Through the ring perhaps the identity of the man in white could be learned. Griffin caught himself smiling at the thought. As soon as he got home he'd ask Grace to track down all those awarded a ring by the Order of Maximilian the Younger.

★

"Where were we, Mr. Gilmore?

"You were about to show me some pages you pulled from the box, professor."

"Yes. My Mom put this list together from my birth father's notes. Done on a manual typewriter, that's how long ago I turned eighteen. It's a list of those who served in the Special Task Force For Music and yes, Hans Baeder survived the war. There's no asterisk next to his name. My Mom said my father told her that he wrote notes of sympathy to the families of those killed – and many were killed. Look at all these asterisks."

He showed Griffin page after page of German names, dozens and dozens with asterisks.

"I'm not surprised to hear about your father writing to the families," Griffin said. "He sponsored Hans Baeder coming to the United States a few years after the war. That's in the dissertation as well."

"My Mom said Dad sponsored a number of the men. Many of them settled in the Baltimore area for that reason."

Griffin returned to the photo. The shattered looks on the faces of the men held him.

"See the hollowness of their eyes?" Professor MacGregor asked. Griffin did. "Haunting, isn't it? These men were musicians, not soldiers. Must have been hellish for them."

"Did your father ever mention Hans Baeder?"

"He may have to my Mom. I was too young to remember. Sorry."

"Hans Baeder was wounded outside the German city of Ulm. An air attack. The last summer of the war. Do you happen to know anything about the air attack?"

"That I can help you with. My father was wounded that same morning. I can tell you the date: August 17, 1944. My father could never play the violin after that day. Six of the violinists were killed that day. Of 24 in the *Sonderstabe* of violinists. Even more were wounded, including my Dad, who lost his left arm below the elbow."

"The American planes surprised them. There was some delay so their train had to travel in daylight. Otherwise, they only traveled at night. The Special Task Force men were defenseless against the planes. Their train cars were stuffed with instruments, not weapons."

"Dr. MacGregor, what happened to the trainload of stolen musical instruments when the planes attacked? The dissertation does not say. I've learned the air raid is officially listed as 'partially successful.' Did the instruments survive?"

"I asked my Mom the same question. Apparently many of the instruments were destroyed. Only a few were saved. Collateral damage, they'd call it today."

Next Griffin asked a question he knew the answer to. He was trying to double check the accuracy of what Professor MacGregor was telling him. If the professor admitted this, he was likely telling the truth as best he knew it: "Was your father a member of the Nazi Party?"

He nodded. "My partner's not Jewish, but I know this shoe box makes him uncomfortable. It's Nazi memorabilia, as far as he's concerned. It's a link to my father, as I see it. That's why I keep the box here, not at our Charles Village condo."

"Do you know why he joined the Nazis? Was your father political?"

"God, no. He was a musician. Worshipped Mozart, as does his son. The men in the Special Task Force For Music had to join. It was very important to my mother that I understand that. They had to join or they would be killed."

"I spoke to Hans' longtime girlfriend. Her name is Miriam. She says your father recruited Hans – his former student at the Dresden conservatory – for the Special Task Force. She said your father did that to keep Hans from serving in the regular army. She believed by doing that your father saved Hans' life."

"I hope that's true. I'd like to think my father saved someone's life."

The phone on Professor MacGregor's desk rang.

"I'll have to take that call, Griffin."

"Hans' girlfriend told me that the day Hans was wounded – your father also – Hans had with him a violin more valuable than any Stradivarius. Could that be true?"

The phone rang again.

"I've got to take this." He smiled wryly. The phone kept ringing. "Not that I want to."

"Which violin could it have been, professor? Hans built a special crate to protect this violin. He never did that for any other violin and he and the Special Task Force looted violins all over Europe." He spoke more rapidly over the ringing phone. "Hans was especially good at judging the worth of violins. Which violin was it, professor?"

"Good afternoon," he said into the phone, "this is Professor MacGregor. How can I help you?"

To Griffin he made a motion like he was writing on paper. Griffin found a pad of paper on the desk. He handed the pad to the professor, along with a pen.

"Yes, Mrs. Sikorsky," the professor was saying, as he wrote on the pad. "I was the judge in today's competition."

He wrote a few words on the pad and tore off a piece of paper, which he handed to Griffin.

Griffin, somewhat to his surprise – delaying intellectual gratification was not his strong suit – never glanced at the paper, which he pocketed. He leaned across the desk to shake hands with Professor Michael S. MacGregor.

The professor may not have noticed. He had turned off the office lights again. He was verbally backpedalling already: "Yes, Mrs. Sikorsky...yes, I know my ass from my elbow..."

Twenty Nine

Rush hour was over, but with the endless repair work to Charles Street, traffic poked along. Griffin turned right onto 33rd Street, but traffic here was more congested. He got stuck through two green lights at 33rd and Greenmount, the surliest intersection in Baltimore, in Griffin's driving experience. None of which troubled him. He needed time to think about his next step after meeting with Professor MacGregor.

Griffin hadn't yet shared Alexandra Webb's dissertation with any of the others. He wanted to settle into the details first. By the time Griffin turned onto York Road, Griffin knew his next step was to make copies of the dissertation for Annie, Kit, Bobby, and Saif. He wanted each of them to answer the question he'd asked the professor: Which violin did Hans Baeder try to save during the Ulm air raid all those years ago?

He stopped at the Staples on Goucher Boulevard to run off four copies of the dissertation. When he got home Annie was not there. She'd left a message that Grace called. Grace had finally gotten the passport information Griffin requested. Had either of the ladies at Future-Ride traveled to Europe? Annie's message was that Grace had learned De-BOR-ah Miller had never been to Europe. Alexandra Webb had gone to Germany 11 times.

"Confirmed," Griffin said aloud. He walked through the back door toward Kit's garage apartment. The apartment door was partially open, to catch a soft evening breeze. Griffin watched, unobserved, as Kit sprawled sideways on a chair. Kit was writing on a pad of paper. Griffin knew Kit was compiling some kind of list.

The first list Griffin had ever seen Kit make was in kindergarten, when he ranked his favorite colors. At that time Kit could print letters, but not whole words. The list, in its entirety, consisted of: Y, R, B, O. The "R," now that Griffin thought about it, was reversed and the "Y" upside down.

He knocked and stepped into the apartment.

"Here's Alexandra Webb's dissertation." He handed a copy to Kit. "Can I take you from whatever you're listing and ask you to read this?

"Kit, remember when I told you what Miriam Freitag said? That during the air raid on the Special Task Force For Music train outside Ulm, Hans wanted to protect one particular violin?" Kit remembered. "Here's what I'd like you to think about while reading the dissertation — which instrument did Hans have? To put it differently – which violin stolen by the Special Task Force is the most valuable?"

"Valuable means which is worth the most money?"

"An excellent question. Define 'valuable' any way you want. Money or whatever else. Which instrument is she after? It's a safe bet the man in white is after it too, but for now we focus on Alexandra Webb and her dissertation. I'll ask Annie, Bobby, and Saif to read the dissertation also.

"I'll do the same. I just came back from asking a violin professor at the Peabody Institute the question. I've got his answer in my pocket. I haven't read it yet. I want all of us to approach the question without influence from anyone else. We'll get together tomorrow night for dinner to compare answers."

"Sure thing," Kit said. The two looked at each other a few seconds. "Since you so obviously want to know," Kit told Griffin, "the list I'm drawing up is the greatest guitar riffs of all time."

"Did "Layla" make the list?"

"That goes without saying. See you for dinner tomorrow night."

★

Griffin called Bobby, who agreed to meet him at the Dunkin Donuts on 41ˢᵗ Street in Hampden. Bobby wore his Marlon Brando clothes – tight jeans, plain white tee, leather jacket.

"Read this, if you would," Griffin requested, handing Bobby the dissertation. "Tell me your answer to this question: What is the most valuable instrument Alexandra Webb discusses? When I handed Kit his copy he made the fine point that 'valuable' may mean different things to different people. Define it any way you'd like. After this, Saif gets his copy; then Annie. They'll answer the question. I'll do the same."

"What's in it for me?" Bobby wondered.

"Dinner tomorrow night. At the restaurant of your choice."

"How about a Russian restaurant? I may be auditioning for a part in Chekov's Cherry Orchard next week."

"Russian it is, then."

A young mother of two, she couldn't have been more than 19 or 20, pushed a stroller into the Dunkin'. She carried a squalling infant. A two year old clung to his mother's legs so fiercely the woman struggled to open the door. This child was crying even louder.

"I must away," Bobby announced, in his baritone Shakespearean voice. He hustled over to help the young mother through the door. His sudden appearance startled the two year old into silence. Bobby flexed his hands repeatedly in front of the boy, as if proving to the child the hands were empty.

"Watch closely," Bobby instructed, in his loudly confident stage voice. "At no time do my hands leave my arms."

The boy did watch, with wide brown eyes. Griffin noticed the gratitude on the mother's face.

"Holy moly, guacamole!" Bobby announced. While distracting the child by waving his right arm, Bobby slipped his left hand into his belt at his back and pulled out a chunk of honey dip. He performed the move very smoothly. Griffin had a sense of what Bobby was up to and even Griffin could barely see where the piece of donut came from.

"Honey dip for you!" Bobby shouted. "If it's okay with your Mom, that is."

The woman said, sure it was fine, just fine, and, mister, could you maybe be here again tomorrow?

★

Griffin couldn't get Saif on the phone. The Statistics Department secretary, working late, informed him Professor Venkatesan was in the library, getting ready for his doctoral defense. Griffin drove to the Venkatesans' house in Homeland. He slipped the dissertation into the mailbox. On the outside of the envelope he wrote instructions for Saif, explaining what question he should answer. Griffin also mentioned dinner at the Russian restaurant in Towson at six the following night.

Back home, Griffin read the dissertation. Annie did as well, falling asleep around midnight, three-fourths of her way through the 256 page dissertation. For a moment Griffin watched her sleep. He gratefully listened to her steady, reassuring breathing. He turned out the light and went downstairs and stretched out on the couch. Griffin had read the dissertation straight through twice by this point. He had a very strong sense of the violin Alexandra Webb felt was most valuable. For an hour or so he dipped back into the dissertation, checking out various points, to see if anything could change his mind. It didn't.

Around three in the morning he fell asleep. Two hours later Annie came downstairs and slipped onto the couch with him. And then, for a while, for a very nice while, the dissertation and everything else was totally forgotten.

Thirty

June 24
5:09 pm

Everyone drove separately to the Russian restaurant in Towson, even Annie and Griffin. It had not been easy for Griffin to restrain himself from asking Annie which instrument she'd picked. He managed to stay silent by keeping busy with household chores, transforming himself into a true domestic god for the day. The shower grouting never looked as it good as it did by mid-afternoon.

Dinner had been scheduled for six but Griffin pushed the meal ahead to five thirty, then to five, unwilling to wait the extra time.

The restaurant had a small side room and Griffin requested a table there. They had the room to themselves.

"Let's order and then discuss what we came here for," he said, as soon as they were seated. There were nods around the table. Griffin could sense their anticipation, as intense as his own.

Their waiter – Griffin thought the man had an uncanny resemblance to Vladimir Lenin, down to the Satanic pointed beard – took their orders. Griffin went with the Kamchatka shrimp, because the waiter assured him the garlic sauce "had a nice bite to it." Bobby asked for the grilled sturgeon. Saif, after extended internal debate – Kit at one point loudly suggested, "Can't you just flip a coin?" – selected the carp stuffed with mushrooms. Kit got the potato pierogies, and Annie chose the Varenki dumplings. Griffin waited until the waiter disappeared into the kitchen.

Griffin began: "We all remember the assignment. We each read Alexandra Webb's dissertation, 'Establishing the Value of Musical Instruments Stolen by the Special Task Force For Music.' We're here to decide which violin Alexandra Webb considers most valuable.

"Which violin did Hans Baeder have that awful day when the American bombers hit the Special Task Force train? Whichever violin Hans held that day, the man in white wants it as well. His connection to Alexandra Webb remains unknown, but I now have a theory.

"This violin must be why Hans got all those calls from someone on the alcove phone at Future-Ride. That little mystery has at last been cleared up. It was Alexandra, not De-BOR-ah, calling Hans every month for 19 months. She must have been calling to ask him, do you have the violin? If you have it, what do you want for it? If you don't have it, do you know where it is?

"Hans was a man of few words. He couldn't have told her much one way or the other – that's why she kept calling.

"That violin also had to be why Dude broke into Hans Baeder's house during Hans' funeral. He was after a violin. Which one? Which violin is it? Here's the violin I picked."

Griffin placed a piece of paper in the center of the table.

"And here is the violin that Dr. MacGregor, the professor at the Peabody Institute, picked."

That piece of paper went next to Griffin's.

Annie, Kit, Bobby and Saif each placed a piece of paper on the table

Griffin came prepared to defend his selection and had mentally cataloged reasons for his choice. Saif, Griffin saw, was holding a single spaced sheet of paper with his reasons for why he felt this was the violin Alexandra Webb was after. Kit had a numbered list of reasons. Bobby was drumming his fingers on the tablecloth, a sign he was primed for debate.

There was no need for debate. Griffin saw that every piece of paper, all six of them, named the same instrument: the 1742 Guarneri del Gesu violin.

★

Bobby spoke first: "Alexandra Webb's dissertation was the product of a young scholar on her way to a doctorate in economics, right? Not surprisingly, the text is littered with equations. Fun for Saif conceivably, but indecipherable to me. So I opted for a different approach. Reading her dissertation, I asked myself, 'Self, what gets Alexandra Webb most excited?'"

"Did yourself have a good answer to your question?" Griffin asked.

"Naturally. Alexandra Webb opened her dissertation with backgrounding. The facts about Alfred Rosenberg and the Special Task Force For Music. She covered much of the same information as Kit did in his presentation on the back porch. Except her work was at greater, obsessively footnoted length. This section, despite its thoroughness, gave off a whiff of having been dutifully done. To me, at least."

"Me too," Annie threw in. "Like a child working through dinner just to get to dessert."

"Well said," Bobby agreed. "Kit was righteously incensed by Alfred Rosenberg. But Alexandra Webb simply presented the facts, without judgment. Did you notice that she rarely even mentions the Nazis? Griffin, it's obvious how troubled you are that Hans Baeder was a Nazi."

"He had no choice," Griffin replied, with some force.

"Alexandra? None of that mattered to her. Her interest is elsewhere."

The waiter arrived with a basket of rolls. Kit speared an onion roll before the basket hit the table. Then he wolfed down a sesame. Bobby stayed quiet until the waiter returned to the kitchen before resuming.

"Because Alexandra was studying economics, the second section of the dissertation is an extended analysis of the estimated value of the many stolen pianos, cellos, and all the instruments other than violins. As you told us, Griffin, the loot was staggering. The Special Task Force kept very busy."

"The term for her type of economic analysis is econometrics," Saif said, with a verbal shudder, as if he'd said "maggots" or "sludge."

Bobby kept going. "The list of estimated values for the stolen instruments went on for page after page. To be honest, I skimmed a lot of this. Alexandra didn't seem particularly interested in this part of the dissertation either. I inferred she produced it to satisfy her economics professors at the Sorbonne."

Annie took a sesame roll and passed the basket to Saif, who, after reflection, selected a slice of banana bread. He passed the basket to Kit, who, with no time for reflection whatsoever, helped himself to another onion roll and a garlic parmesan. By the time the basket got to Griffin, it was empty. That day Griffin hadn't stopped researching to eat and his knife was already buttered in anticipation of a roll.

Watching from the doorway, the Lenin lookalike waiter saw this. He brought a second basket of rolls. This time Kit waited until the basket actually made contact with the table before taking a roll. Once the waiter was out of earshot, Bobby continued.

"Alexandra saved her passion for the third and final section of the dissertation. Here she focused on stolen violins. Naturally Stradivarius I had heard of. But she discussed other violin makers of apparent world-renown. Like Amati."

"Andrea Amati," Saif volunteered. "Sixteenth century Italian, did most of his work for King Charles IX of France."

"And Antonio Stradivarius," Kit said, "the best known violin master of all time."

"In a seventy year career," Annie added, "he made more than 650 violins."

"And of course Guarneri del Gesu."

This was Griffin. He motioned for someone to pass him the basket of rolls. By the time Kit did, the basket was again empty.

"Oh, did you want one?" Kit asked Griffin slyly. Kit waved to the waiter, who carried over a third basket.

Griffin grabbed the roll on top, pumpernickel it turned out to be, and as he buttered the roll he asked Kit, "What made you pick the Guarneri del Gesu? What led you to that decision?"

"I asked myself, what does an economist care about? The answer, of course," Kit proclaimed, "is money. Remember the nine page inventory of stolen violins in the dissertation? Alexandra wrote pages and pages about that."

"That list is the only inventory of instruments looted by the Special Task Force to survive the war," Saif pointed out.

"For every violin in that nine page inventory," Bobby said, "Alexandra Webb assigned an estimated value in 1987, when she wrote her dissertation. She listed the estimated value of every violin in that one big chart of hers."

"And in the other column of her chart," this was Annie speaking, "was her projected value of the instruments twenty five years later. Five years ago now."

The comments were flying so quickly around the table that Griffin, to his pleasure, felt like he was watching a four way tennis match.

Bobby: "I went online to different sites to see if Alexandra Webb's estimated values for the instruments three years ago were accurate."

Kit: "So did I. They weren't even close to accurate."

Saif: "The estimated values of the instruments were far too low."

Annie: "Amazing, isn't it, how many websites are devoted to the 1742 Guarneri del Gesu."

Griffin: "It is amazing. Oceans of digital ink have been spilled on that one instrument."

The waiter arrived with their dinners and conversation about the dissertation ceased.

★

What did they talk about during dinner? Afterward, Griffin had no recollection and he guessed the others didn't either. They all shared their entrees with each other. Griffin raved about Bobby's grilled sturgeon and Annie's dumplings, but in truth he did not taste anything. Until this – quest, is that what this had become? – was over, Griffin's taste buds would be on hiatus.

Once dinner was over and the dead plates cleared away and after the waiter had brought their coffee and desserts and departed, discussion of the Alexandra Webb dissertation resumed.

Griffin asked, "Did any of you notice any mention of Hamburg or Ulm in the dissertation?"

"None," Saif agreed. "I saw that as well. Alexandra Webb, for as thorough as she was in everything else, avoided mentioning anything about the possible location of the instruments stolen by the Special Task Force For Music. I realize that question was not central to her analysis, but..."

"But it's not like the lady has no interest in the question," Kit stated. "She's devoted enormous effort through the years, trying to track down the del Gesu."

"Trips to Hamburg and Ulm," Bobby threw in.

"Calls to Hans Baeder," Annie added.

There were a few moments of quiet broken when Griffin said, "I was stunned to see what some of the Guarneri del Gesu violins are bringing in." This time it was Kit first to speak. "Six million dollars for one auctioned off in 1999."

Saif added, "In 2001, a group of sixteen investors got together and formed a corporation to purchase a Guarneri del Gesu for three and a half million." Saif poured milk into his coffee as he explained, "They lease the instrument to a violinist for the Tucson Symphony for twenty years. He pays twenty thousand annually for maintenance and insurance, just for the chance to play the thing."

Kit finished up Saif's story. "At the end of those twenty years, the investors plan to sell the violin, when its estimated value should exceed twenty million after taxes. And none of these violins are from 1742, the truly golden year for the Guarneri del Gesu violin."

Annie said, "The 1742 del Gesus are such a big deal that the one owned by the city of San Francisco has its own name,

The David. When it's not being played it's kept in a glass case in a museum."

This exchange was bouncing around the table even more rapidly than their talking before dinner.

Over his coffee cup Griffin said, "Guarneri del Gesu, first name Giuseppe, made 13 violins in 1742. Twelve are accounted for. The remaining one went missing in the Second World War."

"The philosopher Karl Wittgenstein's family," Saif mentioned.

"That's right," Kit agreed. "Remember the deal the Wittgenstein family cut with the Nazis to stay out of the concentration camps? Alexandra Webb has a full section on it in her dissertation. The Nazis got all the money. And the Nazis got the Wittgensteins' musical instruments – most importantly, a 1742 Guarneri del Gesu. In exchange, the Jewish Wittgensteins were permitted to stay in Vienna and out of the concentration camps."

"Which probably saved their lives."

"Yes, Bobby, which probably saved their lives."

"The Wittgenstein Del Gesu wound up in a Paris violin shop after the war," Saif said, picking up the story from Kit. "The owner later died. His widow said she didn't remember how they acquired what has to be the most valuable violin in the world. And she says she doesn't know what happened to the violin. The shop no longer had it. How could she not know that?"

"As I recall," Griffin answered, "Alexandra Webb wasn't convinced either. She predicted the violin would someday be offered on the black market."

"So where does that leave us?" Griffin asked, accelerating his voice as the waiter banged through the kitchen door carrying another coffee pot. "A 1742 Guarneri del Gesu violin may have survived the war. Alexandra Webb placed the value of a 1742 at what, Saif?"

He held off answering until the waiter departed. "Forty five million, as of five years ago."

"But we all agree she undervalued the instruments."

"Absolutely," Saif concurred. "In my research today I determined that three of the instruments in her dissertation chart have been recently auctioned off. Two Stradivariuses and an Amati. A Spanish collector bought the Stradivariuses; a billionaire in Brazil purchased the Amati. Each time the auction price of the instrument exceeded, substantially exceeded, the value Alexandra Webb predicted years ago when she wrote the dissertation."

"So: your estimate of a missing 1742 Guarneri del Gesu?"

Saif: "Fifty million."

Bobby: "Got to be more."

Kit: "Ginormous."

Annie: "Who could say?"

They sipped their coffee in awed silence.

"No way," Griffin said, breaking the quiet.

"No way what?" someone asked.

"No way could I do this without all of you."

There were a few more minutes of coffee soaked silence. From his spot by the kitchen door the waiter looked over at Griffin. The waiter stroked his Lenin-like beard and waved the check in Griffin's direction. Griffin shook his head. They weren't done yet.

"As Miss Paulette would tell you – eagerly tell you – I know next to nothing about classical music," he said. "Can anyone tell me what is so remarkable musically about the 1742 del Gesu?"

To Griffin's surprise it was Annie who answered.

"I read a wild explanation about that today. Would anyone like to hear it?"

Everyone would.

"The explanation is from a Hungarian violinist who has played violins from different parts of Guarneri del Gesu's career. The Hungarian said, 'The tone of a Guarneri del Gesu is so rich that playing one other than the 1742 is like drinking the finest glass of wine you've ever tasted in your life. Playing a 1742 is like being served the wine by your mistress, naked.'"

★

"We've got to get going, but I have to ask – in your reading of Alexandra Webb's dissertation, do any of you recall her discussing the rich tone of a violin?"

"No, but she's an economist. Tone isn't what economists care about," Kit answered. The others nodded their agreement.

"True, but..." Griffin had thought extensively about this issue, but was only now coming to a conclusion. "Doesn't it feel like the dissertation could be about diamonds or petroleum futures or any commodity? Instead of musical instruments stolen during the war, don't you get the feeling she'd be just as interested in anything that turns a profit? A violin exists to make music, not money."

"You got a point in there, Griffin?" Kit wanted to know.

Griffin answered, "My point is that Alexandra Webb and the man in white – whoever he really is – may be after the same violin, but they have very different interests. I think he's the buyer and she's the seller. We've never known the connection between the two. The connection is certainly there. We all saw the security tape Grace sent us of the man in white calling Future-Ride from Arazzo Castle.

"I think that's their connection: buyer-seller. I figure they have an arrangement. He wants the violin. She gets a commission for obtaining it. She made all those trips to Ulm and Hamburg trying to find where the Special Task Force For Music had stashed its loot. She called Hans Baeder every month for 19 months. She must have hired the thug who Timothy Dean called Dude to break into Hans' house. Dude was looking for the del Gesu violin. Her commission? Say twenty percent."

"Of forty five million or more?" Saif suggested. "Not a bad payday."

"But, Griffin!" Annie demanded. "Did Hans Baeder have the del Gesu, do you think? I agree Alexandra Webb wants that to be true."

"As does the man in white," Kit added.

"But did Hans actually have the del Gesu? Did he have it that day outside Ulm when the American planes attacked."

Griffin answered quickly. "I think Hans did have a del Gesu. Miriam Freitag convinced me of that. That's the violin Hans got wounded saving. The much bigger question of course-"

"Where is that del Gesu now?" Annie finished for Griffin.

"Exactly. Where is it now? I don't know. There is one thing we know for sure."

"Which is what, Griffin?" Bobby asked.

"Alexandra Webb and the man in white don't know either."

Everyone rose from the table. The waiter handed Griffin the check. The amount nudged into three figures; Griffin had only $98. They were pursuing a violin worth tens of millions of dollars and Griffin lacked the cash for dinner and tip.

Annie reached into her purse and handed Griffin a twenty.

"The change is yours," he told the waiter.

The waiter stroked his Lenin-ish beard.

"Everyone in your party seemed to be enjoyin' themselves tonight, I'm thinkin'," he said, in a thick Baltimore accent which decapitated every "g" at the end of his words. The man may have resembled a Russian revolutionary, but he'd grown up inside the beltway. "What're you folks doin' next?"

"I may have an idea," Griffin replied.

Thirty One

June 26
8:33 am

Two days later Grace called Griffin. He told her, "Grace, if I didn't know you better, I'd say you were positively giddy."

"Mr. Gilmore," Grace started and stopped and Griffin could tell she was struggling to dampen the delight in her voice. She couldn't quite. "You have done us a huge favor."

"Because?"

"Because you asked me to track down everyone awarded a signet ring by the Order of Maximilian the Younger."

"Which I found out about from Mike MacGregor, the violin professor at the Peabody Institute. There can't be all that many recipients of rings from the Order of Maximilian the Younger."

"Mr. Gilmore," Grace repeated in a cheerleader's cheeriness Griffin couldn't help but grin at. "It turns out that in the two centuries of that award, there have been 33 recipients. Learning their identities was easy. We knew that within hours of your phone call Wednesday night. But it took our people four days to determine that of those 33 rings, the whereabouts of only 32 can be accounted for."

"And the one unaccounted for, Grace?"

"The one ring that isn't accounted for must be the one you saw on your man in white, the night you met in the Baltimore Museum of Art."

"So you know who he is?"

"We do, Mr. Gilmore. After all this time we do. And that is why you have done us a huge favor."

"Who is he?"

The excitement in her voice still evident, Grace began her backgrounding.

"Your man in white's name is Roberto Ruiz. Born 1954, Barcelona, Spain. Ruiz was his mother's name. His father remains unknown, even to Roberto, it seems. His mother was a prostitute in Barcelona, a heroin addict who died of a drug overdose when her son was nine. Roberto pretty much raised himself on the streets. He slept in an abandoned school bus. Dinners he often retrieved from a dumpster.

"Are you at your computer?" Grace asked him. "I'd like to send you an email attachment with the only known picture of Roberto Ruiz as a child. His nickname was Chico."

"Which is Spanish for boy," Griffin pointed out.

"With an unmistakable condescension to the name," Grace clarified. "Roberto detested being called Chico. He boasted that someday he'd be a man of respect. No one would call him Chico again, which is what happened. Here comes the picture."

Griffin was in his backyard beneath a pine tree, laptop on a folding table. It was the morning after their dinner in the Russian restaurant. He felt eyes on him. Over his shoulder he spotted Dr. Eckleburg staring at him from the kitchen window.

"Got the email," he told Grace.

★

Griffin opened the email attachment. She'd sent a class picture, old enough to be in black and white.

"Seventh grade," Grace informed him, anticipating Griffin's question. "Roberto Ruiz is in the back row, tallest kid in the class."

"Skinniest too," Griffin said.

"See the other kids in the class? Smiling. Happy for the break from the regular school day. Not our Roberto," remarked Grace.

"No. He's humiliated. Look at his clothes compared to the other kids and it's not hard to see why."

Roberto's pants stopped about mid-shin. The cuffs were frayed. Roberto wore a short sleeve shirt worn through in places. All the other seventh graders were in long sleeves, even sweaters. Christmas decorations in the back of the classroom placed the time of the picture as December. It wasn't hard to imagine the twelve year old Roberto, alone in the world, without the money for decent long sleeve shirts or a sweater.

"Smartest kid in his class," Grace told him. "Do you recognize your man in white from this picture, Mr. Gilmore?"

Griffin studied the picture of Roberto Ruiz at twelve. Griffin could not help but sympathize with the child's plight.

"No." He looked some more, before continuing. "No. I honestly cannot see any connection between this tragic, undernourished kid with the sunken eyes and the man who took the key from me in the museum."

Griffin remembered the comment Bobby had made about the man in white – Roberto Ruiz – while they were watching the security camera footage from Arazzo Castle. Bobby, with his actor's eye for a performance, confidently stated that the aristocratic air with which Mr. Ruiz carried himself was merely a role. Bobby believed the man had not been born to wealth and advantages. Bobby, Griffin understood now, was very much right.

"What do you know about Roberto Ruiz today, Grace? Why is he so important to you that you're so knowledgeable about the details of his early life?"

"Most of what we've learned comes from Interpol. Some is from CIA sources. There's quite a lot on Mr. Ruiz. He's attracted a good bit of attention in a number of countries through the years. Mr. Ruiz is an international arms dealer. He makes his living – and a very good living it is – supplying guns, ammunition, and explosives to various groups around the world.

"I've studied up on him. I've learned that the Basque separatists are a steady customer. The IRA once was. The Balkans were good to him. Parts of the old Soviet Union are now. He started out supplying both sides of the Iran-Iraq war. In Ukraine too. Africa? If it weren't for Roberto Ruiz, Africa might not be the Garden of Eden, but it would surely be a lot less bloody."

"How about the United States?"

"The Mafia has used his services on occasion. He's not some wild-eyed, idealistic Sixties revolutionary. This is what he does for a living."

"That explains the Makarov," Griffin said.

"The pistol he pointed at you in the museum," Grace added.

"He did more than point the thing at me," Griffin reminded her. "As I recall, you were a bit surprised he used such an elderly pistol. But you also said the Makarov was often the weapon of choice for those needing to smuggle a gun through security. Which is what he likely did, coming in from Spain.

An arms dealer would appreciate the virtue of a Makarov while traveling."

"That's why you've done us a huge favor, Mr. Gilmore. We want Roberto Ruiz. We want him out of the arms business. It'd make the world a far quieter place."

Next Grace said, "When Senor Ruiz started out in his chosen profession, he had two partners. One Serb and one individual with an organization that was a precursor of Al Qaida. Those gentlemen have not been seen or heard from in many years. It is highly unlikely either of those gentlemen is still among the living. Did they cross him? Cut into his profit? Whatever the explanation, he's a self-employed entrepreneur these days. You ready for the next picture? It's a mug shot, the only mug shot ever taken of Roberto Ruiz."

★

Moments later, staring back at Griffin in the mug shot was a man with dark hair, defiant dark eyes, and a gaunt face. The determination in those eyes was unmistakable. He wore an expensive looking creamy silk shirt over a torn white tee shirt.

"This mug shot was taken in Amsterdam, twenty five years ago. Ruiz was then late thirties. On a tip, the Dutch police grabbed him at the airport. He was arrested and booked. Put in a holding cell. Then he disappeared. The jailer was bringing dinner and found the cell unlocked and empty. To this day no one can explain how Ruiz slipped out of custody.

"At some point in his escape he must have been injured. He acquired a limp in Amsterdam. He limps to this day, as you know. Recognize your man in white yet?" Grace wondered.

"Not yet. Almost," Griffin answered. "The facial features? Sure, I can see that face becoming the face of the man pointing a gun my direction at the art museum. But this guy I'm looking at-"again Griffin glanced at the mug shot, "this younger version lacks the man in white's confidence and continental sophistication. His aristocratic bearing. That's still in the future. But it's on its way."

"Know what he was doing in Amsterdam?"

"Buying or selling guns, I would assume."

"No. He did not travel to Amsterdam on business, Mr. Gilmore. This was pleasure. He was there to buy a stolen painting by Van Gogh. By this time Roberto Ruiz had begun his own little art collection. An Impressionist painting here; a Roman artifact there. If what he wanted was for sale, he'd purchase it legally through an intermediary. If the object was not for sale, he would arrange to have it stolen."

"But he's not just another collector, is he?" Griffin insisted. "Those objects he buys? There're not just a rich man's equivalent of collecting salt and pepper shakers or whatever, are they?"

"I've reached that same conclusion, Mr. Gilmore. Along the way Ruiz taught himself several languages. He became a gourmand. Extraordinarily knowledgeable about the history of European nobility. This was all part of his journey. Along the way Roberto Ruiz started referring to himself as Roberto de Ruiz."

"'De' is a Spanish honorific. The Germans do the same thing with 'van' in their names. It's a recognition of a certain status."

"Clearly," Grace concluded, "that status matters to Roberto de Ruiz."

"The clothes and the culture are a kind of validation," Griffin noted. "Proof he's no longer Chico Ruiz from the streets. He's Roberto de Ruiz. He has escaped his past to become a man of substance."

"He's told people he's related to Mozart. Since Ruiz's father is unknown the claim is, I suppose, theoretically possible. Still the claim seems extraordinarily unlikely."

Griffin considered the information for a moment.

"That's why he has the signet ring from the Order of Maximilian the Younger, isn't it, Grace? For the same reason he claims to be related to Mozart. He replaces his shameful ancestry with a glorious one."

Again, by Grace's silence Griffin could tell she concurred in his judgment.

"How did he obtain the ring?" he asked.

"He got it in Munich. Three years ago. There was a museum display of the life of musicians in 19th Century Bavaria. Sound familiar? The ring was in the museum display one day and gone the next morning. Someone spotted a car leaving the museum late at night. Roberto Ruiz was seen in that car, with his latest acquisition, the ring."

"The prostitute's son who raised himself on the streets of Barcelona has successfully buried his past behind a life of culture, wealth and acquisitions, even a prestigious name."

"All of which is built on bloodshed. Don't lose sight of how that cultured façade was obtained, Mr. Gilmore," Grace ordered, in her stiffest voice. The giddy cheerleader who had so amused Griffin was gone. "Remember the individual who provided that tip which led to Ruiz's arrest at the Amsterdam airport?"

"Yeah?"

"He was found the next morning floating face down, throat slit in one of Amsterdam's famous canals. One last picture. Taken six years ago."

★

The picture had been taken at some distance with a high powered lens. Roberto Ruiz was stepping into a car. He was dressed entirely in varying shades of white: hat, suit coat, shirt, tie, slacks. The only color in his attire was the gold band in his Panama hat. The band glittered in the sun.

"The years since the Amsterdam mug shot have been kind to him," observed Griffin. "See how the face is fuller. He's no longer missing any meals. And that's haute cuisine not Lean Cuisine he's been having. The clothes are so much more expensive. Tailor-made, I would bet. That's the man from the museum."

"The car he's getting into is a Bentley," Grace said. "It too was tailor-made."

"Now *that* is the man who stole the key from me," Griffin said. "He has acquired not just the trappings of wealth, but that aura of nobility. You can see it in the picture. I saw it in the museum. I didn't notice he was six-five, but I couldn't help but be aware of his sense of power and prestige. It's understated but unmistakable. Where was the picture taken?"

"Spain. He has a villa, a compound really, in the Pyrenees," Grace replied. "That's where he spends most of his time. That's Basque country and they protect their arms supplier. If you look closely, you can see guards with machine guns in the background of the picture. He keeps other apartments and houses around Europe – Geneva, Berne, Palermo, Kiev. Those are the ones we know about. He stays under the radar screen in his day job of arms dealer. Uses different aliases; keeps moving.

"This is as close as anyone has been able to get to him in years—half a mile away. We've never been able to get any closer, though we would dearly love to. The Brits would as well; the French and Russians also. There aren't many issues those countries and Interpol agree on, but taking out Roberto Ruiz is one.

"The only time he surfaces is for his acquisitions of culture, which is where he lives large. Paintings, artifacts, musical instruments. But only the best."

"Only the very best," Griffin emphasized. "He's after the very finest musical instrument in the world, Grace. It's worth fifty million dollars, possibly more. Me, Annie, Bobby, Kit, Saif, and Mike MacGregor, the violin professor at the Peabody all agree: he's after the 1742 Guarneri del Gesu violin. That's why he went into the dungeon of Arazzo Castle. He believed the violin might be there. He's after the 1742 del Gesu.

"Alexandra Webb of Future-Ride is as well, though her connection to Ruiz remains uncertain. I believe he's the buyer; she's the seller, working on commission, helping him obtain the ultimate proof of his journey from Chico to Roberto de Ruiz."

"Then that is how we're going to take him out, Mr. Gilmore." The giddy cheerleader's voice was back, even giddier than before. "We'll likely never get him in his day job. He's too cautious, too protected, too experienced. He's got too many connections in the arms trade who want him to stay in business. I doubt we'll put him out of business in his line of work.

"But we might just entice Roberto de Ruiz, your man in white, here, with the chance to obtain the ultimate proof of his cultural achievement – the 1742 Guarneri del Gesu violin."

"The violin will be the bait, Grace?"

"Exactly. The bait is the del Gesu violin he obviously wants so desperately. A violin which, now that I think about it, you do not have."

"We'll have to work around that."

Grace plowed on, her chipperness returned in full force.

"With the violin as bait, we convince him to leave the security of his Pyrenees villa, and come to the United States. And he'll be arrested. And the world becomes a good bit less dangerous. I'm hoping you will help us. Can we count on you?"

"Sure." Griffin started to say something more, then stopped. He couldn't bring himself to ruin Grace's mood. What Griffin was about to say, but didn't, was: *The violin won't be the bait, Grace. I will.*

Thirty Two

June 26
8:39 am

"I'm on my way to class," Saif told Griffin, whose conversation with Grace had ended seconds before. "You'll have to make it quick."

"Quick it is, then. Go online," Griffin requested. "Soon as you can after class."

"Looking for?"

"Looking for websites devoted to selling musical instruments. Find the best two or three websites not connected to an official organization. We don't want to be dealing with the Vienna Philharmonic or whoever. Find the websites that act as electronic bulletin boards. Websites where some people list instruments for sale; others list the instruments they're looking to buy. Doable?"

"Doable, certainly." Saif replied. His voice had the rushed pace of someone speaking into a phone while walking quickly. "Excuse me for a second," Saif morphed into professorial mode. "Tiffany," he said to one of his Hopkins student he'd apparently run into, "you misapplied the T Statistic on your last assignment. ...Sure. ...Just get the revised assignment to me by the end of the week....Don't mention it. Griffin, you were saying?"

"Pick out the sites you think are best. They could be the sites which get the most traffic. They could be the sites which appear most professionally arranged. Use your considerable judgment. Saif, I can't think of anyone more qualified to make this decision."

"I'll do it right after class. Got to jump, Griffin."

"Go teach. Get back to me once you've made your decision."

As soon as Griffin ended the call he headed out the backdoor for Kit's garage apartment.

★

Kit was leaning against the wall, still in his pajamas, sprawling across his unmade bed. The bed was normal-sized and Kit barely filed half of it. He was writing on a pad of paper when Griffin entered.

"What are you listing?" Griffin wondered.

"Best TV dads."

"Is Rob Petrie on the list?"

"Needless to say. Whazzup this morning?"

"Kit, can you pick up a box that would be used to ship a violin? Through the mail, say? Go to Fed Ex, UPS, places like that. We could ask Professor MacGregor at the Peabody. I saw the one he had. I'd rather keep him out of this if we can."

"I'll get on it right now. What do you need it for?"

"We'll worry about that later. Can you just get the box?"

Kit agreed he would. Griffin turned to leave, but stopped.

"Did Marcia Brady's Dad make your list?"

Kit showed Griffin the paper with MIKE BRADY in oversized block letters and underlined, at the very top of the page.

265

★

Next, Griffin called Bobby.

"Ah, Mr. Lowell," Griffin began. "Did I wake you?"

"I'm getting ready for an audition. What's going on, Griffin?"

"I wondered if you'd be available later today, post-audition. We're starting to set the trap. I'm going to ask you to reprise your starring role as Dr. Walter Briggs, legendarily eccentric investor. Dr. Briggs will be making a call."

"Sure. I can bring him back for the sequel. Who's Dr. Briggs calling?"

"Future-Ride."

"I've decided to invest with Alexandra Webb and the stunningly distasteful De-BOR-ah Miller?"

"To the contrary. You are telling the ladies of Future-Ride that you have decided to invest your money elsewhere."

"With another company?"

"With a musical instrument."

"Ah. Would that be the 1742 Guarneri del Gesu?"

"Don't worry about that now. Will you be around later?"

Bobby promised he would.

★

Annie was out; buying nails and chatting with Miss P at Kenilworth Mall, Griffin assumed. How would he stay busy until Saif and Kit got back to him? He cleaned some more shower grouting. He edged the front walk some more. Mostly, he glared at the kitchen clock, furious the time would not move more quickly.

★

At 11:30 Saif finally called. Griffin was scrubbing the kitchen floor when his phone rang. He dropped the brush, which tumbled into the bucket of dirtying water with a *plooop* sound. By the second ring he'd yanked the phone from his pants pocket.

Saif told him, "I think I've got the best three websites for serious collectors of classical musical instruments."

"Can buyers and sellers communicate about offers?"

"On all three websites. They all have message boards which are surprisingly active. Just yesterday on one site there was a new posting of a Stradivarius offered for sale. Another site has a listing for a trumpet from Paris, mid-18th century. The trumpet's history – its provenance – is suspiciously vague. There's a gap during the years of the Second World War. Buyers presumably wouldn't notice or care. I was only aware of the gap because of everything we've learned about the Special Task Force For Music and the man in white's interest in the 1742 Guarneri del Gesu."

"The man in white's name is Roberto de Ruiz," Griffin said. He recapped for Saif the conversation he'd had with Grace, where she detailed the story of Chico Ruiz's rise to become Roberto de Ruiz.

"You need anything else, Griffin?" Saif asked, in a rush. "I've got to go study for my doctoral defense."

"Go study. But can I call if we need you?"

Saif paused, though even the pause was hurried.

"This is all coming to a head, isn't it, Griffin?"

"I think it is, yes."

"I wouldn't miss it. Call me if I can be of help."

★

A bit later Kit appeared at Griffin's front door, carrying a Fed Ex-ish box.

"Looks just like the one Professor MacGregor had in his office," Griffin said, ushering Kit inside. "About, what, three feet long, one foot wide, and a foot deep. Well played."

"What should I do with the box?"

"Hold onto it. Now, next step. Go online. Find out how much an 18th century violin typically weighed. If you can find out how much the 1742 Guarneri del Gesu weighs, better still. Figure a couple extra ounces to account for the weight of foam pads that would protect a violin shipped in a box like this."

"And then?"

"And then, Kit, stuff that amount of weight into the violin box. Be as exact to the weight as you can. Buy a scale. Then, when you have placed the exact same weight of whatever you're using to stuff the box, and it weighs the same as a violin, seal the box up."

"Okay," he answered, "But stuff the box with what?"

"Stuff it with whatever you'd like," Griffin answered. "We want someone who's extremely knowledgeable about violins to be convinced there's a violin inside that sealed box."

★

Griffin spent most of the next hour on the couch, petting Dr. Eckleburg, that spot under the chin she liked so much. At 1:15 he abruptly stood up, sending Dr. Eckleburg tumbling off the couch. Griffin thought for a few seconds, searching for the right words. When he had them, he called Saif.

"Here's what I came up with," he told Saif, without much of a hello. He was getting as bad as Grace. "This is only the opening move in the chess match. We don't want to show the cards in our hand. To mix metaphors atrociously. I need you to post a message. All three websites. I'm trying to keep our message both simple enough and vague enough.

"Here's the message for you to send: 'Attention: My client has recently come into possession of a renowned 18th century string instrument. Serious buyers only please.' Don't sign it with my name or anybody's. That'll increase the mystery. Post it on the message boards of all three websites you selected."

"I'll send the message-"

"But not over your professional electronic address, Almost-Doctor Venkatesan. I am counting on you to maintain an unbridgeable gap between your professor's life and what we're doing here. Remember the firewall we talked about when all this was starting?"

"No one at Hopkins can know I'm consorting with the likes of you."

"That's more true than ever, my friend. You're not even one week or so away from becoming Dr. Venkatesan. Stay off the university server. You have a personal lap top. Use that."

"I will. But, Griffin? In your message you're not specifying the asking price or the kind of string instrument. Could be a viola, could be an Aeolian harp, could be a hammered dulcimer, could be a six string guitar, all of which are currently for sale on these websites. And without an asking price? You are likely to get a great many responses."

"That's okay if we do. There are only two we're interested in."

"Alexander Webb and Roberto de Ruiz."

"Alexandra Webb and Roberto de Ruiz."

"You're setting out the bait, aren't you, Griffin?"

"That's the idea."

"Maybe one of them will nibble."

"Better still, both of them. And better yet – they both don't just nibble, but take the bait, hook, line and proverbial sinker. Saif, can you check the websites every hour or so, between classes and prepping for your doctoral defense?"

"No prob."

"Call me as soon as you get any nibbles."

★

At 10:30 the next morning Saif did exactly that.

Griffin was on the couch with Dr. Eckleburg when the phone rang. When he saw it was Saif calling, Griffin got to his feet so quickly Dr. Eckleburg took another tumble to the floor.

Saif's voice was rushed, not with the demands of a crowded schedule but with excitement.

"We've had dozens of responses on the websites to our notice," Saif began. "Including Alexandra Webb, I'm pretty sure."

"Not that I doubt you, but what makes you say that?"

"One reply email came to the website from De-BOR-ah Miller's address at Future-Ride. So I called up there, pretending to be tech support. I'm no actor like Bobby, but I can fake it as a techie."

The delight in his voice was unmistakable. Griffin thought back to that first night when they discussed the man in white over pizza. How had Saif described Griffin, Annie, Bobby, and Kit? You're off road guys. Clearly Saif was enjoying his time off road.

He said, "Guess what? De-BOR-ah Miller's been out sick all week. Alexandra Webb used her email account. I assume without her knowledge. Why would she do that, do you think?"

"If our offer somehow blows up on Alexandra, she'd claim she knew nothing about it. She'd say De-BOR-ah went rogue on her. I don't know if buying a violin stolen by the Nazis is against American or international law; I do know it's not the sort of activity the CEO of a Manhattan investment firm wants to be caught engaging in. She's using De-BOR-ah as her fall girl. Talk about throwing De-BOR-ah under the bus? Alexandra Webb would be willing to toss her associate under the bus, jump behind the wheel, and stomp on the accelerator.

"De-DOR-ah has all the likeability of the flu, but she deserves better than that. No question about it – anyone trusting Alexandra Webb is taking a huge risk. What did she say in the email?"

"Four words, Griffin: 'Which instrument? What price?'"

"Sounds like the lady of the dissertation, doesn't it? Money-driven and to the point. Remember that Alexandra Webb probably has a commission arrangement with Roberto Ruiz?"

Saif did. He said, "The websites say twenty percent is typical for commissions."

"A twenty percent commission of the forty five million-"

"Or more."

"Or more. Whatever the Guarneri del Gesu sells for is her payday," Griffin agreed. "But that's all this is for her. A payday, nothing more. For Roberto de Ruiz, the del Gesu is something else entirely. Speaking of – any word from our man in white, Roberto de Ruiz?"

"I don't think so, Griffin. Not yet anyway."

"I'd be surprised if he replied right away. He's too careful. It's a safe bet he's aware of our initial offering. But for now he's sitting tight.

"Even if he didn't notice the posting," Griffin went on, "Alexandra Webb certainly did and will tell him about it, if she hasn't already. This is the first step for her in gaining that ginormous commission for obtaining the del Gesu. She's got to be feeling extremely fortunate right around now. All those months of calling Hans Baeder without result. The many fruitless trips to Ulm and Hamburg. Instead, the object of all her searching suddenly appears to be for sale.

"Can I call you this time tomorrow, Saif? It's my sense we need to keep this moving quickly. I don't think we should just shoot Senor de Ruiz an email with all the necessary information. Instead, he'll get a series of emails, each with another piece or two of information. Let's keep him wriggling on the hook, anxious and guessing a bit.

"But before then, our favorite actor has to step back on stage."

★

"I'm calling from a pay phone? And, I'm calling collect?"

"Bobby, you're Dr. Walter Briggs, who is not only frugal, but weirdly so. Trust me. Alexandra Webb will take your call."

"How do we even know she's still in the Future-Ride office at quarter after five in the afternoon?"

"Grace has helped us with that at my request. She had someone on her staff call Future-Ride. The staffer claimed she has heard such wonderful things about Future-Ride. She wants to invest with the firm. A 1.32 million dollar investment. She's going to call Future-Ride about financials and discuss investment strategy. This all takes place at 5:30, today. Alexandra Webb won't be leaving early today."

They were standing by a pay phone at a 7-11 on The Alameda. The store's only customers were a pair of twelve year old boys filling a Big Gulp cup with every flavor available. The twelve year olds wore hoodies and shorts so oversized they seemed destined to wind up around their ankles.

"Bobby, you tell Alexandra Webb you won't be investing with Future-Ride after all."

"That's it? I'm, sorry but-"

"You're not sorry at all! Dr. Walter Briggs wouldn't care about disappointing anyone. It's a simple fact you're imparting. You won't be investing with Future-Ride. Remember when we were in the Future-Ride offices in Manhattan? Almost the last words Alexandra spoke to me were to ask we call her, whatever our decision on investing. That's why you're calling her now."

"She'll ask why."

"Of course she will. We're counting on that. That's the real point of the call. Your explanation why you're not investing in Future-Ride. We're planting a seed in Alexandra's greedy brain.

"Bobby, you're going to tell Alexandra Webb you have decided to invest every dime you own and every dollar you can borrow to buy a musical instrument. You do not identify the instrument. You do not name the seller. You're a man of mystery. Nor do you mention the price. You do tell her the asking price for the instrument is so high you are part of a consortium of buyers going in together on the instrument. Your role is simply an investor. The point man for the purchase is your lawyer."

"That's you," Bobby said.

"Me, indeed," Griffin said. "You don't know all the specifics of the investment. You're Dr. Walter Briggs, inventor and above such trivial concerns. But you've been assured your lawyer will, soon after the sale, turn around and resell the never-named musical instrument for a sizeable profit. This is all about making money. That Alexandra will get."

Bobby watched the two boys leaving the 7-11, passing a Big Gulp cup back and forth. They got on their bikes and pedaled away, still passing the Big Gulp back and forth.

"Bobby? Bobby, you sure you got all that?"

★

Bobby did; he absolutely did. The entire conversation – a virtual monolog for Bobby – took less than two minutes.

The worry "sorry" never crossed Bobby's lips. He did not apologize for investing elsewhere. He let Alexandra Webb know that any disappointment she might be feeling simply did not show up on his radar screen. He was marvelously mysterious about what instrument he and his consortium were buying. Alexandra obviously kept pressing on that point, but Bobby never deigned to answer her anxious questions.

"My lawyer knows that," he said several times, with just the right mixture of condescension, annoyance, and intellectual's befuddlement.

"My lawyer knows that," he said one last time, before ending the call.

"Oscar worthy," Griffin told Bobby. To himself, Griffin muttered, "Now comes the tricky part."

Thirty Three

June 28
10:39 am

Griffin called Saif.

"Let me close the door to my office," Saif said. A few seconds later he returned to the call, asking, "What's our next step?"

"Next, we let Alexandra Webb and Roberto de Ruiz know we're offering the biggest prize of all. Send out another email on all three websites. Reply directly to all who contacted us and post it for all others. Here's the message: 'Attention: Appraised value of the violin we are offering is $45 million. No intermediaries. We will deal only with buyer directly. Our client wants sale consummated in Baltimore-'

"Griffin, many of those responding live abroad. They wouldn't necessarily know where Baltimore is."

"Not know where Baltimore is!" Griffin shouted in mock dismay.

"Hard to believe, I know. Better you add, 'Maryland, USA.'"

"Okay. Where was I? 'Our client wants sale consummated in Baltimore, Maryland, USA by July sixth at a location of our choosing.'" Griffin continued. "The $45 million price tag should keep out the hoi polloi."

"The hoi polloi?" Saif laughed. He really was enjoying himself. "Who are the hoi polloi?"

"You are. I am. Kit, Bobby and Annie are. Everyone who doesn't have $45 million to buy a violin are hoi polloi. This is too rich for the hoi polloi. But not too rich for Alexandra Webb and Roberto de Ruiz.

"Alexandra will of course recognize the $45 million as the value she placed on the 1742 Guarneri del Gesu in her dissertation. Senor de Ruiz will as well. He hired her; he knows her credentials. The violin is no doubt worth substantially more than that. But we're making a point for Alexandra and Roberto. No one else is of interest to us. Let's knock on their doors, see if anybody's home.

"One last detail." Griffin opened the door to the Malibu. "Say, 'Replies to this offer must be received within 24 hours.'"

"That's a tight time window, Griffin. What if Alexandra Webb or Roberto de Ruiz don't see the notice?"

Griffin slid into the driver's seat.

"They'll respond," he said. "Both of them. In their very different ways, the 1742 Guarneri del Gesu simply means too much to let slip by. They'll respond."

"Is this the time to mention that we don't actually have a 1742 Guarneri del Gesu to sell?"

Griffin started the car's engine.

"No, it's not the time to mention that."

★

Saif called back the next morning. When the phone rang Griffin was on the front porch, Dr. Eckleburg sunning herself on his right thigh. This time the cat moved more quickly than Griffin and avoided getting tumbled to the floor.

"He replied, Griffin! He bit the bait," Saif announced, in a voice loud enough that for him it qualified as joyous shouting. "I was just checking the message boards and I saw he replied."

"Roberto de Ruiz?"

"Roberto de Ruiz himself. I'm certain of it."

"Not that I'm doubting you, but how can you be so sure it's him, Saif? I assume he didn't sign his name."

"He was hardly foolish enough to do that. He signs his posting simply 'Buyer.' Still, I'm certain he is the one who answered our posting. Here. I've got the reply up on my screen. Let me read it to you.

'Price accurate. I desire to inspect the 1742 del Gesu-'"

"We never specified the make of violin."

"Exactly, Griffin. Exactly. The answer goes on to say, 'I desire to inspect the 1742 del Gesu to establish its authenticity. If acceptable, payment to be made at time of sale.'

"And, Griffin? The website requires those leaving messages to do so through email. The Europeans have a system which allows you to trace emails to the country, even city of origin. I can tell the email was routed through Berne, Switzerland."

"Berne's where Grace said Roberto de Ruiz keeps one of his apartments. I'll let her know. She'll have Interpol try to grab him, but I can't imagine that will happen. It's a safe assumption he's since departed the premises. He's good at moving quickly."

Griffin went on, "And Roberto Ruiz is referencing the Alexandra Webb dissertation when he says of the $45 million price tag, 'price accurate' and not 'price acceptable.' Any other buyer would say, 'price acceptable.' How many people in Berne would know about Alexandra's dissertation? Think how long it took us to track it down and have it translated."

"It's an inductive leap," Saif concluded, "but I'm confident Roberto de Ruiz sent this."

"Give yourself a pat on the back, professor. You got time for our next step?"

"I really should study for my doctoral defense," the dutiful son and student replied. A few seconds later the friend and off road wannabe overruled himself. "But I wouldn't miss this for anything. What do you need me to do?"

"Our next step is to respond to Mr. Ruiz. Here's our message, kind of good news-bad news for him: 'Buyer: Your price is acceptable. We will consider no other offers. However, the client desires this transaction take place July Fourth.'"

"Griffin, the previous message said July sixth."

"I know. We're accelerating the pace on him."

"You definitely are. July Fourth is only six days away."

"We need de Ruiz rushed, a bit off balance, hopefully. He'll have to scramble making travel and other arrangements on the crowded holiday weekend."

"Aren't you afraid he'll feel too anxious and rushed and won't agree to our terms? Maybe he'll just stay home."

Griffin did not hesitate. "No, he'll come. He's the hooker's son, who's spent his lifetime making the long climb from Chico Ruiz to Roberto de Ruiz. For the 1742 Guarneri del Gesu? For him, this is the ultimate prize. This isn't merely a Van Gogh, like the one he picked up in Amsterdam. And for that matter, he's not just any buyer – de Ruiz is a man who tells the world he's related to Mozart. He wears a ring – one of fewer than three dozen in existence – of the Order of Maximilian the Younger. A 1742 Guarneri del Gesu? For that, he'll be here."

"But we don't have the violin," Saif insisted.

Griffin ignored the point. "End the message with this: 'Buyer will be contacted with precise location and time and instructions for payment. Buyer must establish a private means for us to communicate.'"

Griffin heard a distant knocking at Saif's end.

"I'll send the message," Saif said, over the knocking. "Should I provide a deadline for reply, like we did before? When he's got to get back to us by?"

"No timeline. Let's see how quickly he gets back to us. That'll be a measure of how anxious he is. The quicker the reply, the more anxious he is. The more anxious he is, the better for us."

Griffin heard more knocking, a little louder.

"That's my student at the door, Griffin. Malik's late as usual. We've got to wrap this. What should I do about Alexandra Webb? She answered as well."

"What did she say?"

"Her answer's kind of a stall. 'I need to contact my buyer. Do not complete any transaction until then.'"

"Tell Alexandra: 'We have made other arrangements.'"

"But, Griffin? She's got to be following the website exchange with Roberto de Ruiz same way we are."

"I agree."

"She'll know our other arrangements are with him."

"So? The only reason we bothered with Alexandra Webb was as a kind of insurance policy, in case Roberto de Ruiz never saw our offer on his own.

"You know, I had Bobby pretend to be Dr. Vernon Briggs again, in a call to Future-Ride. Without coming out and saying it, Bobby strongly implied to Alexandra Webb that he was part of a consortium of buyers looking to sell the 1742 Guarneri del Gesu. The point of the call was to help convince Alexandra that the del Gesu was now available. I knew she would then tell Roberto Ruiz, in order to get her commission."

"So Ruiz gets the violin on his own. Which means Alexandra Webb doesn't get her commission. She's out nine million dollars, more."

"That's also right."

"She won't like it."

Griffin picked up Dr. Eckleburg and returned the calico to his thigh.

"No," he agreed with Saif. "I don't think Alexandra Webb will like that at all."

★

Half an hour later, Griffin was on the front porch, sipping orange juice with Kit and Annie. Dr. Eckleburg was there too, sprawled on her back, dog-like, enjoying a shaft of sunlight on her belly.

Griffin recounted for Annie and Kit what he'd learned about Roberto Ruiz. He explained the emails Saif had been sending to lure Ruiz with the promise of the del Gesu violin. When his phone rang, Griffin grabbed the phone before taking the time to see who was calling.

"I'd say he's anxious," were the first words he heard.

"Is this Saif? Who's anxious?"

"Roberto de Ruiz, of course. He's already replied. He's provided a private channel for communication, as you insisted. He did it with passwords and encryption. Very cleverly done, too," Saif commented, in a respectful tone. "It's secure. He can communicate with us and we can with him – and no one else will know what we're telling each other. As soon as he knew the channel was secure, he sent us a message."

"Saif, I'm on the porch with Kit and Annie. Give us a quick sec to go into the dining room and fire up the speaker phone."

Once that was done, Griffin asked, "What exactly did Senor de Ruiz's message say?"

"He wrote, 'Date acceptable. I need time, location, and payment information immediately.' I'd say he's eager. Griffin, do I reply to Mr. de Ruiz? He said we should respond immediately."

"Not yet. Why don't we let him get a bit more anxious."

"How long should I wait?"

Griffin thought a moment. "Five hours. At two o'clock send him a reply on the secure channel he's set up. Two our time is eight o'clock his. The Spanish dine late. It'd be nice if we interrupted his dinner, keep him off balance a bit.

"Now, if I'm selling the del Gesu for the money, as we want Ruiz to believe, my first concern would be arranging payment. So, here's the text: 'Buyer: Payment is to be made at time of sale on July Fourth. Exact time and location of our meeting to follow.'"

Griffin then asked Saif, "Can you be here at three tomorrow afternoon?"

Saif agreed he could, "Though I'll be cutting it close. I've got a late lunch scheduled."

"Who with?" Griffin asked, assuming the answer would be someone at the university or on his doctoral defense panel.

"Janice Singh."

"The gorgeous Janice! She's the one who came to my door looking for you. I wouldn't let you run away from her, as I recall."

"I'm glad you didn't."

"First date?"

"Second actually."

"Better still."

A few moments of pleasurable silence ensued, broken by Saif asking, "Griffin, you need something more from me?"

"Just this. Did de Ruiz say anything else?"

"He did. He again insists on inspecting the del Gesu before forking over $45 million. Sounds reasonable. You are aware we don't"-

"I know, Saif. I know. We don't have a del Gesu to sell him."

★

Still on the speaker phone, Griffin next called Grace. He detailed for her the exchange of emails. As always, she proved a skilled listener, interrupting seldom but inevitably with an insightful question.

At one point she asked, "Mr. Gilmore, as far as de Ruiz knows, you're in this for the $45 million, right? You have no other agenda, like helping your government capture an international arms dealer, correct? You understand that he can't very well put this on the plastic. I don't think a check that size would clear any bank." Griffin granted all that was right. "He won't have that kind of cash to hand you, obviously. How do you expect payment to be made?"

"Off shore bank account, you think? But as far as details are concerned, I'm way in over my head with that, Grace," Griffin admitted. "How are these things typically set up?"

"There is no typical," Grace responded. "I can set up an account in the Cayman Islands for you. We've done that in stings before, most often for money laundering."

"It'll have to be a real account. Routing number, account number, however it works. We can assume he'll check that out as best he can. If he sniffs anything phony, he won't leave Europe. He's very cautious."

"It'll be a real account," Grace assured him, almost boastfully. "It'll pass any sniff test. You should also understand that from here on out we'll be checking the passenger manifests on all international flights arriving at BWI. Newark, LaGuardia, and Dulles as well. Everyone arriving from Europe at an airport in this part of the country will be checked.

"We've got a fairly recent picture of Senor de Ruiz – the one getting in his Bentley outside his Pyrenees villa. The picture will be circulated to every airport in the country. We know that he's used various aliases and false passports. Those names will be on a watch list. "With any luck at all, we'll grab him at the airport." Grace kept on; Griffin could almost see her checking off numbered items on a legal pad. "You will need to set up a meeting with Ruiz, Mr. Gilmore. He must believe he's getting the del Gesu violin. Even if he manages to avoid us at the airport, we'll grab him on the way to the meeting. I don't believe Roberto Ruiz will get within a mile of you. You are doing your country a service, Mr. Gilmore. The violin is the bait with which we bring Roberto de Ruiz to justice."

Grace spoke with her usual supreme confidence, which Griffin did not share. He thanked her and was about to hang up when a thought occurred to him.

"Grace, didn't you say Interpol has an interest in bringing Mr. de Ruiz to justice?"

"A very serious interest."

"Are they willing to put their money where their mouth is?"

"How's that, Mr. Gilmore?"

"Is there an Interpol reward for assisting in the capture of Roberto Ruiz, wanted international arms dealer?"

"There is, and has been for some years. He is a very wanted man."

"Drawing on that reward, just in case this all works out – can you cut four checks in equal amounts for Robert Lowell, Saif Venkatesan, Covington Carson, and Miss Anne Knaack."

"Not five checks? Nothing for you?" Before Griffin could reply Grace answered her own question. "For you, this isn't about money."

"No, it's not."

"It's about payback."

"Not going to deny it."

He was again about to end the call when another thought occurred to him. The question had been gnawing at the edges of his brain for some time.

"Grace, what do you know about Hans Baeder's emigration to this country?"

"Only the information I sent you in the Fed Ex package." From memory she recited, "Hans Baeder arrived in the United States from Germany, September 4, 1954."

"Did he emigrate directly from Germany?"

"We can find that out. That would be part of the paperwork in his visa file. It was assumed that nothing happening to Mr. Baeder between Germany and the United States could be of interest. Is that assumption incorrect? Why do you want to know?"

"Just curious."

Grace wasn't taken in. "I'm not certain I believe you, but I'll get the information."

Griffin thanked her again and ended the call. He looked at Kit and Annie and said, "I'll call Bobby. I need us all here tomorrow at three. Coffee and donuts. We're moving into the endgame."

Thirty Four

When Griffin passed around coffees in the living room, Annie immediately noticed the sixth cup of coffee.

"Who's that for?" she wanted to know.

"He said he'd be late."

"Who he?" Annie asked, but the he remained unidentified.

"Here's where I think we are," Griffin began. "Grace has promised that if this works out, there is a share of the Interpol reward for each of you. For aiding in the apprehension of an international arms dealer. Roberto de Ruiz. Assuming our sting succeeds."

Griffin summarized de Ruiz's career, mostly for Bobby, who knew none of the details.

"Roberto de Ruiz believes he is about to purchase a 1742 Guarneri del Gesu. For him, the violin is the ultimate prize in his long journey to escape his humiliating past."

Saif started to object.

"Yes, professor, I know we don't actually have the violin," Griffin recognized. "But what we do have," he turned to Kit, "is the kind of box a violin would be kept in. The box is sealed and filled with whatever is in there to match the weight of a violin."

Kit explained, with some pride. "The weight is precisely the weight of the 1742 del Gesu."

Griffin pressed on. "Grace is in the process of setting up an offshore bank account. Roberto de Ruiz has agreed to pay $45 million into that account for the del Gesu. He will wire the money into the account at the time of our transaction."

"What about Alexandra Webb?" Annie asked. "She's been after the del Gesu too."

"For many years, she's been pursuing the del Gesu," Griffin agreed. "But she's out of the picture now."

"She's out of a commission as well," Kit reminded everyone. "I can't imagine she's all that happy about losing out on what we figured was her nine million dollar commission."

"We don't all that much care about Alexandra Webb," Griffin replied. "We do care about Roberto de Ruiz. He is a criminal our government and a number of other governments want. We'll help them capture de Ruiz and each of you will enjoy your reward when we do.

"Over the last couple days Saif has sent a series of emails to de Ruiz. We've told Senor de Ruiz the price – $45 million – and date – July Fourth – of the sale of the del Gesu. We have not, however, specified the exact time or location where the transaction will take place. We'll take care of that today."

There was a knock at the door and Griffin stopped speaking.

★

Griffin heard the knock quite clearly; he realized he must have been anticipating it. Grabbing the sixth cup of coffee from a window sill, he walked to the front door. He opened the door and said to the man on the porch, "Coffee, cream and sugar okay?"

"That'd be just fine," Sergeant Ahearn said, accepting the cup. Before taking a sip he approached Annie.

"A pleasure to see you again, Ms. Knaack."

Griffin was delighted the man remembered the proper pronunciation of her last name, with two syllables.

"Mr. Covington, Mr. Lowell," Sergeant Ahearn said, shaking hands with Kit and Bobby.

"And, Sergeant, this is Saif Venkatesan, another former high school classmate."

Sergeant Ahearn stood in the middle of the living room, looking around.

"This is the house you got in exchange for our activities last December?" Griffin and Annie agreed it was. "You certainly deserve it."

He peeled back a chunk of the plastic lid and sipped.

"I have information from Grace," the Sergeant began. "Then I know you wanted me here to ask me something.

"Mr. Gilmore, an offshore bank account is being set up in the Cayman Islands," he explained. "Once that's done, Grace will call later today or tomorrow. She'll give you the phone number and contact person at the bank. Someone will be standing by from midnight July Fourth on, in the event you and de Ruiz have your meeting. De Ruiz can call that number in the Caymans and ask for a Mr. Robert Jordan. With Mr. Jordan's assistance and the password Grace will give you, de Ruiz can actually transfer the forty five million into your account. For deposits that large a password is necessary.

"Sorry, Mr. Gilmore – and Grace asked me to stress this – you won't be able to keep any of it. That money belongs to the American taxpayer."

"Grace made a joke?"

"Never intentionally," Sergeant Ahearn replied.

"Long before any of that happens, however, I'm confident the feds will grab de Ruiz. Likely at an airport. As it has been explained to me, an enormous amount of federal resources are being devoted to this. Personnel are stationed at every airport east of the Mississippi handling international flights. The list of passengers for every flight coming into this country from abroad is being checked. You're dealing with a very wanted man, Mr. Gilmore. Extraordinary precautions are being taken. Now what do you want to ask me?"

★

Griffin knew what he had to say, but couldn't say it, not immediately. He knew that once he spoke to Sergeant Ahearn there was no turning back. No one else in the room – not even the sergeant, with all his years on the streets – quite grasped the danger Griffin was about to place himself in.

They had not met Roberto de Ruiz. Griffin had, and understood how lethal the man could be. Griffin had no doubt that de Ruiz, despite his cultured polish, would have shot him in the museum if he needed to. If Griffin's death had been the price for obtaining the key which de Ruiz thought would be bring him the 1742 del Gesu – then Griffin would be dead. Griffin knew that at the time. Standing in his living room, that realization crashed back to him with full force. He feared for a moment he might vomit up the coffee.

He kept the coffee down and spoke to Sergeant Ahearn:

"Sergeant, we need to propose a place where I meet Roberto de Ruiz. A meeting needs to be set up by email, as though I am arranging to sell him the del Gesu. Otherwise, he'll never leave Europe. He'll know he's being set up. This guy is very thorough and very smart."

"I agree with all that. A meeting needs to be scheduled with Ruiz to persuade him you really are going to sell him the violin. It's part of convincing him of your bona fides. If he's not convinced, as you say, he never leaves Europe. Every meeting needs a time and place. What time would you prefer to meet? Have you considered that?"

"I was thinking 5:30 in the morning of July Fourth."

"Why so early and why the Fourth of July?"

"The Fourth of July is a holiday. Most folks will be sleeping late. We don't need anyone else around if at all possible.

"I want to go with 5:30 because I'll be carrying a good sized box. I don't want some concerned citizen spotting me with the box thinking I just burglarized some nearby house. We don't need that complication. There will Fourth of July parades all day and cookouts and people about and fireworks at night. Best to get this done before any of that. That's why the early meeting."

"Next question of course is place. Where do you think the meet should happen?"

"I was hoping you could help with that."

Sergeant Ahearn thought a good while, weighing, then rejecting, possible locations for the meeting. "All right," he said finally. "This place worked once before for a sting. Should work again.

"You know Rodgers Forge? Row house neighborhood by York Road and Stevenson Lane, south of Towson?" Griffin did. "On Dumbarton Road in Rodgers Forge are an elementary and middle school. The schools are side by side. They share a playing area for Little League, soccer, softball, lacrosse. You know those fields?'

"Sure. Annie played softball there."

"Why don't you arrange to meet Ruiz there on the Rodgers Forge fields? We can have cops in a couple of the row houses lining the fields on Dumbarton. You'll be under surveillance the entire time. With the Baltimore County PD all over the place for your meet in the Rodgers Forge fields, he'll be walking right into a trap. We'll be there for you."

"Will you be there, Sergeant?" Annie asked.

"Unfortunately not, Ms. Knaack. The county PD has budgetary concerns about overtime and I have maxed out mine. I won't be working for the rest of the week. Truth be told, I can use the time off. But, chances are – and I cannot stress this enough – he never gets anywhere near you.

"Mr. Gilmore?" The sergeant's voice was suddenly softer, barely audible. "You don't have to show up for the meeting. That's something else Grace insisted I tell you. I'm saying it to you too. If you have any doubts, any fears at all? Just bail. You don't have to be there. You hear me, Griffin?"

"I hear you, Sergeant, but I am going to do this." He was stating a simple fact, a fact as unquestionable to him as the atomic weight of some element in the periodic table. "I have to be there, and be there holding a box which Ruiz will think has the violin he wants inside. Ruiz is too smart and too cautious. He won't walk into a trap without the violin box – which means me, carrying the box – in the middle of it."

The sergeant's soft, kindly voice vanished. "Dammit!" he shouted at Griffin. "You don't have to do this. You hear me, Griffin?"

"As always, Sergeant. Thank you."

"Does he ever listen to you, Ms. Knaack?" the sergeant asked Annie. The question was accompanied by a throwing up of his meaty hands.

"Not always, no,"

"Relax, Sergeant," Griffin told him. "This might just work."

"Tell you what," Sergeant Ahearn said. "I'll be there. The department's overtime budget shouldn't stop me. I'll bring Officer Fernandez. We'll be there. Can't let you have all the fun."

★

Griffin watched Sergeant Ahearn walk through the sharp afternoon sunlight and get into in the car parked in front of the house. It was an unmarked police vehicle. Griffin appreciated that the cop had driven an unmarked car rather than a police cruiser, which would have left neighbors gossiping.

Only after the man had driven out of sight did Griffin turn around. Saif was already at the dining room table, laptop open.

"Ready to send the email whenever you are," Saif said. "I crafted language which gives the location and time for the meeting you and the Sergeant agreed on. Should I send to Roberto de Ruiz?"

"Send it."

Griffin looked at each of them again, starting and ending with Annie. Then he said, "I'm going to need your help."

Thirty Five

July 2
8:30 am

"Still no sign of Roberto de Ruiz," were Grace's first words when she called Griffin. "Under any of his many aliases. I'll send you the list, just so you'll have it. We'll keep checking passenger manifests. We've got someone stationed at 55 airports. He doesn't know what he's up against."

"Yeah, he does," Griffin said, after hanging up.

★

July 2
12:30 pm

"No word from Roberto de Ruiz," Saif explained in his call to Griffin. "He has not replied to the email I sent setting out the exact time and location of the meeting. His silence could mean that he's not going to go through with it. It could mean he's traveling right now. Could mean a lot of things."

"It could mean he's trying to make me anxious. And I have to say it's working. Saif, will you be able to keep an eye out for de Ruiz's reply? I know you're especially busy these days. What with your teaching, your doctoral defense July 5th. And of course now there is the gorgeous Janice to keep you occupied."

"I'll check online every hour."

★

July 2
2:00 pm

"We've got an ID on Dude, Mr. Gilmore," Sergeant Ahearn explained when he called that afternoon. "The guy Timothy Dean got high with at the biker bar in Essex? His name is Cleveland Dumont. He is a Sparrow's Point native. Your age. You've heard of someone with a record as long as your arm? This guy's record's as long as both arms and maybe a leg or two. He's a veritable role model for recidivists.

"Mostly he's done crimes against property, several burglaries we know about. To that we can probably add the break in at Hans Baeder's house, though we'll never get him for that. He's been arrested for a few bar fights. He's a car thief. It's my sense he'd do just about anything for money.

"Cleveland Dumont's father and grandfather put in their thirty years working on the line at Bethlehem Steel. Honest, hardworking men all their lives. Cleveland has never worked an honest day in his life."

"How'd you get his name?"

"I leaned on the Belair Road therapist. Remember Timothy Dean said that's where he met Dude? At court-ordered counseling for his drug addiction. I don't know that we could use the ID of Cleveland Dumont in court. A defense attorney could keep it out of evidence as coerced. But I knew you'd want to know. And another thing, Mr. Gilmore. Remember the business card we found in the glove compartment car Timothy Dean was driving?"

"What about the card?"

"You may recall that our handwriting expert" – Sergeant Ahearn delivered the last two words with sufficient sarcasm Griffin could just about see quotation marks floating around them – "our expert said she just couldn't be sure whether the 5722 Gist Avenue written on the back of the card had been written by a man or a woman."

"My memory is that you weren't happy with her for that."

"I'm not quite so angry now. I thought she was just being a bureaucratic weenie, afraid to make a decision. I chatted with her today. There are characteristics of both a man and a woman's handwriting. It's such a small sample, and a confusing sample. I can't fault her reluctance to decide."

★

July 2
4:45 pm

On the phone Grace told him: "Mr. Gilmore, all the details on the Cayman Islands offshore bank account have now been finalized. If need be, de Ruiz can call, give this password to the contact at the bank, Robert Jordan, and money can be wired into the account that has been set up. The password is PERSEPHONE."

"Queen of the underworld," Griffin knew from his reading on mythology. "And all the riches to be found there."

"Mr. Gilmore, you do understand that you cannot-"

"Keep the money. Yes, I get that."

After the call Griffin realized he was smiling, slightly. Not at Grace's attempt at humor – she had all the joke-telling skills of an undertaker. She must have heard the tension in his voice and tried to relax him. He appreciated that. Not that it worked.

★

What did Griffin do all day, between calls?

He went into the basement armed with a wire brush and putty knife Annie had picked up for him on a trip to the mall. The basement walls were stunning in their clashing ugliness. Two walls were painted the faded green of bronze statutes exposed for years to rain and snow. Two walls were painted a shade of red Griffin knew was Kermes, which first appeared in Persian carpets 2500 years ago. That anyone could paint that terminally clashing combination on the walls of the same room baffled Griffin.

He began scraping the paint. There were several coats of paint to scrape away, which required Griffin to work long stretches in the same spot. A shower of the dull green and deep red paint chips began covering the basement floor. The slow progress was fine with him. It gave him time to think.

★

July 2
9:35 pm

"Sorry to call so late," Sergeant Ahearn apologized. "Hope I didn't wake you. Only now did I learn that our tech guys had finished their work."

"You didn't wake me, Sergeant," Griffin replied, doubting sleep would be an issue at all. "What work did your tech people finish?"

"I'll be by tomorrow to give you a tracking beeper. It's only slightly larger than the size of a pinhead. It is to be taped in your armpit. The technology is amazing. The beeper is warmed by your blood. There is no need for a power source. The beeper will allow us to track your whereabouts at all times in the meeting with Roberto de Ruiz – a meeting I remain convinced will never occur."

★

July 3
9:15 am

"Still no word from Roberto de Ruiz, Griffin," Saif said, calling the next morning. As Griffin listened, he picked a thumb-sized red paint chip from his hair. "Maybe the man is bailing. Maybe he senses he's being set up."

"He probably does know he's being set up," Griffin answered. "But for the del Gesu? He'll come anyway."

Something inside Griffin's left ear itched. With his index finger he scooped out a green paint chip.

"How is it possible to get a paint chip in your ear?" he wondered aloud.

"I have no idea."

"And you call yourself a professor."

★

July 3
11:05 am

It was Annie who called next.

"I'm at the mall, Griffin," she told him. "Is there anything here you need?"

"Is Miss P there?"

"She is, why?"

"Is the mall open on July Fourth?"

"It is, why?"

"Can you ask Miss Paulette if she'd mind if we met her there at the mall? You, me, Kit, Bobby, Saif? Say eight in the morning July Fourth?"

Annie said she would and asked why Griffin wanted to speak to Miss P.

"Annie, I've been thinking about those notes on Hans Baeder's wall. The notes that stutter and the notes that are a bit off, remember? I want to ask her about those. Would she be around, you think?"

"I can ask her. Anything else?"

"Hurry home as fast as you can."

★

July 3
12:12 pm

Grace called.

"Mr. Gilmore, I had hoped to tell you we know Roberto de Ruiz is on his way to us, but I can't. Not yet I can't. I called because I have some information you asked for earlier."

Griffin looked at his hands. The palms of both hands were blistering from the scraping. "Which is?"

"You asked about the travel of Hans Baeder when he left Germany for the United States, summer 1954."

"Yes, I want to know if Hans stopped anywhere between Germany and the US. He sailed here, I assume. I cannot imagine Hans had the money for a plane ticket, which must have cost a good bit in those days."

"As you figured, he sailed, on a cargo ship. He worked as part of the ship's crew in exchange for passage. That was sometimes done in those days, for those who lacked the money for the ticket."

"Sailed from where?" Griffin scratched his eyebrows. A snowfall of tiny green and red paint chips descended. "What was Hans' point of departure for the US? Germany?"

"No, France. Mr. Baeder left from Le Havre. In the Fifties, Le Havre was the point of departure for most folks sailing from France for the United States."

"Can you tell, Grace? Can you tell if Hans went through Paris on his way to Le Havre?"

"That cannot be determined. The record doesn't reveal travel within European countries. However..."

"However what?"

"However he almost certainly had to go through Paris. He'd have no choice. All the train lines to almost every city of any size in France in those days ran through Paris. Hans almost certainly could not have afforded a car to drive straight through to Le Havre from Germany. I doubt he even had the money for gas, let alone rent or own a car."

"He never got a driver's license in this country. He didn't drive. He had to go to Le Havre by train," Griffin answered. "I'm confident he must have gone through Paris on his way to America."

"Why is that important? Whether he went to Paris?"

"I'll let you know."

298

★

July 3
1:48 pm

"Let's see if it works, Mr. Gilmore," Sergeant Ahearn said. "Tape the tracking beeper into your armpit the way I showed you. We put it in the armpit so the beeper won't be noticed in an ordinary frisk. Once the beeper is in place, walk around the house."

As he promised the day before, Sergeant Ahearn arrived at Griffin's house with the beeper. The Sergeant was now calling on a phone from his unmarked car parked out front.

Griffin did as ordered. He taped the very small beeper under his left armpit and walked from the upstairs bathroom, down the steps, through the dining room and kitchen, out the back door, onto the back porch, and into the yard.

"Had you the whole way," Sergeant Ahearn said. "It's almost a shame to waste this technology, since this meeting's not much likely to happen."

★

July 3
2:17 pm

"I know I sound like a broken record, Griffin, but no word from Roberto de Ruiz."

"Keep checking, Saif. I'm not in the habit of disagreeing with Sergeant Ahearn –who is convinced the meeting will never happen – but I believe de Ruiz is on his way for the del Gesu."

"Hey, Griffin?"

Griffin was looking at his bare feet. He'd been working in the basement without shoes or socks. The feet were filthy and decorated with paint chips and dust.

"What is it, Saif?"

"I've been wondering. Is it possible Roberto de Ruiz knows it's you offering the violin?"

"I've been wondering that as well. I suspect he does know it's me."

"Is that a problem?"

"Shouldn't be. If he knows who I am – and he addressed me as Mr. Gilmore in the museum – then he knows I was arrested as a thief and very nearly did time. That a thief would somehow get a hold of a violin and be willing to sell it for the biggest score of a lifetime? That fits my profile."

"Does he know about your link to Grace? If he knows about her, he may know you're linked to the federal government. That might scare him off."

"No," Griffin answered firmly. "I don't think he knows about Grace. All the Duke and I talked about were the logistics of recovering the key and his family's honor. That and endless lectures on grapes and wine. Whichever blonde the Duke was with then? Who was getting paid off by Roberto de Ruiz for information on my plans? She wouldn't know anything about Grace. I never told the Duke about Grace.

"And, Saif? I'm convinced that even knowing about Grace wouldn't discourage Ruiz. He's after the del Gesu. It matters too much to him. He's coming here, no matter what."

★

July 3
2:31 pm

Grace was nearly shouting in her excitement.

"Guess who bought a ticket for a flight arriving BWI tonight?" She sounds like a child unwrapping a present Christmas morning, Griffin thought. "A gentleman by the name of Salvador Caballero. Recognize the name?"

"Isn't that one of the names on the list you sent me of aliases used by Roberto de Ruiz?"

"It is indeed. Senor Caballero bought a ticket at the very last minute. And the ticket was not purchased under his own name but through a travel agent. He was attempting to avoid detection. He likely would have succeeded except the Spanish government is working with us on this. They would love to take out the man supplying explosives to the Basque separatists. The Spanish contacted us."

"What time does the flight arrive at the Baltimore airport?" Griffin asked. He was studying his blisters, which had started to bleed.

"Due at BWI at 7:11 this evening."

"You'll have some people there?" Griffin wondered.

"Some people and me." Griffin studied his bloody blisters in silence. "Mr. Gilmore?"

"Let me know how it goes, Grace. I've got to get back to my scraping."

★

As he scraped, Griffin thought about the notes on Hans Baeder's wall. Why did he change the composition of his beloved Mozart? Why add notes Miss Paulette described as a little off and stuttering? While he was dying? Griffin scraped and considered the questions.

★

July 3
3:47 pm

"Griffin?"

By Saif's tone Griffin knew why he had called.

"He responded, didn't he? Roberto Ruiz replied."

"Yes. He has emailed that he'll be at the time and place of the meeting you propose. He has the money. He expects you to have the 1742 Guarneri del Gesu. That' a problem, isn't it?"

"I'm trying to finesse that."

"There's one other thing." Griffin asked what that was. "De Ruiz is somewhere in the United States. Unlike email sent from Europe, with email sent in this country it is not possible to tell where the message originated. I know he's here in the US. More precise than that, I can't say. You want me to forward the email to Grace? The feds have the technology to trace the point of origin."

"Don't bother. Ruiz is very good at moving quickly. He'd be long gone by the time anyone showed there."

"All we know is that de Ruiz could be anywhere from Maine to California."

"Or Baltimore. He could be in Baltimore right now getting ready for our meeting."

★

July 3
7:27 pm

"He never showed, Mr. Gilmore," Sergeant Ahearn explained. "Grace asked me to be here for the arrival of the flight here at

BWI. I volunteered to make this call, since I wanted to give you the bad news myself. Roberto Ruiz never showed. The seat on the plane was empty. The ticket went unused. I'm sorry."

"Don't apologize, Sergeant. I knew de Ruiz wasn't on that flight. He's already in this country. Maybe already in Baltimore. It's my belief he is."

Somehow, by the silence, Griffin could tell that Sergeant Ahearn, a man not easily surprised, was startled by that news.

"I guess it would be futile, Mr. Gilmore, to remind you that you do not have to do this. We can set the trap without you."

"You're right, Sergeant. It would be futile. I'll be there tomorrow morning at 5:30."

"You know I'll be there as well."

"Actually, Sergeant? I'd like to see you before then. Here at my house? It's kind of important."

Thirty Six

July 4
3:20 am

Eventually Griffin and Annie gave up even pretending to try to sleep. They did not talk much; there wasn't much that needed saying. The day was planned. Griffin knew planning would only go so far. Annie, he suspected, knew that as well.

At quarter after four Annie told him, "Might as well get it over with" and they both got out of bed.

Griffin and Kit drove in Griffin's Malibu to the Rodgers Forge fields. Griffin carried the box stuffed with whatever Kit had put inside – it certainly was not the 1742 del Gesu violin. Griffin waited there for a sign from Roberto de Ruiz. The sign was a phone ringing by the softball field.

On the phone, Griffin listened to Ruiz's instructions about getting to Stevenson Lane with the box in less than sixty seconds. If not, "I keep driving. If the del Gesu is damaged in any way, there is no sale."

Griffin said, yes, he understood the terms. Roberto de Ruiz then informed him, "Put down the phone. Hold onto the box. Start running, Mr. Gilmore, You have sixty seconds."

Griffin did as instructed, though he did not put the phone down, he tossed it. It landed somewhere in the dirt of the infield. He headed back up the hill he had descended.

Gritting his teeth against the pain in his legs from all that scraping in the basement, he reached Stevenson Lane. A pair of headlights went on and a voice called out for him to get into the car. From his suit coat pocket Ruiz pulled out a small box with four switches. With a push of each switch there was an explosion. Parked cars loudly blew up on both sides of the fields.

"A bit of a distraction," Robert Ruiz said. "Now you must be frisked."

The two men got out of the car. As he frisked Griffin, Roberto Ruiz said, "You moved more slowly than I anticipated, Mr. Gilmore. While crossing the fields."

"My legs are sore from scraping red paint and green paint from the walls in the basement of our house the last two days," Griffin answered, at unnecessary length. "My hands took a beating too."

He showed Roberto Ruiz his hands, palms up. Ruiz stopping frisking to look at Griffin's hands. Even in the uncertain morning light it was obvious Griffin was not exaggerating the toll the scraping had taken on his hands. Blisters and welts were visible, parts of several fingers were worn raw in places, and there were band aids on each hand.

The frisking resumed. The beeper Sergeant Ahearn had taped inside Griffin's armpit was smaller than a dime but this frisking was so thorough Griffin knew it was inevitable the beeper would be discovered.

When he found the beeper Roberto Ruiz said, "A beeper in the armpit is standard procedure, Mr. Gilmore. I am afraid your law enforcement associates will hereafter be unable to track your whereabouts."

That, Griffin knew, was right. The feds, Sergeant Ahearn and Officer Fernandez, whatever personnel Grace had detailed – none of them would know where Griffin was going. He did not either.

They pulled away from the curb.

"Two more stops," Roberto Ruiz said. "Then we shall transact our business."

Thirty Seven

July 4
5:40 am

They drove west on Stevenson Lane down the big hill toward Bellona Avenue. Strange, the thoughts that occur under stress, Griffin decided. As they reached the bottom of the hill he remembered that the novelist Scott Fitzgerald had once lived very near this spot.

No, Griffin ordered himself. You cannot allow your thoughts to bounce around right now. Focus.

They arrived at Bellona as the light went red. Griffin heard another car explode behind him. De Ruiz did not wait at the light, but turned right immediately. He then took a quick left on Haddon Avenue, a shortcut only a block long and one that would be unknown to anyone who had not spent some time in preparation. Griffin guessed de Ruiz had been in Baltimore a couple days getting ready.

When they reached Charles Street, de Ruiz turned right, then right again soon after. They entered the parking lot of a grocery store still closed for the night. They left the parking lot and crossed into a small area behind a nondescript brick office building. They were now hidden from passing Charles Street traffic.

In all Griffin's years of traveling on Charles Street, he had never noticed the building since it was set so far back from the street and was tucked behind a convenience store. In the rear of the office building were trees, a small lot for employees, and dumpsters. De Ruiz pulled into a space between the dumpsters. Griffin heard a pair of police sirens roll past on Charles Street.

De Ruiz parked beside a new black SUV. The car the two men had been in was an old grey Tercel half the size of the SUV.

"The authorities may have spotted the grey car we are now vacating. We shall be more comfortable in this vehicle. Make haste, please." De Ruiz gestured for Griffin to step into the SUV. Pointing to the box, de Ruiz said, "And do be gentle with the del Gesu."

★

De Ruiz drove the black SUV out of the parking lot and back onto Charles Street, as if he had all the time in the world. Griffin knew de Ruiz did. No more than seven minutes had elapsed since Griffin had staggered to Stevenson Lane, with his legs hurting.

The police had no reason to stop this SUV, whose existence they could not even suspect. De Ruiz drove north on Charles Street. Somewhere to their right Griffin heard the siren of a fire truck. By now 911 calls must be pouring in from terrified Rodgers Forge residents. The cops there would have their hands full dealing with people streaming out of their homes screaming. There were fires to contend with and possibly more cars exploding. No one in law enforcement would be helping Griffin, even if they knew where he was. Which they didn't.

De Ruiz put on a CD. Griffin recognized the music from Miriam Freitag's apartment.

"Mozart," he said. "*Eine-*"

"*Eine Kleine Nacht Musik.* I knew you to be an American of some culture. A man like myself, Mr. Gilmore. Unlike that thoroughly disagreeable Cleve, whose services I required.

"I regret I was forced to engage Cleve these past days to obtain the needed vehicles and other chores. He was recommended me by an American woman working for me. Fortunately, after tonight I will never be required to deal with him again. Truly an unpleasant man. His aftershave is no substitute for regular showers. I have advised him so repeatedly. He would also be well-advised to reduce his intake of whiskey."

"Cleve would be Cleveland Dumont? He drove you from the Baltimore Museum of Art. Isn't that correct? Mr. de Ruiz."

Roberto de Ruiz gave Griffin a long, appreciated glance.

"You are truly a bright and no doubt persistent man, Mr. Gilmore." De Ruiz reached over and touched the box resting between Griffin's knees. "And if the 1742 Guarneri del Gesu is inside that box, then you are about to become a wealthy man as well.

"And if it is not inside the box?" de Ruiz slid upward the right cuff of his white slacks to reveal an ankle holster.

"A Makarov?"

Another appreciative glance.

"A weapon with which I have demonstrated some expertise in the museum, you must acknowledge."

As they drove north on Charles Street, Ruiz continued addressing Griffin: "Your reference to our time together in the Baltimore museum reminds me, Mr. Gilmore. I have been remiss."

He reached inside the pocket of his white suit coat and pulled out an object which he handed to Griffin, who recognized it immediately.

"The Duke's key."

"It is of no value to me," de Ruiz said. "You might return it to its rightful owner."

Griffin promised he would, wondering if he'd survive this morning to get the chance.

After half a mile de Ruiz turned off Charles Street, putting them back on Bellona Avenue. As they were completing the turn, in the side mirror Griffin spotted another police car hurrying down Charles toward Rodgers Forge. The siren faded into the distance.

"You've been here a few days?" Griffin asked.

The morning had lightened enough Griffin could see de Ruiz's face. There was an unmistakable look of expectation on that face. When he learned the box did not contain the del Gesu, de Ruiz would not be at all pleased.

"Can I ask, Mr. de Ruiz? How'd you get to Baltimore from your villa in the Pyrenees?"

"You know of my villa, Mr. Gilmore? Should you seek employment in the future? My organization can always use someone of your obvious talents."

"Thanks. How did you get here?"

"Prior to my arrival here," he replied, "I flew from Barcelona to Munich, then to Rome. From there I flew to Mexico City. From Mexico City I traveled Mexicana Airlines to Albuquerque. Another flight to Pittsburgh. Where I was met by Cleveland Dumont, who drove me here.

"I wore lifts in my shoes, which rendered me almost six foot eight. It is possible to be so obvious no one notices, I have learned. Arriving in America I wore a false beard, like the beard of your beloved president, Abraham Lincoln. Who would question … Honest Abe, he was called? Getting here presented no insurmountable difficulties."

And, just like that, Griffin thought, in a handful of sentences Roberto de Ruiz described how he eluded the best efforts of Grace and the federal government.

"Now, Mr. Gilmore. I must ask you." They were almost down the long, winding hill of Bellona Avenue, the light rail tracks to their left. Ruiz was keeping strictly to the speed limit, neither too fast nor too slow. Griffin know no cop was about to stop the SUV. "I must ask. How did you ever obtain the del Gesu?"

★

Instead of answering, Griffin said, "You went into the dungeon in Arazzo Castle, Mr. de Ruiz. You needed the Duke's key to open the door to the room in the back of the dungeon. The room proved to be empty."

They were stopped at the intersection of Bellona and Ruxton Road, where Ruxton Road humpbacks over the light rail tracks. While waiting for the light to turn green, Ruiz gave Griffin his longest look yet. The Mozart played on softly.

"You continue to impress me, Mr. Gilmore."

"Mr. de Ruiz, going to Arazzo Castle made sense. The Special Task Force For Music had stayed there."

"True. The surviving record of their travels during the war is severely and tragically limited. Nonetheless, that much is known. I thought a del Gesu might have been kept in the unopened room all that time. Alas not."

Griffin said, "Arazzo Castle made particular sense because the Special Task Force went there within days after they were attacked in an American air raid at Ulm, Germany. It was in this air raid Hans Baeder was wounded. He was wounded trying to save the del Gesu. The del Gesu stolen by the Nazis from the family of the philosopher Wittgenstein. In exchange

311

for the violin, the Nazis spared the Wittgenstein family from the death camps."

Ruiz turned off Bellona into the parking lot of Grau's Market. The lot was empty except for a Hummer sitting in the far corner.

"I recall Hans Baeder's name. He is mentioned in the dissertation by Alexandra Webb. You know of her?"

"We met, in New York."

"Alexandra Webb was the one who hired Cleve Dumont to assist us. In her dissertation Alexandra states that Herr Baeder was an acknowledged expert on the value of violins. Surely he recognized the greatness of the 1742 Guarneri del Gesu. You say he was wounded while protecting the instrument?"

"Yes, he was."

"He sounds a brave and impressive man."

"He must have been," Griffin agreed. "Mr. de Ruiz? From your response can I conclude you did not order the break in of Hans Baeder's house?"

Robert de Ruiz parked the SUV next to the Hummer, which was a bright orange color.

"I could not have done so. I have no idea where this Hans Baeder lives."

Griffin had no doubt de Ruiz was telling the truth. If de Ruiz did not order the burglary of Hans' house, then it must have been Alexandra Webb.

That would at least explain the Future-Ride business card with Hans' address on the back in handwriting having both male and female characteristics. Alexandra knew Cleve Dumont was working for Robert de Ruiz; she was responsible for hiring Cleve in the first place. She must have imitated de Ruiz's handwriting as best she could. With the card as evidence of de Ruiz's intentions, she ordered Dumont – who Timothy Dean referred to as Dude - to break into Hans' house. But the del Gesu was not to be found there.

If events had played out as Griffin was now assuming, it meant Alexandra Webb could be playing a double game – working for commission on Robert de Ruiz's behalf while pursuing the del Gesu for herself.

"Mr. Gilmore?" de Ruiz was asking, eager for Griffin to resume his explanation. The Mozart kept playing.

Griffin continued: "The Special Task Force was in Arazzo Castle on August 20, 1944. That much is, as you know, confirmed by the record. It is my belief Hans Baeder, either as part of the Special Task Force or on his own, then went to Paris. He must have gone immediately after Arazzo, since Paris was liberated by the Allies on August 25, 1944."

Griffin went on, "Hans went to Paris because he had a French classmate at the Dresden conservatory he had attended before the war. The classmate lived in Paris. In Paris the classmate had a shop which sold musical instruments."

"By any chance, Mr. Gilmore, was this the music shop which may have had the del Gesu after the war?"

"The very same shop, I am convinced. During the war Hans helped out his old classmate, who was Jewish and living in Paris, with the Nazi authorities."

"How do you know this, Mr. Gilmore?"

Thinking appreciatively of Miriam, Griffin said, "I have spoken to someone who knew Hans very well. I trust we can respect this woman's privacy, since she herself never knew more than the most general details of the del Gesu. She certainly had no idea of its location."

"Of course."

"It is my belief that in his gratitude, Hans' classmate agreed to keep the del Gesu Hans left with him in August

1944. The man ran the Paris shop with his brother. By 1950 both were dead. The man's widow carried on the shop, though her knowledge of musical instruments was minimal. This is why her account of having the del Gesu is discounted. The assumption is that no one running a music shop could possibly be ignorant of the del Gesu's extraordinary worth. I believe it was not only possible, it happened."

"How did the del Gesu get from the Paris music shop to that box you have now?" Ruiz asked next.

"Hans Baeder immigrated to America in the summer of 1954. He may have wanted to get back to the Paris music shop before that, but in the wretched poverty of post-war Germany never got the chance. We will never know.

"But in that summer of 1954 he went into Paris before coming to America. It is my belief he picked up the del Gesu at that time. The widow running the Paris music shop by then certainly would have remembered Hans' aid during the war. She would not question his taking the del Gesu. If Hans Baeder asked her to remain silent about his getting the del Gesu, in her gratitude for his helping her husband, she would do so."

"How then did you come by the del Gesu you are holding?"

"I found the violin where Hans, who died one year ago today, hid it."

"An amazing story, Mr. Gilmore."

And all of it true, Griffin was thinking, as best I know – except for the last detail that I have the del Gesu with me. De Ruiz could have been reading his thoughts.

"Mr. Gilmore, I trust you understand my desire to inspect the del Gesu before arranging payment to your bank account. I will need more room to open the box. Let us step into the parking lot. After our transaction I will depart in this vehicle," he pointed to the orange Hummer, "so huge and brightly painted no one will notice."

De Ruiz grabbed his Panama hat from the back seat. They climbed down from the SUV, Griffin clutching the box. Once they were standing in the parking lot he leaned the box against his legs and looked at his hands.

"The box, Mr. Gilmore?"

Griffin looked at his hands some more.

De Ruiz repeated his request, his gentlemanly tone ebbing. "The box, if you would. Now."

Griffin saw no way around handing de Ruiz the box. Thinking of the Makarov in its ankle holster, Griffin picked up the box and handed it to de Ruiz. De Ruiz held the box lightly, by the sides, judging its weight. He smiled and Griffin knew Kit had done his job well, stuffing the box with whatever to match the weight of the del Gesu.

De Ruiz was beginning to open the box and in fact had torn open a few inches of the thick cardboard, when a car engine started up on the side street just outside the parking lot. By de Ruiz's reaction Griffin knew this was not part of the Spaniard's elaborate preparations.

A car starting up on a Ruxton street a little after six on the morning of July Fourth could of course be a coincidence unrelated to the del Gesu. Griffin strongly doubted it. De Ruiz looked at him. Griffin shrugged.

"I have no idea," he said. He didn't either. The car did not sound anything like his Malibu, which Kit was driving, or the Mini Cooper Annie, Saif and Bobby were in. This car could be a Ruxton homeowner off to work or to an early coffee. Griffin did not think so and could tell de Ruiz did not either. De Ruiz reached down to the ankle holster.

The car was a small and sleek convertible, with a driver and passenger. Griffin and de Ruiz watched in silence as the car moved down the side street. The car turned left onto Bellona and then quickly left again into the Grau's Market parking lot. Without looking at him, Griffin could sense de Ruiz's growing alarm. De Ruiz slipped the Makarov into his right hand.

The car went directly at the two men, headlights on high beam, leaving Griffin and Roberto de Ruiz shielding their eyes from the overwhelming lights. Twenty feet away, the car stopped. Still blinking in the headlights, the men heard a woman say, in the sweetest Georgia drawl, "Why Roberto. And Mr. Wales, didn't you say your name was? Though I doubt it now. What a pleasant surprise."

Thirty Eight

July 4
6:19 am

Roberto de Ruiz was as shocked by Alexandra Webb's arrival as Griffin, but he recovered nicely.

"Alexandra, the pleasure is all mine." De Ruiz gave her a courtly nod. "Thank you for your concern, but I am quite capable of handling this transaction alone."

"I don't think so, Roberto." She stepped out of the car. Someone remained in the passenger seat. "I have worked too long to let you keep this all to yourself."

Roberto de Ruiz maintained his composure, though Griffin could tell the man was scrambling.

"Fine," he agreed. "As always, you are most persuasive. You have convinced me. Shall we say the standard arrangement? Twenty percent?"

"The standard arrangement won't do it."

"Fine. Can we augment your compensation to, let us say, ten million?"

"Roberto, my friend, you're just not getting it. I won't settle for ten million. I've already had two offers exceeding sixty million for the del Gesu. I'll let the two compete against each other. The high bid will be multiples of what you're offering me.

"A man in your line of work will hardly be in any position to go into court to recover the violin, Roberto. Whoever Mr. Wales really is, makes no difference. My ticket out of the country is already purchased. Once the bidding on the del Gesu is done, I am beyond everyone's reach."

Roberto de Ruiz bounced back smoothly. "Fine. Fine. You will allow me to counter offer?"

As he spoke de Ruiz was drifting almost imperceptively to his right. Limping, he moved slowly. Griffin saw what de Ruiz was attempting – he was moving out of the blinding stab of the car's headlights. Griffin noticed de Ruiz was keeping the hand with the Makarov behind his back.

"Fine," he repeated. "Shall we say-"

By this point de Ruiz was outside the headlights' glare. The morning was light enough Griffin, Roberto de Ruiz and Alexandra Webb could all see each other clearly. Two of them now noticed de Ruiz was holding the Makarov, pointed in Alexandra's direction.

"Alexandra," he said in a cold, clear voice, "you will have your associate in the car hand me the car keys and you both will walk away. Otherwise, I shall place a bullet between your lovely eyes."

"No, you will not, Robert de Ruiz." She said the "de" with disdain. "Your pistol is no threat without a working firing pin, a detail Cleve here took care of earlier today. While the two of you were busy preparing for this morning's events, at my orders he has disabled your weapon."

Ruiz pointed the Makarov at one of the car's headlights. He pulled the trigger, but only a dry click resulted.

"Cleve doesn't much care for you, Roberto. He was more than happy when I paid him to tell me your arrangements, including the location of the Hummer. He has been in my solo employ for some time."

From the front seat a voice with a strong Baltimore accent said to Ruiz, "I don't like you correcting my sentences. I don't need all your crappola about culture and showers."

Alexandra Webb reached into her purse and pulled out a gun of her own. No doubt de Ruiz could identify the make; Griffin had no idea, only that the barrel seemed enormous.

"I may lack your skill with a weapon, dear Roberto, but from this distance I can certainly place a bullet or two in your chest. And that of the man standing to your side. You would be well advised to remain precisely where you are." Turning toward Griffin, she said, "You as well, whoever you are."

Griffin did not have to be told a second time. He would have done his best to stop breathing, if ordered.

"Cleve," Alexandra ordered to the car's passenger, "would you retrieve the shopping cart you left by the back of the Hummer?"

Cleveland Dumont exited the car, bringing with him a waft of whiskey and Aqua Velva.

He walked to the back of the Hummer and returned with a shopping cart. He shoved the cart across the lot to Griffin.

"You," Alexandra Webb ordered Griffin. "Take the box from Mr. de Ruiz." *De* with disdain again. "Put the box in the cart."

Griffin did as told.

"Now, push the cart over to me."

Griffin was about to do exactly that, when, from just outside the parking lot, came the sound of singing.

"*Oh, I wish I was in Dixie!*"

Griffin knew immediately it was Bobby, singing as he walked closer.

"Away! Away!
"In Dixie Land, I'll make my stand."

Bobby entered the parking lot, singing as he went. Behind Bobby, Griffin could see Annie and Saif approaching.

Bobby had a fine voice, tinged just enough with a Southern accent.

"To live and die in Dixie."

He tipped an imaginary hat to Alexandra. "Mornin', ma'am."

She waved the pistol in Bobby's direction. Graciousness disappearing, she screeched at him, "Get the hell over there with those two, Dr. Briggs."

Bobby bowed.

"Ah, Dr. Briggs. One of my finest roles, if I do say so myself.

"Griffin, the tracking beepers in the band aids on your hands worked fine," Bobby went on, speaking as if he couldn't be bothered with Alexandra's boorish interruption. "We knew where you were at all times. It's just that all the craziness with the cars exploding in Rodgers Forge slowed us down following you. Cops and fire trucks are everyplace."

Alexandra Webb's graciousness had vanished entirely. "Shut up," she yelled at Bobby. To Griffin, she said, "Push the cart to me."

Griffin did, but deliberately pushed the cart too lightly, leaving it half way between her and the three men.

"Too late for you, my dear," Bobby said, glancing to the parking lot entrance.

All eyes watched as Kit behind the wheel of the Malibu turned into the lot. He banged around a very tight turn at thirty plus, accelerating as he approached. He headed directly at Alexandra Webb. Griffin saw the look on Kit's face and it was gleeful and positively demonic.

She might have gotten away, but Alexandra's greed exceeded her sense of self-preservation. Rather than turn and run from the parking lot, she stepped forward to the grocery cart. She got her hands on the box.

As she did, Kit crashed into the shopping cart with enough force the cart acted like a missile impaling Alexandra's midsection. She was sent flying backwards and when she landed she did not move or make any sound.

The contents of the box, which turned out to be pieces of paper, went flying, confetti-like around the parking lot. Griffin saw the pages were Top Ten lists Kit had compiled over the years. Griffin snagged one mid-air. It was a list of the ten greatest movie trailers of all time.

He turned to look at Roberto de Ruiz, but all that was left was the white Panama hat.

Thirty Nine

July 4
8:38 am

"Sorry we're late, Miss P," Griffin said, as he, Annie, Kit, Saif and Bobby converged on their old music teacher. She was waiting in the parking lot of the Kenilworth Mall. "Some things came up."

Miss Paulette looked at each of them, arranged in a rough semi-circle. Her gaze stayed with Saif until she recognized him, one of hundreds of her students through the years. "You're Venkatesan. Saif." He nodded. "What in the world are you doing with these people?"

Saif smiled brightly. "Going off road."

Griffin said to her, "Stay right where you are, Miss P. Be back in a sec."

Griffin walked to the trunk of the Malibu. He returned with the six pictures of the music notes penciled onto Hans Baeder's wall. He also carried a red highlighter.

"I remember these pictures," Miss Paulette said. "You showed me the pictures when we met by the fountain in the mall. Some of the notes are Mozart's. Most are not."

"That's exactly what I want to ask you about. This will probably work best if we spread the pictures on the hood of

Annie's car. I have arranged the pictures as they appeared on the bedroom wall of a gifted violinist named Hans Baeder. He studied in Germany, as you concluded.

"Hans Baeder did this while he was dying. A man who survived the horrors of the Second World War made the effort to write these notes on his wall while he was dying. You can see how shaky his hand got as he was finishing. I do not believe this was nothing more than a time-killing activity for Hans. These notes are on that wall to tell us something. Miss P? What are they trying to tell us?"

Griffin handed Miss Paulette the red highlighter.

"Miss P, as I recall, you told us that a lot of these notes are Mozart. Some entire lines are Mozart, some parts of lines."

"That's correct."

"Can you cross out those notes which you know to be Mozart?"

She studied the pictures one at a time.

In the first picture she crossed out almost all the notes. In the second and third pictures most of the notes were crossed out. In the next two pictures about a third of the notes had a red line through them. In the last picture every note had a red line through it. Griffin estimated about 45% of the notes were Mozart's.

Miss Paulette needed about five minutes. Griffin picked up the sixth picture, with all the music notes red lined, leaving five pictures on the hood of the car. Miss Paulette looked up, a smile tugging at the corners of her heavily lipsticked mouth. The Mozart was a pleasure for her.

"Now, Miss P. Didn't you also say some of the notes were, in your phrase, 'a little off.'?"

"I don't recall the precise phrase, but yes, there are notes here which don't quite make sense. Here, for example, there's a half note where you'd expect a quarter note."

"I'll take your word on that. When we talked before, you were convinced this was not by accident or by incompetence."

"I don't know what caused it, but neither of the causes you give explains this."

"Could you put a red line through those notes? The ones which are a little off."

This was a far slower process. After ten minutes Miss Paulette had crossed out every note in the first picture. Griffin took the picture off the car hood. In another ten minutes the fifth picture was in Griffin's hands as well. Each of the remaining three pictures had more notes crossed out than untouched.

"Finally, you said some of the notes were like a stutter. The same note repeated. A record skipping was the phrase you used."

"Cross out the repeating notes?"

"Please."

This she did rapidly. Two more pictures were now in Griffin's hands. A single picture remained on the hood of the car.

"Miss P? How many notes are left in that one picture? These are the notes which are Hans Baeder's, not Mozart's. And these are the notes that flow best with the original composition, not a little off and not notes like stutters or repetitions."

"Fourteen," she answered quickly.

"Is the number fourteen special to Mozart in any way? Or particularly relevant to violins? European music? Anything along those lines?"

She considered the questions for more than a minute.

"Not to my knowledge."

"Now, Miss P, remembering that I am not musically talented-"

"I'll pass up the chance to make an easy joke."

"Much appreciated. Doesn't each line in these scores have a corresponding letter? Wasn't it EGBDF – Every Good Boy Deserves Favor?"

"That must have been from one my few classes you didn't cut. Yes, that's how lines in a score are identified."

"If you assign one of the EGBDF letters to each of the 14 notes that aren't crossed out? Do the remaining notes spell anything? Words? Music terms? Abbreviations you recognize?"

This got a quick, "No."

"How about if you turn the picture upside down? Reverse the EGBDF. Spell anything now?"

A quicker, "No."

"Does it spell anything in German?" This was Saif.

"I can't read German but I cannot imagine it would. There aren't enough vowels."

The six of them stared at the one picture on the hood for some time. Then Griffin winced. "Oh. Oh, I see it. I see it now.

"This isn't a code. Nothing is being spelled out, not in any language. Which was a smart decision by Hans, since he couldn't know if the person trying to decipher his notes could read music or read English or German."

"What is it, Griffin?" Kit asked.

"It's the outline of a picture. An upside down, L-shaped connect the dots picture."

He took the red highlighter and connected the dots.

"I still don't see it," said Annie.

"How about if I add some stars and stripes to the rectangle at the top. Can you see it now? It's a flag blowing in the breeze. How about now?"

Now everyone saw it too.

★

Once Miss P's car was out of sight he turned to Kit.

"Can you find Hans Baeder's house again? 5722 Gist Avenue?" Kit said he could. "Bobby, I know you said you have a gig later today. And, Saif, you have to prepare for your doctoral defense tomorrow – though the outcome's a forgone conclusion for sure. But, can everybody meet at Hans Baeder's house? Everyone drive separately. Follow Kit. I've got to stop home to pick up something. We'll meet in Hans' front yard."

★

Griffin arrived at 5722 Gist Avenue last, carrying a shovel. Annie, Kit, Saif, and Bobby were standing in the front yard, grass thigh-high in places. Kit was ending a phone call as Griffin stepped into the yard.

"That was Grace," Kit announced. "Giving us the scorecard.

"Alexandra Webb is still in intensive care but her injuries are not life threatening. She is not licensed to carry that gun she pointed at you, de Ruiz, and Bobby in the parking lot.

"Cleveland Dumont is also in the hospital. After he fled on foot into Ruxton he apparently decided he needed transportation back to Essex. Tried to steal a car. Cleve really isn't the sharpest tool in the shed. Turned out the car the he went after is owned by a police captain, who didn't exactly appreciate the attempt. Like Alexandra, after release from the hospital he'll be arrested."

"Roberto de Ruiz?" Griffin inquired.

"Whereabouts still unknown."

"No surprise," Griffin said. "Even with that limp he is very good at moving quickly."

He walked to the center of the yard, eyes searching the grass as he spoke.

"On the subject of Roberto de Ruiz. Interpol has a long standing reward offered for anyone assisting in the capture of

Roberto de Ruiz. Grace agreed if de Ruiz is brought in, that reward will be split four ways, equal shares for the four of you."

"Split five ways," Annie corrected him. Grace called me and we agreed the money will be split five ways."

Griffin looked up, at each of the others. "Thanks, but truthfully? I doubt we're going to see any of that money. I think de Ruiz is long gone.

"On the upside? He gave me the Duke's key. Our arrangement with Duke Ferlingheti is half of the fee upfront. We've been paid that. And half of the fee on delivery of the key. He wants that key. He'll pay us. I'm certain we all agree that amount should be split five ways, to include Saif. So, we've got some payment for our efforts. Though, I have to say again: it was never about the money."

Annie asked, "So why the shovel, Griffin?"

He answered her question with another question. "Kit, remember the other time we were here? You tripped over something in the grass."

"It's right here, what I tripped over," Kit answered, kicking at something. "The metal stump of a flagpole."

"Griffin, you think Hans buried something under the flagpole?"

"I do, Annie."

Griffin walked over to where Kit was standing. He slammed the shovel into the ground next to the circular metal flagpole base.

He winced in the effort and dropped the shovel.

"My blisters from scraping," he explained.

"Here, amigo," Bobby said. "I'll dig. I have experience at this, you know." He took the shovel from the unresisting Griffin. "I played the gravedigger scene in Hamlet. My role was First Clown." Bobby talked as he dug. The morning was hot and he quickly worked up a fair sweat. "In our Hamlet? The director was obsessed with realism. In the gravedigger scene I really dug real dirt with a real shovel. Piled the real dirt on stage. Realistic it was; good theater it wasn't. We closed over the weekend."

In a few minutes Bobby had dug deeply enough that with the shovel he could leverage the metal flagpole base and the cement underneath it out of the ground. Saif and Kit dragged the metal and cement to the side. Bobby kept digging.

While Bobby continued his digging, Griffin said to Kit: "Remember when CJ the real estate agent showed us this house? CJ said Hans used to spend hours sitting on his porch in the glider that's still there. What better place to keep an eye on whatever's buried beneath the flagpole. That was the point of the notes on his bedroom wall: to direct someone to the flagpole that was here all those years. CJ said the flagpole only came down a couple years ago and by then Hans was too ill to replace it."

Bobby dumped another shovelful of dirt into the grass and said, "In the gravedigger scene in Hamlet I kept digging until I hit a skull. There's no chance of that happening here, is there, Griffin?"

"I don't think-"

Bobby's shovel struck something that was very un-dirtish and un-rockish and certainly not skullish sounding.

"You sure that's not a skull?"

"Bobby, be careful, please," Griffin implored.

Bobby gave little jabs with the shovel.

"A wood box, I think," Bobby said. Some more soft jabs of the shovel. "Four feet or so long, not that wide."

"Did the First Clown use his hands to dig?"

"No," Bobby replied, getting down onto his knees. "But I'll ad lib."

★

For the next ten minutes no one spoke. Bobby cleared away the dirt a handful at a time.

Eventually Bobby told Kit, "Hey, amigo, you get at one end and I'll be at the other. We pick up the box slowly. Very slowly."

They pulled the mud-caked rectangular box from the ground. Bobby sat on the side of the now sizeable hole examining the box, which rested on his sweat-stained jeans.

"The box is made of thick, solid wood," he said. "I see wood screws at the corners to hold the box together. Looks like the box has been in the ground a long time, but it's built well enough it's holding together."

"Hans Baeder, by all accounts, was a fine carpenter."

"Griffin, there's no latch to open it. I'll use the edge of the shovel."

"Bobby?"

"I know, Griffin. I know. You don't have to tell me to be careful. I can see it in your face."

Bobby was careful. He slowly worked the edge of the shovel until the lid loosened enough for him to peel it away.

Inside the box were pieces of thick canvas, grey but not muddy. The box had withstood the years, protecting its contents. The canvas pieces had not been thrown into the box like packing, but had been carefully arranged, like blankets around an infant.

Bobby pushed the canvas to the side. His fingers shook with anticipation. Inside the canvas was another box, smaller, of deeply varnished wood. This box appeared worn, but not damaged, more like it had been sitting on an antique shop shelf than underground. Hans' precautions had done their protective job.

This second box had a latch, which Bobby, on his third try, opened.

"And there it is," he said. "The most valuable violin ever made." He laughed, exhilarated. "It's like being served the finest wine by your mistress, naked."

"But why, Griffin? Why bury the del Gesu?" Annie insisted, with surprising passion. "Why would Hans Baeder bury this? Of all people, he knew what the del Gesu was worth. Not what it was worth in money. I know he didn't care about that. But what about the music?"

Griffin had considered the question and had his answer ready. "Hans was ashamed of his role in the Special Task Force For Music. You remember Miriam Freitag telling us that. He never forgave himself for stealing the violins. So he buried the del Gesu. He couldn't bring himself to destroy it, so he buried it. Then he left directions on where to find it in the notes on his bedroom wall. We were the ones to follow the directions.

"Kit? Can you to take that to Grace today?" Griffin asked. "She'll have experts evaluate it, but that has to be the 1742 Guarneri del Gesu."

★

Later, Griffin and Annie were alone on the steps of Hans Baeder's house.

Bobby had left for his gig, after bestowing on Griffin a "Well played, amigo." Kit was in his latest lease, a silver Jag, DC-bound, to deliver the del Gesu to Grace. Griffin hoped Kit was not driving too insanely. Saif was off to his last day of prep for his doctoral defense.

"So," Annie began.

"So," Griffin agreed.

"So, what are your plans for this fine holiday?"

"I thought at some point we should visit Woodlawn Cemetery. Pay our respects to Mr. Hans Baeder, who died one year ago today."

"And?" Annie asked, getting up from the steps.

Griffin got up from the steps also. "Kit won't be back from delivering the del Gesu to Grace for another couple hours."

Annie began walking in the direction of her Mini Cooper. "And Bobby is busy with a gig for the next few hours."

Griffin headed toward his Malibu. "And Saif has to study."

Annie broke into a jog. "Whatever will we do with ourselves for the next hour or two?"

"Shower grouting?" Griffin suggested, starting to run.

"Bookcase building?" Annie offered, moving faster.

"We can think of something, I'm sure," Griffin said.

And they raced each other to their cars and home.

About the Author

JC Sullivan is a Baltimore writer. He has written for the *Chicago Tribune*, *Christian Science Monitor* and the *Wall Street Journal*. His first article in the *Journal* led to an appearance on C Span, testifying before a Congressional committee. His short stories have appeared in literary journals in Massachusetts, Florida, New York and Bangalore, India. *Shark and Octopus* is his first novel.

JC got the idea for *Shark and Octopus* years ago watching a trailer for the movie "Ocean's Eleven." Remember the Brad Pitt-George Clooney series of movies set in Las Vegas, where a gang gets together to plan and pull off a complicated heist? JC got to thinking about writing a heist novel – but instead of the glitz of Las Vegas, how about his very unpolished hometown of Baltimore? And what if the gang has to manage the heist without anyone learning the prize was ever missing? *Shark and Octopus* is that novel. It's a comic caper, a mystery, and a thriller as well.

JC Sullivan has lived in Baltimore all his life and has no plans to move. He survived growing up the youngest of four boys in a rowhouse. The techno-thriller author Tom Clancy lived a couple streets over. JC's father was an FBI agent who did some counter-intelligence work, chasing Soviet spies during the Cold War. As a result, no one in the Sullivan family was allowed by the American government behind the Iron Curtain. The Berlin Wall came down without JC's help.

He attended a private high school but spent most of his time there on the basketball court. When his knees gave out JC decided he'd better become a more serious student. About that time he started writing fiction.

He has been a lawyer for more than three decades, working mostly on behalf of construction companies. He has taught English as a second language and tutored the SAT (Verbal section only, math was never his strong point). He has two daughters Kira and Meredith, both Quaker-educated. *Freeze Tag*, the prequel to *Shark and Octopus*, is nearly completed. You can follow his blog https://wordpress.com/view/jcharles-sullivan.wordpress.com.